MORE
VIEWS
~ from the ~
BOUNDARY

Brian Johnston joined the BBC's Outside Broadcasts Department immediately after the war and worked first on live radio broadcasts from theatres and music-halls all over Britain. He was one of the first broadcasters to work both for television and radio and began his long association with cricket commentary in the summer of 1946. Between 1948 and 1952 he also presented the live feature 'Let's Go Somewhere' for the popular Saturday night programme *In Town Tonight*.

From 1946 until the end of the sixties he covered all the televised Test matches for the BBC and was a member of the television commentary teams for the funeral of King George VI, the Coronation and Princess Margaret's wedding.

He became the BBC's first Cricket Correspondent in 1963 and held this post until his retirement in 1972. Since then he has continued as a regular member of the *Test Match Special* team, and has broadcast from 265 Test matches over the last forty-six years.

He took over presenting *Down Your Way* from Franklin Engelmann in 1972 and continued for fifteen years, presenting exactly the same number as Engelmann – 733 – the last coming from Lord's Cricket Ground.

He has had two autobiographies and twelve other books published, including *It's Been a Piece of Cake* and *45 Summers*.

Brian Johnston died in January 1994.

by the same authors

Views from the Boundary

also by Brian Johnston

Let's Go Somewhere
Stumped for a Tale
The Wit of Cricket
Armchair Cricket
It's Been a Lot of Fun
It's a Funny Game
Rain Stops Play
Brian Johnston's Guide to Cricket
Chatterboxes
Now Here's a Funny Thing
It's Been a Piece of Cake
Brian Johnston's Down Your Way
45 Summers
Someone Who Was

BRIAN JOHNSTON

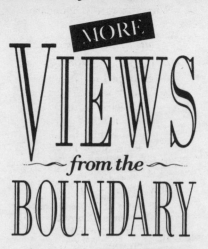

MORE VIEWS from the BOUNDARY

Celebrity interviews
from the commentary box

Edited by PETER BAXTER

BBC TEST MATCH SPECIAL

Mandarin

A Mandarin Paperback
MORE VIEWS FROM THE BOUNDARY

First published in Great Britain in 1993
by Methuen London
First published in paperback 1994
by Mandarin Paperbacks
an imprint of Reed Consumer Books Ltd
Michelin House, 81 Fulham Road, London SW3 6RB
and Auckland, Melbourne, Singapore and Toronto

Copyright © Brian Johnston and Peter Baxter 1993
The authors have asserted their moral rights

Introduction copyright © Mandarin Paperbacks 1994
Line illustrations by Rodney Shackell.
Photograph of Harold Pinter © Ivan Kyncl;
of Peter O'Toole © Mohamed Ansar;
of Alan Ayckbourn © John Haynes; and of
Brian Johnston © Pauline Johnston.
All other photos supplied by individual contributors.

A CIP catalogue record for this book
is available at the British Library
ISBN 0 7493 1615 2

Printed and bound in Great Britain
by Cox & Wyman Ltd, Reading, Berks

CONTENTS

Foreword		1
Introduction		5
Leslie Thomas	*The Oval 1981*	7
Michael Charlton	*Headingley 1984*	16
Leslie Crowther	*Old Trafford 1985*	26
Sir Bernard Lovell	*Old Trafford 1987*	35
Peter Scudamore	*Headingley 1989*	46
John Kettley	*Old Trafford 1989*	56
Max Jaffa	*The Oval 1989*	66
Eric Idle	*Trent Bridge 1990*	74
George Shearing	*Lord's 1990*	87
John Major	*Lord's 1990*	99
Vic Lewis	*Old Trafford 1990*	109
Harold Pinter	*The Oval 1990*	122
Lord Runcie	*Lord's 1991*	133
Max Boyce	*Trent Bridge 1991*	145
Graham Taylor	*Edgbaston 1991*	158
Peter O'Toole	*The Oval 1991*	165
James Judd	*Edgbaston 1992*	177
Ian Richter	*Old Trafford 1992*	192
Alan Ayckbourn	*Headingley 1992*	206
David Shepherd	*The Oval 1992*	219

The 'Biter' Bit:
   Ned Sherrin interviews
   Brian Johnston
	Lord's 1992	232

FOREWORD

IT HAS BEEN SAID by many, including John Major, that not only will Test Match Special not be the same again in 1994 and beyond, Summer will not be the same either. When Brian Johnston died early this year, he left an indelible mark and a void no-one will ever be able to fill completely.

Nor should anyone try, because he was unique. The game, thank God, will go on and so will the programme. It remains to be seen whether the Saturday lunchtime conversations which Brian used to conduct with a wide variety of cricket-loving celebrities can ever have quite the same air of relaxed spontaneity.

I took over from B.J. when, believe it or not, he retired as BBC Cricket Correspondent in 1972. Thank God, he never retired in reality and he was as sparkling as ever right up to his last season in 1993. He set the tone for Test Match Special, imbuing it with his irrepress-ible sense of humour. Those Saturday interviews were no exception, as the collection in this book frequently demonstrates.

Life for him was fun and his vitality radiated to everyone around him. Everyone he met – and many he never even met – felt like his friend. He was the most natural broadcaster of them all, a born entertainer and a kind and generous soul. It was because these qualities were conveyed to all these listeners that no-one, so far as I know, ever refused a chance to come to talk to him in the box. They wanted a slice of that unique atmosphere, as well as of the chocolate cake.

The selection of conversations which make this a book to treasure are full of examples not only of Brian's wit but also of his not inconsiderable erudition. That word is often used in connection with academics, but Brian would have been the last person to call himself a scholar. What he had was natural intelligence, a retentive memory, a great interest in people and wide general knowledge.

He would never pretend to know something he did not know, however, (a dangerous thing for anyone to do on the air) and he was quick to spot something which might confuse the listener as well as himself. When Eric Idle, the comedian, whom Brian found harder to talk to than some – perhaps because that sparkling wit had only a mild interest in cricket – mentioned that the motto of the Cambridge Footlights is 'ars est colare artem' Brian's characteristic response was 'Oh, quite. You needn't translate for me, but for the listener, would you mind?'

The answer, in case your Latin like mine (and Brian's) has long since gone, is 'the art that conceals art' and how well that familiar phrase applies to his skill at the microphone: apparently so natural and easy, but actually acquired through hard work and experience as well as through a God-given gift of the gab.

The joy of this book lies mainly, however, in the wit and experience which Brian's beguiling charm drew from those to whom he was talking. You will learn more here about every one of his subjects, even the (naturally very guarded) Prime Minister. More about

cricket, too. To whet your appetite, here is Harold
Pinter:

'People – particularly foreigners – tend to say
cricket is a peaceful game. It's not. It's a very,
very violent activity, I think. A lot of people are
bowling very hard and trying to hit the ball hard
and the feeling is incredibly intense. The thing
that always continues to amaze me about cricket is
that every game possesses tremendous tension and
drama.'

It happened that I read that soon after Michael
Atherton and Devon Malcolm had in their turn been
peppered by red-hot fast bowling from Courtney
Walsh during the Jamaica Test on England's tour
of the West Indies early in 1994. It characterised
the passionate nature of the game in the Caribbean
and I don't suppose Pinter could better his choice
of words if he were to hone them for one of his
plays.

The interviewees come very well out of this collection, but then they had a masterful and kindly
inquisitor whose objective was the very opposite of
a sixteenth-century Jesuit with a heretic. 'Put them
at their ease,' Brian would have said if ever he had
analysed his own method, 'and they will give of
their best.' Come to think of it, he would have
made a very good manager of England cricket teams,
whose players so often seem too tense for their own
good.

Whatever was happening to England on the field
these interviews, expertly culled by the Test Match
Special producer Peter Baxter, were conducted in an

atmosphere of enjoyment and I am sure you will feel part of it when you read them.

CHRISTOPHER MARTIN-JENKINS

INTRODUCTION

UP TO THE END of the 1992 season we had invited seventy-five people to give *their* 'View from the Boundary'. It all started during the first Test against the West Indies at Trent Bridge in 1980, when dear old Ted Moult was our very first guest.

Three years ago the BBC published twenty of these Saturday lunchtime conversations in *Views from the Boundary*. Now Methuen are publishing another twenty-one in this collection called *More Views from the Boundary*.

These conversations – *not* interviews – are with well-known people who have a love of cricket, though they don't necessarily play it. We invite them to spend a Saturday of a Test Match in the commentary box with us on *Test Match Special*. We try to give them a little sustenance, usually a glass or two of champagne, reinforced by a tray lunch – airline style.

During the luncheon interval, after the news, we have about twenty-five minutes to talk. It is live, unscripted, uncensored(!) and with no prior knowledge of the questions. It is a most rewarding exercise to learn from such a variety of people something about themselves, and to find out just what cricket means to them and why they love it so.

In this new edition we certainly have a mixed variety of professions as proof that cricket is a link which knows no barriers of class, occupation nor background. In alphabetical order we offer you: an actor, an Archbishop, an artist, an astronomer, an author, a band leader, a broadcaster, a Chancellor of the Exchequer, three comedians, a conductor, a hostage, a jazz pianist, a jockey, two playwrights, a political commentator, a soccer manager, a violinist and a weather forecaster.

So now please join me in the commentary box. No champagne I'm afraid! But I do hope you enjoy yourself.

BRIAN JOHNSTON

LESLIE THOMAS

LESLIE IS AS hilarious in real life as are his characters in his many novels. I suppose he does sometimes stop talking but I have never experienced it! He is a very funny man with a tremendous knowledge of so many things. His time in the Army, his travels round the world, his spell as a writer on the *Evening News*, his collection of antiques and of course, after a late start, his love of cricket. He worships cricketers and enjoys nothing better than playing cricket alongside old England players for the Lord's Taverners. He may not be a great cricketer but he takes it very seriously, and tries like mad. In September 1992 I was umpiring in a Taverners' Charity Match on a lovely little school ground in the Close at Salisbury, where Leslie now lives. He caught a sizzling catch at deep mid-wicket, made it look very easy and tossed the ball up in the air like a true professional. I'm glad to say – though perhaps *he* was disappointed – that the Taverners did *not* rush up and kiss him!

He is a permanently busy man. When he joined us at the Oval in 1981 he had come up especially from Somerset and was off the next day to play cricket at Arundel. He had just returned from travels abroad, was preparing to launch his fiftieth novel, *The Magic Army*, in October and had already begun yet another book, *A World of Islands*. I started by asking him how much he enjoyed his travelling all round the world.

THE OVAL, 29 AUGUST 1981

LESLIE THOMAS   The trouble is, going to these places abroad you miss the cricket and I have to try and find you on the overseas service and all I get is the Top Forty – whatever that may be.

BRIAN JOHNSTON   Were all those novels on the Army based on your actual experiences when you were in the Army?

LESLIE   Yes. My entry in *Who's Who* says, 'rose to the rank of lance corporal', which is all I ever did.

BRIAN   Were you stationed abroad?

LESLIE   Yes, in Singapore, where we played cricket. I remember getting off a plane in Singapore once and asking the taxi driver to take me to the Padang, where they played cricket, and I sat under the same tree where I sat as a soldier when I was eighteen years old and watched cricket – and I swear it was the same two batsmen still in.

BRIAN   When did cricket start in your life, then?

LESLIE   Well, I never told anyone this, Brian, but very late. I was telling my son last night that at the age of twelve I didn't know how many men were in a cricket team.

BRIAN   Oooh – sacrilege!

LESLIE   I know, it's a terrible thing to say, but I was brought up in wartime in Newport, Mon., which was not a centre of cricket, despite what Wilfred Wooller told me recently, that they did play matches there, and I honestly didn't know anything about the game until I went to live in Devon – and it was March and I was batting in the nets and another batsman got behind me because I was missing so many of the balls.

BRIAN   Where was this in Devon?

LESLIE   In Kingsbridge.

BRIAN   Very nice – on the river down there.

LESLIE   Yes, in fact my novel, *The Magic Army*, is set at that period during the War in Devon. It's about the huge invasion army waiting to invade Europe.

BRIAN   And did you develop into a batsman in the end?

LESLIE   No, I never did. Actually, this is a fraud. I've played cricket all my life and frankly I've never been much good, except I've always been very enthusiastic. I love the game. I love playing it, watching it, reading about it – everything about it. When I was in my teens, if I made a duck on a Sunday I couldn't sleep the whole week and it made me miserable, but now, you see, I go out for the fun and strangely enough I do get some runs. I've had a couple of fifties and I made ten not out for Prince Charles' XI.

BRIAN   Not on a horse.

LESLIE   Well, almost. It was on the polo ground at Windsor – the first time cricket had ever been played there.

I was playing golf yesterday with a great friend called Ben and he's very tough and he thinks cricket's a poof's game and he told me so. So I said I'd send Lillee round to see him and he said, 'There, I told you – Lily.'

BRIAN   Are you any good at golf?

LESLIE   So-so. I played with Peter Alliss on television a couple of years ago and I did reasonably well. I think that some days I play like Arnold Palmer and some days like Lili Palmer.

BRIAN   You did that *A Round With Alliss*. How many holes did you get through?

LESLIE   Oh, about five. I had a two on one hole, it was terrific. But I think he's a tremendous man.

BRIAN   What about cricket, though. Have you supported Glamorgan?

LESLIE   Do you know, I've just been asked to write a chapter for a book that's coming out next year in which each chapter is about a different county and I'm writing about Glamorgan – about the daffodil summer, the summer they won the championship. I went to see Wilfred Wooller the other day, had lunch with him and he was terrific. I'd never met him before. I love cricketers, you know. Sir Leonard Hutton is a great friend of mine, because I used to write a column for him when I was on a newspaper. I saw him at Lord's the other day and I'm always so pleased to see him and I think it's mutual; we really like each other.

BRIAN   You wrote his cricket column for him?

LESLIE   Years ago, yes. I was on the *Evening News* and it was headed 'SIR LEONARD HUTTON SAYS' and underneath in very small type 'as told to Leslie Thomas'. But I didn't mind, it was a great privilege.

BRIAN   Did you learn a lot from him?

LESLIE   Tremendous, yes. Terrific sense of humour. He's a singular man. Some people think he's a very hard man, but he isn't. He's one of the most interesting men I've ever met. We were at Worcester and on the first day

I bought lunch. On the second day he bought lunch – he was getting about fifty thousand quid more than me – and on the third day he brought sandwiches. I'd got a little packet of crisps and he said, 'Those crisps look OK.' So I said, 'Well, help yourself.' And he delved into the crisps, ate a handful and then said, 'They're better with salt.' So I said, 'There's some salt there somewhere.' He had some more and by the time he'd finished there were three crisps in the bottom of the packet. So I said, 'Well, you might as well eat them all now.' And he said, 'No, lad, you eat them. They're your crisps.'

(Sir Leonard Hutton died in September 1990 at the age of 74. Ed.)

BRIAN You say you didn't know about cricket till you were twelve. Who did you watch? Who were your heroes?

LESLIE Oh, R. S. Ellis of Australia in the Australian Services team in 1945. Spin bowler. I modelled my bowling on R. S. Ellis. A blank look's come on your face. R. S. Ellis – same team as Cristofani and Miller. The first cricketer I ever saw, in fact, was Keith Miller – at the Leyland Ground at Kingston-on-Thames. He was reading a sporting paper and I asked for his autograph and he said, 'Have you got anything good for the four-thirty?'

BRIAN That's typical Miller.

LESLIE You know, to sit up here today is absolutely wonderful for me. It's so cosy, isn't it? And you get drinks and eats.

BRIAN But you kept so quiet there.

LESLIE Well, I did for once in my life, because I was fascinated. You can actually see the ball moving and I know that all this stuff you do on the radio is absolutely true.

I live in Somerset now, where they're all cricket barmy – men, women and children – and when Botham was making his runs at Headingley, we had a house full of workmen and one got so excited he fell down the ladder.

(This conversation took place six weeks after the famous Headingley Test of 1981, when Ian Botham's innings of 149 not out enabled England to beat Australia by 18 runs after following on 227 behind. Ed.)

BRIAN   Why have you gone to Somerset?

LESLIE   My son's going to Millfield. That's the sum total of it. And we want him to go as a day boy. I want him to be able to spell. I think he'll have a wonderful time there.

BRIAN   Can you spell?

LESLIE   I'm not bad. I always think spelling is something you can get from a book. People say to me, 'Who actually writes your books? Do they put the full stops in?' Because they think I couldn't possibly do it.

BRIAN   Can you listen to Test Match commentary going on as you write, or do you have to shut yourself away?

LESLIE   I sneak off every now and then and turn the television or the radio on.

Something happened to me last year which I just couldn't believe. I went to the Centenary Test Match Dinner and I was sitting next to Bobby Simpson and I went out for something or other and when I came back he said, 'There's a young man over there would like your autograph.' So I said, 'Why didn't he ask?' He said, 'Oh, he's very shy.' So I signed the autograph and asked, 'Who is it for?' He said, 'That chap over there, Kim Hughes.' I thought, my God, I should ask for his autograph.

(At this time Kim Hughes was the Australian captain. Ed.)

BRIAN Have you ever thought of writing a book with cricket as a background to it?

LESLIE No. Cricket does tend to creep into a lot of my books. *The Magic Army*, which I've just finished – it's a very long novel, about a quarter of a million words – as the armies go off to invade Europe, there's a village cricket match taking place. I checked the local papers down there and on 6 June there was a cricket match. There's the story of a titled lady who was absolutely shocked as she was coming back from Dover at the time of Dunkirk with troops and wounded and everything on her train and as they went past Wimbledon there were fields full of cricketers in white.

BRIAN It all goes back to Sir Francis Drake. 'The Armada can wait; my bowels can't.' Isn't that what he said?

LESLIE Is that what he said?

BRIAN They said he was playing bowls, but he had to rush off when he saw the Armada coming. But your book – a quarter of a million words!

LESLIE It took three years.

BRIAN Do you do a wadge and then sort of correct?

LESLIE I do about a thousand words a day. In fact the BBC have done a television documentary about the writing of this book. It's in three parts. They followed me around and they filmed the writing and the research and all that sort of thing.

BRIAN Do you keep yourself to a thousand words a day or do you do as many as you feel you can that day?

LESLIE The worst mornings I sit there – just as you have to come here when there's no play and it's raining – and I put my hands on that typewriter and I write a thousand words whatever. That's being professional, I think.

BRIAN Yes, it is, but supposing you don't get that inspiration.

LESLIE Oddly enough, the morning you don't get the inspiration, if you just press on and press on, it's frequently the best morning that you have.

BRIAN You get these marvellous comic scenes. If they're not taken from life, how do you conjure them up?

LESLIE Well, a lot of them are taken from life, because life's very funny, I think. If you look at it from a certain angle and see the amusing things – even in the most dreadful tragedy. I saw the most grotesque thing in Spain. We were having dinner in an open-air restaurant by a road that was just like a killer track. There were accidents all the time along this stretch of road and there was the most frightful crash just below us. There was a man in the restaurant playing one of these little organs and he switched to the Dead March. There were people lying about everywhere, but that's the sort of grotesque humour that does happen in life.

BRIAN What about your time in Fleet Street?

LESLIE I worked on the *Evening News* when it sold a million and a half copies a night – no thanks to me – but it was a great newspaper then and I had a wonderful life. I went to about eighty countries. I travelled with the Queen and the Duke of Edinburgh and I went all over the world. In fact, when I wrote my first novel, *The Virgin Soldiers*, and it became a best-seller, it was a double-edged thing, because it meant I had to leave Fleet Street and in fact I went back and got an office in Fleet Street, because it was home. Now I only miss Fleet Street at lunchtime.

BRIAN One of the things they say you're interested in is antiques. Is that so?

LESLIE Yes. My wife had an antique business for some years and we have a sort of collection of bits and pieces. We had a stall in Portobello Road at one time. It was great fun. People used to come down and see me standing there in the morning and think, 'Oh he's down on his luck, poor fellow.' I used to go and buy bits of china and if we made ten pounds at the end of the day or twenty pounds – this is some years ago – we were so happy. More than all the royalties. I suppose it's ready money.

BRIAN Now what about the winter? You wouldn't be tempted to follow a team round on tour?

LESLIE No, I've seen relatively little cricket abroad, strangely enough. I saw a Test Match once in Trinidad. I came straight off the boat, went to the day's play in the Test Match and got straight on the boat again and went away. It was when Cowdrey made a big score.

BRIAN Well, you're going to watch the rest of the day with us, I hope.

LESLIE You bet. This is where I'd like to come every time I come to the Oval.

MICHAEL CHARLTON

MICHAEL CHARLTON was unusual. He was an Australian cricket commentator with a 'Pommie' accent during the 1950s. He also introduced the Australian equivalent of BBC TV's *Panorama* called *Window on the World*. Sadly – for us – he deserted cricket to become a political commentator and interviewer full time, coming over to work in England, where he still lives. He was a splendid contrast to the normal Australian cricket commentator, with a delightful sense of humour portrayed with a friendly chuckle. He was the ABC commentator over here in 1956 and we started my conversation with him with a clip from his own commentary during the Old Trafford Test in 1956 – Laker's match. He described a unique wicket – Burke caught Cowdrey bowled Lock 22. It was unique because it was the only wicket Tony Lock took during the match, Jim Laker taking the other nineteen.

HEADINGLEY, 14 JULY 1984

MICHAEL CHARLTON It was remarkable, wasn't it. Two world-class spinners, one of whom gets nineteen wickets and the other gets only one.

BRIAN JOHNSTON Tony Lock's still trying to work it out. Laker got all his wickets from the same end – the Stretford End. Locky bowled from that end as well.

MICHAEL Yes, so it was the same for both. I remember going out to the wicket when it was all over and what I shall never forget is a small circle on a length on off stump in which it looked as if a whole series of two shilling pieces had been put down – and that was Laker. He'd bowled absolutely on this spot. I thought he was just about unplayable.

BRIAN Well, now, travelling round with the team you get to know all their feelings and inner secrets. Publicly they said the pitch was made to measure for Laker, although in fact England made 459 on it.

MICHAEL It was the same for both sides, wasn't it? There was a lot of controversy about that pitch. I think the Australians thought they'd been taken for a ride. They thought that that pitch at Old Trafford that time was not the traditional one. Some new soil had been put on it and all that kind of thing, but it was the same for both sides. Not a happy tour all round, I think, that one for the Australians. They were on a down-swing that time. I think also that they weren't as well led as they might have been and I think there was a general feeling – certainly my own feeling – that Keith Miller should have captained that side.

BRIAN Let's just remind people that the first Test of that 1956 series was drawn at Trent Bridge and then the second one at Lord's Australia won.

MICHAEL   Yes, Miller won that. Extraordinary figure he was. I remember him as he came off the field throwing a bail to somebody.

BRIAN   There's a picture of him, it's been captured and I've seen it in books.

MICHAEL   He had a flair for that, didn't he?

(Miller took ten wickets in the Lord's Test. Ed.)

BRIAN   Then England won the third Test by an innings here at Headingley and then they won the Old Trafford one by an innings and the fifth was drawn.

Let's talk about Miller for a second, because you say he should have been captain. How good a captain do you reckon he was?

MICHAEL   Well he was a very fine captain of the state side of New South Wales, because I think he was an inspirational captain. He was not a man to speak coherently and explain things in detail before matches began. He wasn't that kind of player, I think we all know. But he could inspire great loyalty in a side and I think that young side in New South Wales absolutely worshipped him. He could do as he liked and he had great luck of course. I think whatever it was Horatio said about Hamlet, had he been put on he was likely to have proved most royal. He was a most inspiring figure.

BRIAN   But he had this lovely, casual approach in everything he did.

MICHAEL   Jimmy Burke, who died so tragically, told me of a match we were all at at Newcastle. It must have been a country match and Miller was captain of the New South Wales side and they walked out in the morning under rather a hot sun. Miller's eyes were shielded against the sun this particular morning and Burke said to him, 'Excuse me, Nugget [they all called him Nugget], there are twelve men.' And Miller, without turning round, said, 'Well somebody bugger off, then.' And just kept on – didn't even look round.

BRIAN Jimmy Burke was a great character. He became a very good commentator, didn't he?

MICHAEL Well, that was long after my time. He was a wonderful tourist, a great mimic, a very amusing boy. He was a happy character when I knew him.

BRIAN And he could imitate somebody throwing when he bowled.

MICHAEL Yes, he had the most dreadful action.

BRIAN I don't think people minded much because it wasn't very effective.

(J. W. Burke, who played 24 Tests for Australia between 1950 and 1958, committed suicide at the age of 49 in 1979. Ed.)

BRIAN What actually was your period of commentating? We knew you in 1956, when you came here.

MICHAEL Round about '52 I was doing Sheffield Shield matches and then I did the '54 tour, England's tour of Australia – Len Hutton's tour. Then there were some in India.

BRIAN You were there in 1958/59, my first time when I came out to Australia.

MICHAEL Yes, I remember you getting bowled over in the surf at Bondi and Jack Fingleton laughing.

BRIAN Yes, someone shouted, 'There's one out the back,' or something. What's it called? I was 'dumped'.

MICHAEL You were dumped, yes. I remember you striding heroically into the surf and appearing like a torpedo about five minutes later, belching sand and salt water.

BRIAN You were a bit extraordinary to be a commentator in Australia, because you had what they used to describe as a slightly Pommie voice.

MICHAEL It's always difficult to explain, but my parents were New Zealanders and we were always brought up very strictly at home not to speak the colonial twang, as my father called it. So it's an environmental thing, largely, coming from my father. We always called England 'home'. In fact, when I came here in '56, they wanted me to sound more Australian. They were a bit disturbed by that.

BRIAN But you were a bit different. The average Australian commentator is not quite as light-hearted as we are and certainly you were light-hearted. You saw the fun in it.

MICHAEL Too often, perhaps. Yes, I always looked for that myself. I think it's the most marvellous witty and amusing game. We were brought up, of course, in the Bradman era and they always said about him that he'd be trying to get a hundred against the blind school. It was a serious business in Australia. I think Don Bradman's seriousness of purpose rather overlaid it, you know. It sat upon its soul like a mountain for many years.

BRIAN Why did you give all this up, then, because you obviously love cricket so much?

MICHAEL Well, I very much ask myself that. The best years I had were undoubtedly going round the world with cricketers and cricket teams. I loved it and I felt quite tearful coming back here this morning. I haven't been here, to this ground, for twenty-eight years. I had the most marvellous time. I suppose because of the rather puritan background, I wondered, at the age I was – mid-twenties – if one was going to go on doing this for the rest of one's life. Oddly enough, it was through cricket that my life was pretty much changed to politics because I was in Delhi once, doing a Test Match there on the Australian tour – Richie Benaud's tour – and I sat next to Nehru, the Prime Minister of India. And I interviewed him on the strength of this later and I got a bit of a taste for this and I ended up doing that ever after.

BRIAN Why did you decide to come over here? We're very glad you did.

MICHAEL I was invited, Johnno. They asked me to come and I've been here ever since.

BRIAN I want to take you back now to perhaps one of the most exciting matches you ever did. The tie in 1960 at Brisbane.

MICHAEL I brought my tie to show you. Specially for you I wear it.

BRIAN That's the famous tie. Is it everyone who was there who can wear it?

MICHAEL Any one of the players or correspondents who were there can wear it. It's a rather unimaginative thing, as you see. It's the West Indies colours and the gold and green.

BRIAN What's this insignia?

MICHAEL Well, you might well ask. Fingo designed this – Jack Fingleton – and it's a golden tied knot. It's the tie for what must be – I don't know, a lot of water's gone down many rivers since then – the greatest Test Match ever played.

BRIAN I think it must have been. And yet the strange thing is, we hear very strange stories of how – it wasn't you – but one of the Australian commentators who was on at the end, didn't realise what the result was and I think said it was a draw and the next day had to go back and do a cod commentary for the archives with some people applauding in the box.

MICHAEL Well, I've not heard that. We all left

the ground in the dawn next morning. Nobody went to bed that night – players, public or the travelling press. There was confusion at the end. It was the last over, last day and the last couple of balls of the Test Match and you know those huge tropical sunsets in the north in Australia – it was like a scarlet ribbon. It was quite hard to see the scoreboard. And the scoreboard panicked, because of all these run-outs at the end, because you very nearly had completed runs. Everybody had their hands on the trigger. Everybody was saying, 'It's all over. They've won.' And it wasn't won, because all these hairline decisions for run-outs were being given. I'd done the commentary period just before the Test Match ended, the penultimate twenty minutes. Clive Harburg did the last session and I was down on the field just as they came off and Joe Solomon thought the West Indies had won and Worrell, the captain, thought they'd lost. It was quite confusing. The ABC scorer kept his head. He was marvellous. He had it right.

BRIAN No names, no pack drill, but certain well-known commentators and ex-Test cricketers writing for newspapers had left the ground and heard the result when they arrived by air in Sydney.

MICHAEL They had indeed. There were those – and we dare not speak their names, even now – who left before the last hour or so, assuming that Australia were going to win. It would have been a remarkable Test Match even if it hadn't had the finish that it did. There was a wonderful innings by a glamorous young Australian in the first innings – O'Neill made 181. There was an absolutely superb innings by Sobers – 132. And there were two shots in that innings in particular. He hit something through mid-wicket – a pull shot, but the trajectory of that shot I can still see. It never rose more than about five feet above the ground. I thought it must have been like that at Trafalgar on Nelson's ships, with a cannonball carrying away the rigging. It went straight over the fence like a rocket and it mowed down the crowd. Then he hit something that hit Colin McDonald at very deep mid-off on the shoulder. An off-drive off Benaud, I think, and it hit McDonald on the left shoulder as he put a knee down to field it and it hit the sight board. That was Sobers. Anyway, it all came down to this. Australia had to get 233 to win in 300 minutes and it looked as if they would do it easily. *(A seventh wicket stand between Benaud and Davidson had taken them from 92 for 6 to 226 for 7. Ed.)*

And it got down to this last over at four minutes to six, I remember, in this blood-red sunset and almost hysterical excitement. Australia had to get six runs off eight balls and there were three wickets to fall and Benaud had batted marvellously throughout the afternoon. I was talking to Richie, whom I hadn't seen for years, only this morning and he said that Frank Worrell went over to Wes Hall, who was to bowl this last over, and said, 'No bouncers, Wes.' So the first thing Wes Hall did was to bowl a bouncer and Benaud hooked it – and I have Richie's authority to say this – he said it should have been six, but he got a top edge and it went miles high and Alexander, the wicket keeper, caught it marvellously over his head.

(Benaud out for 52 – five runs needed to win off six balls. The new batsman, Meckiff, was nearly run out taking a bye off his second ball. Four were needed off four balls. Ed.)

Wally Grout hooked the next one from Hall – skied it to mid-wicket. Now, Wes Hall was soaked with sweat. He was bowling like a hurricane and his shirt was flapping all over the place. I remember the umpires kept having to stop him and tell him to tuck his shirt in, because this billowing sail, this spinnaker, was obscuring everybody's view. The umpire couldn't see. Anyway, Wally Grout skied this to Rohan Kanhai at mid-wicket and Kanhai had all day and all night to get underneath this, except that Hall, who was doing all his own fielding, changed course and I swear he was doing fifty miles an hour. He galloped across and he barrelled into Kanhai, knocked him flying and it went to ground. They got a single. Three were needed off three balls. The four thousand people who saw this are the members of the most exclusive and boring club in the world.

BRIAN I've never heard it in such detail.

MICHAEL So Meckiff let fly at the next ball from Wes Hall and he hooked him far out to deep mid-wicket, on the far mid-wicket fence and again you could hardly see in this terrific sunset.

BRIAN A four would have won the match.

MICHAEL Of course. And they rushed off. They took the first two. Wally Grout turned for the third and Conrad Hunte – he was a beautiful player, Hunte – he threw. It must have been the throw of a lifetime. He was travelling round the boundary, right on the boundary line. He scooped it up and he threw it over the top of the stumps and Grout was flying for these last few yards. He hurled himself along the ground. He skidded on his stomach – out by half a foot, something like that. He got up covered in red dust and people were hysterical by this time. Kline came in and he hit the first one to forward short leg and Joe Solomon threw Meckiff out from side on. And so there was this enormous confusion, you see, with people running around. I think the official attendance that day was four thousand and I shall never forget, like Colonel

Maitland at Waterloo – you must know this, Johnno, as a guardsman – 'Stand up, Guards!', that crowd stood up as one man and they came over that fence like a wall and they rushed the pavilion. Frankie Worrell came off and I remember him saying, 'Man, this is a game for cool fools.' And Bradman, who was below us, he had a newspaper in his hands and the thing was in tatters, it was twisted so much. Like a stage magician with a torn paper act.

BRIAN And the celebrations that night.

MICHAEL The West Indians sang calypsos all night. The crowds were out in the streets. I've never seen anything like it.

BRIAN Well, happy memories and how could you really have left that for a world of interviewing kings and prime ministers? Is it fun?

MICHAEL Well, yes it is, but it's a different kind of amusement.

BRIAN Do you get a few laughs?

MICHAEL I wouldn't say there are many laughs, no. I would say it's a fairly detached sort of amusement. It's not the generous, carefree, likeable world that you all happily reflect here.

LESLIE CROWTHER

SADLY ON 3 OCTOBER 1992 Leslie had a horrendous car accident. His Rolls Royce veered off a motorway into the embankment on the side of the road. It turned completely over, with Leslie still inside. Miraculously – thanks no doubt to the solid bodywork of the Rolls – he was able to get out and, still conscious, was even able to crack jokes with his rescuers. However, after being taken to hospital, he had a severe relapse and went into a coma which was to last for six weeks. He was transferred to Frenchay Hospital in Bristol where he underwent two operations on his brain. At first, when he came out of his coma, due to tracheotomy he was unable to speak, but could write things down. There are two delightful stories about this. His wife Jean opened a letter addressed to him from No. 10 Downing Street asking if he would agree to accept the award of a CBE. She whispered into his ear that he *must* sign his acceptance and it was the very first thing he wrote. On another occasion one of his daughters was exercising his brain by asking him to identify and point at various shapes – circles, squares etc. She felt he was not concentrating so reprimanded him gently and said, 'Come on, Dad, concentrate, and try harder.' He immediately reached for his pencil and paper and hastily scribbled just one word: 'Bollocks'. Recovery was under way! As I write Leslie is back home and making steady progress.

I suppose a lot of people think of Leslie as a presenter of *Crackerjack* and his famous 'come on down' in the quiz show *The Price is Right*. But of course he is far more than that. He is one of the top five stand-up comedians in the country, performing in cabaret, pantomime and especially as an after-dinner speaker. He has a fund of stories and jokes, usually topical, and is a great ad-libber with any interrupters.

Besides his work he is a tremendous worker for charity. In 1991 and 1992 he was President of the Lord's Taverners for whom he made nearly 350 appearances at various events, every one requiring a speech from him.

When he joined us in the box at Old Trafford in 1985 it was a wet day. So we had a rather longer session than usual during 'Rain Stopped Play', though he had to leave us in mid-afternoon to go back to Blackpool where he was appearing twice nightly in *The Price is Right*. I mentioned his quick wit as an ad-libber. You will find proof of this with his final remark of our conversation!

OLD TRAFFORD, 3 AUGUST 1985

BRIAN JOHNSTON I got you to sign something just now and you did it with your left hand. Are you a left-hander at cricket?

LESLIE CROWTHER I'm a left-handed bowler. Fred Trueman, who is godfather to our son, Nicholas, describes my bowling as left arm blankety blank over the wicket, which is very accurate. But I bat right-handed.

BRIAN So where did you start your cricket? When did you first become interested in it?

LESLIE I first became interested at the Scarborough Festival when I was in a show called the Fol-de-Rols, which was a concert party, as you know. The Australians were playing and Neil Harvey was over and so were Keith Miller and Ray Lindwall and all that lot.

BRIAN Sounds like '53.

LESLIE That's right, it was. I went along and I suddenly saw all these magical people in real life, as it were, and I became totally besotted and I've followed cricket ever since.

BRIAN Did you play at school?

LESLIE I did, but I was very bad. I wasn't any good at any kind of sports. I had a very strange illness called meningitis.

BRIAN You were lucky to get away with it.

LESLIE In the late forties I was very lucky to get away with it. They diagnosed it as scarlet fever and I was shoved in a scarlet fever ward, so I had to be cured of scarlet fever before they could start on the other.

BRIAN You wear glasses, so that would have affected your cricket – the fact that you're short-sighted.

LESLIE Oh, very short-sighted, yes, but nothing affects my cricket. It's always been bad.

BRIAN So when you started in 1953, which team did you take up as your favourite?

LESLIE England. I thought that was a good team to take up. I didn't bother with a county, just went straight for the country. Lately, of course, I've been following the fortunes of Somerset, because that's where we've moved and it seems a fairly good team with people like Richards and Garner and another chap called Botham.

BRIAN You're near sunny Bath, are you?

LESLIE Yes, about three miles. The Bath cricket festival, of course, is great, now they've sorted out that wicket.

BRIAN It's lovely, isn't it? So who were your heroes after 1953 in the English cricket scene?

LESLIE Oh, Peter May, Ted Dexter, Tom Graveney, Ken Barrington – the really elegant strokemakers. You were saying earlier that cricket and the theatre are very aligned and that there is something in common with the two professions and there is. The thing about cricket, although some people call it a slow game, it's a very very dramatic game and every player gets his entrance and his exit – very often sooner than he wants to – but it's a dramatic game and I love it.

BRIAN There is this affinity and it's partly because cricketers enjoy meeting people from the stage.

LESLIE That's right. When I was in a thing called *Let Sleeping Wives Lie* at the Garrick Theatre, there was a nervous tap on the dressing room door one evening and Johnny Gleeson was ushered in. And apparently, when he came to England to play in that marvellous series with that incredible bowling that nobody could fathom, he went to every single West End show and introduced himself shyly to everybody.

(J. W. Gleeson toured England in 1968 and 1972 and played in 29 Tests for Australia, bowling an enigmatic mix of off- and leg-breaks. Ed.)

BRIAN Back in Australia he was a farmer and used to have to go 120 miles each Saturday to play in his game and he didn't see any theatre. I remember talking to him about it and he literally went to everything when he came here.

LESLIE   He absolutely adored it and so we got to know him very well. There was a wonderful moment in *Let Sleeping Wives Lie* with Brian Rix, who, as you know, is potty about the game, Leo Franklyn – wonderful chap, mad about cricket – and myself and Bill Treacher and there was a Test in the West Indies when all England had to do was draw the last match to win the series.

BRIAN   That was Colin Cowdrey's tour in 1968. Jeff Jones came in to bat for the last over and held out.

LESLIE   That's right. We. had a dresser who was a wonderful guy – gay as a brush – and we got him with a blackboard and chalk at the side of the stage, chalking up the score. The audience must have been absolutely baffled.

BRIAN   That was one of the best matches I've seen. At one time there was no chance of Jeff Jones ever having to bat and the night before he had a very good night out and he wasn't quite prepared for it. It didn't matter, because he didn't hit the ball with the bat. Every single ball hit him on the pad. There were six appeals for LBW. He thrust his leg out and it was the most marvellous last over. It won the series and we had great celebrations in the English Pub in Trinidad that night. Did you ever play for the Stage?

LESLIE   No. I am an old stager. I play for the Lord's Taverners. I've got a photograph of the late and great Kenny Barrington, saying, 'Thanks for helping with my benefit and for taking the greatest catch off my bowling I've ever seen.'

BRIAN   That's rather nice. Wasn't he lovely, though, Ken?

In your career, which do you prefer? Standing up in front of the curtains? Is that your favourite?

LESLIE Anything is my favourite, I don't really mind – in a farce or a play or after-dinner speaking, a variety act, cabaret, pantomime – that's great, because you've got the lot there. Everyone thinks pantomime's easy and it's the most difficult convention.

BRIAN Can I reveal, for the first time in public, that last week I was rung up and offered the part in pantomime of Alderman Fitzwarren this winter.

LESLIE You're joking! Oh!

BRIAN And I think it was going to be at a very nice theatre. I said I'd rather be Baron Hardup, but he said, 'No, you've got to be Alderman Fitzwarren,' and unfortunately this January I've already mapped something out. It's a thing I've been dying to do all my life.

LESLIE You'll have to wear tights, you know, if you're Alderman Fitzwarren.

BRIAN What Fits Warren fits me. But pantomime is hard work, isn't it? You've got to do those twice-daily things.

LESLIE Oh, yes. You clock in at two and clock out at half past ten at night.

BRIAN Have you ever managed to bring cricket into your act?

LESLIE I've got masses of cricket stories. The first time I met Fred, in fact, I was doing a cricket ballet. There was a ballet-dancing wrestler called Ricky Starr, so I did this burlesque. If you can have a ballet-dancing wrestler, why not a ballet-dancing cricketer? I did this thing from *Swan Lake* and ponced about in tights and a box and pads. Sheila Burnett was behind the wicket as the keeper. This was in the Fol-de-Rols.

BRIAN Where are you from originally?

LESLIE In fact I'm a Nottinghamshire man, born in West Bridgford, or bread-and-lard island, as it's called.

BRIAN Not so far from Parr's Tree, then.

LESLIE No, in fact Parr's Tree fell down when I was staying at the Bridgford Hotel, which is now council offices. I was in pantomime and there was this horrendous storm. Down went Parr's Tree and I went down in my pyjamas and dressing gown, got this hacksaw from the night porter and a torch and I climbed over into Trent Bridge. And I still have a branch of Parr's Tree.

BRIAN They turned the rest of it into cricket bats, which they sold at enormous profit, but yours is the genuine branch.

LESLIE There is a poem in the Long Room – or square room, really – at Trent Bridge. It was written in 1938 to mark the centenary of cricket at Trent Bridge and it goes like this:

So small a space, so lost this slip of earth,
When we spread out the map that spans the shire
Only an oasis in a city's dearth,
A spark still left in long extinguished fire.
But men have gathered here and given their praise
To many a battle, many a Notts-shire team,
Stored up great sunlit deeds, then, going their ways
Have seen Trent Bridge for ever more in dream.
They helped to build a game, those cricketers,
The Gunns and Shrewsbury, Daft and Flowers,
Batting and bowling down the golden hours
On this hallowed turf. Surely today
Their ghosts come back where once they loved to play.
No cricket ground had nobler visitors.

BRIAN That is super. Now, who wrote it?

LESLIE   Thomas Moult.

BRIAN   I must tell you, he wasn't reading that. Are you good at memorising lines?

LESLIE   Well, yes, because I started out as a straight actor – a lot of people think I still am!

BRIAN   You've managed to snatch an afternoon today, but how often can you get away to watch cricket?

LESLIE   My agent has arranged it very badly this year, because we started round about the time of the first Test and we finish working long after the sixth Test is over.

BRIAN   You had a match at Blackpool, though.

LESLIE   Oh yes. And what is amazing about coming up here to work is that if you're living down south you do tend to forget, unless you're reminded of it, and there's no reason why you should be, because it's not publicised in the papers, the fact that the Lancashire and Northern and Bradford Leagues – all these leagues – are unbelievably strong, play the most wonderful cricket and all have as a pro. a Test cricketer who just doesn't happen to be playing Test cricket for his country at the moment. There was this cricket festival at Blackpool. It was Geoff Boycott's World XI and an International XI and I just went along and, sure enough, there were twenty-two players plus about eight reserves all of whom were Test cricketers from Sri Lanka, Pakistan, India, Australia – David Hookes was playing – it really was quite remarkable. I was asked to adjudicate the man of the match on the Sunday and there was no doubt about it that it was a guy called Sivaramakrishnan. He was turning the ball square.

BRIAN   When the Indians come over next year, will you come and coach us in how to say that, because you've got it rather well. I'll call him 'Shivers'.

LESLIE   It'll be 'shivers' anyway.

BRIAN   You're wearing the MCC tie.

LESLIE   The old ham and egg. It took me nine years of impatient waiting to get it and I've worn it ever since. I bought it seven weeks ago and I've worn it as a pyjama cord – I just love it.

BRIAN   At one time it was not done to wear that tie until the great Lord Cobham became President of MCC in the mid-fifties and he said, 'What is the point of having a club tie if nobody wears it?' And he began to wear it and now everybody does. I think it's very good.

LESLIE   I think it's a great honour to be a member of that particular club and to wear the tie. I'm not saying that sartorially it is the greatest choice of colours, but it's a smashing tie to wear.

BRIAN   A great honour to be in the club.

LESLIE   You're in the club, are you? You'll make Fleet Street!

PROFESSOR SIR
BERNARD LOVELL

IN THE MID-1980s I visited Jodrell Bank when doing a *Down Your Way* in Cheshire. I was amazed at the gigantic size of the revolving bowl of the telescope. It was not until I had finished my interview with Sir Bernard about Jodrell Bank that, over a cup of tea, I discovered his great interest in cricket. He had not only been a good cricketer but he had also carried out a number of highly technical experiments to try to help umpires in making their decisions. He emphasised that he was only trying to *help* them, not to usurp their powers. They are, and probably always will be, the final arbiters on all decisions.

None of his aids have so far been used in this country, partly due to the large expense involved. We now have a referee at all Tests and overseas there has been a third umpire watching the television replays, who can be called on if either umpire is in doubt about a run-out or a stumping. The difference between this and Sir Bernard's successful experiments, is that his method involves direct, and more or less instantaneous contact with the umpires. With the third umpire watching a monitor, decisions have taken up to 30 seconds as he watches several replays. Personally, so long as TV and the big screens on the grounds show replays, I think the umpires should be given Sir Bernard's aid to decide at least on run-outs and possibly stumpings. I hope you will find our conversation as fascinating as I did.

OLD TRAFFORD, 6 JUNE 1987

SIR BERNARD LOVELL   I was given permission to take equipment to Jodrell Bank in 1945. It was very remote then and we were allowed to stay for a few weeks with these trailers. That was in December 1945 and we're still there. We started building the big steerable telescope in 1951/52. Before that I'd been building bigger and bigger aerials on the ground to try and do certain things and then the desire to make one of these devices completely steerable arose and that led to what you now see in the Cheshire Plain. We began operating in 1957 and this year we shall celebrate the thirtieth anniversary of its first use, which is really quite remarkable, because no one believed that it would be any good. In fact I had the greatest diffi-culty in persuading people either that it would last as an engineering structure for fifteen years, or that it would be useful scientifically, and now it's busier and more in demand than it ever has been.

BRIAN JOHNSTON   Now, don't be modest about it, is it one of the great telescopes of the world?

SIR BERNARD   I think it is. It's still one of the largest

and I think remarkable as a scientific instrument because of its longevity. It cost us £600,000 to build and you may remember I got into a lot of trouble because of overspending. Now you couldn't possibly build it for less than £20 million. So it's one of the great investments of science.

BRIAN What's the greatest achievement you've seen in your time there. What gave you the most pleasure?

SIR BERNARD I think the answer must be, oddly enough, the detection of the carrier rocket of the first Sputnik in 1957 for the simple reason that it was the only instrument in the world that could do this by radar and it was the episode that got me out of trouble.

BRIAN Because it justified the expense.

SIR BERNARD Well, some solution to these problems then had to be found, because this was the first intercontinental ballistic missile. But, on the astronomical side, the fascinating thing is that if you go round the place today, you'll find the students and the staff working on maybe ten different projects and the things they're working on were entirely unknown when we built the instrument in the 1950s. They've been the result of recent advances. So I think the great advantage of the instrument is that it has been so adaptable both to modern techniques and to the new discoveries which have subsequently been made and today it is a front-line instrument.

BRIAN It is a very fascinating thing to see. It revolves completely round, does it?

SIR BERNARD That's right – about 3½ thousand tons, revolving with great precision on the railway track, just taking out the motion of the Earth. And of course the bowl, which is about 1½ thousand tons or thereabouts, is rotated on those columns which are as high as Nelson's Column.

BRIAN What achievement that hasn't been achieved would you like to do?

SIR BERNARD Well, I'd like to put the telescope into space. There's no problem in principle, but we're talking about billions of dollars. One of the next major developments in the subject with which I'm concerned is to put a large radio telescope, like the one at Jodrell, in orbit round the Earth and link it to the Jodrell telescope and to others round the Earth. This would give you the equivalent for some of these experiments of measuring the sizes of these remote objects in the universe of a telescope which had an aperture, instead of the 250 feet of our Jodrell telescope, of 10,000 miles.

(Although the United States have subsequently put the Hubble telescope into space, it is an optical, rather than a radio telescope. There are hopes that a combined American/Russian project may put a radio telescope into orbit by the end of the century and there are Jodrell Bank scientists involved in that project. Ed.)

BRIAN So that's played a big part in your life. Now let's come to cricket. You were educated down in Bristol, so did you play cricket as a boy down there?

SIR BERNARD Oh, very much so. I spent – I was going to say 'wasted'. . . . But I nearly failed all my exams because of my enthusiasm for cricket.

BRIAN We're not modest on this programme; how good were you as a boy?

SIR BERNARD Well, I played for the university. I played as a bowler, but I made a few runs. I then got more interested in work, but I did play during the critical period of my first degree in Bristol. I played for three different teams, including the university. Nowadays, if one of my students told me he was doing that, I would have no time for him.

BRIAN   And did you see some Gloucestershire cricket in those days?

SIR BERNARD   Oh, very much so, yes.

BRIAN   Who particularly?

SIR BERNARD   Hammond. I think I must have seen Walter Hammond play more or less his first match for Gloucestershire. One of my earliest memories is not of Gloucestershire but of seeing Hobbs make his hundredth hundred. That was in Bath, because the boundary between Gloucestershire and Somerset was close to my home. But I was a fanatical Gloucestershire supporter and indeed remained so until I became closely involved here at Old Trafford. Nevertheless, Somerset was also a great interest and then they had these tremendous hitters, Earle and Lyon.

BRIAN   G. F. Earle – Guy Earle.

SIR BERNARD   His bat looked like a toy. I thought of him yesterday, watching Botham. He was much bigger than Botham. But Hobbs – I think that is my earliest memory. I must have been a boy of about ten.

(Sir Jack Hobbs made that hundredth hundred at Bath in 1923. At the time only W. G. Grace and Tom Hayward had ever reached that landmark. Ed.)

BRIAN   He was brought out a glass of champagne or ginger ale.

SIR BERNARD   Something like that – by Percy Fender – and I believe given a cheque for 100 guineas. But Hammond was really the person that was so marvellous to those of us who were young.

BRIAN   I was lucky enough to see him make his 240 at Lord's against Australia in 1938 and I don't think the modern generation really appreciate how tremendous he was.

SIR BERNARD   No, the cricket you see here is stodgy

compared with that. His elegance was quite amazing. I remember one day Gloucestershire were playing Kent and I think either Freeman or Woolley got him out before he had scored and I was quite miserable. I almost went home for the rest of the day.

BRIAN When you came up here, then, what about Lancashire cricket?

SIR BERNARD Well, I came to Manchester and joined the university in 1936 and I discovered that the university was quite close to this ground and I used to get a bus down to the entrance. Where we are now, on top of this executive suite, is more or less on the site of the old galvanised shed. One used to pay sixpence to get in there. I saw quite a lot of cricket.

BRIAN Any particular Lancashire player you'd picked out?

SIR BERNARD Well, Cyril Washbrook, I remember. I've talked to him today and he's full of praise for some of the young people we might get in a few years' time. I remember him not only as a batsman, but also his fielding at cover point, which was quite spectacular.

BRIAN And you have some sort of office here?

SIR BERNARD Well, I was very lucky to be made one of their vice-presidents about five or six years ago. So that's a very nice arrangement.

BRIAN Now, you've taken tremendous interest in the various technicalities of cricket and are trying to help the umpires. We can start with an easy one, because we can see it. There is your light meter, which looks like the top half of a clock. There are two of those on the Wilson Stand. How do they work?

SIR BERNARD We have a photosensitive element, which is transformed by some rather simple electronics into a small motor which drives that clock. The photosensitive element is more or less focused on the region of the sight screen and there you see what the light is. It doesn't pretend to be absolute, but it's relatively accurate.

BRIAN When it's up at twelve o'clock, is that perfect light?

SIR BERNARD No, the perfect light is when it's hard over at a quarter past. These are really crude experimental models. We've got a manufacturing design, but at the moment the TCCB are sitting on that, deciding what to do about it.

BRIAN People always say that you can't have a common thing like that, because the light on each cricket ground is different.

SIR BERNARD Well, of course they're different. But then you adjust this to suit the particular ground and from experience. You can't be absolute, because the umpire has to decide whether he offers the light to the batsman. It depends on the speed of the ball and all that sort of thing. It gives them a guide. You see, in the beginning, I thought it would be interesting to make a permanent recording of the light and about six years ago I had a light meter over the pavilion with a recording device and the intensity of the light came out on a paper chart. This was fascinating, because the conclusion one came to very quickly was that the umpires were rather consistent in the time at which they offered the light to the batsmen, but they were extremely inconsistent as to when they came back again. Very often the light would recover to what it was when they went off and another ten or fifteen minutes would elapse before they came back again. Now you have the recording here continuously. These are very sensitive. A cloud comes over and you will see them . . . in fact, at the moment the light is better at the Warwick Road end than it is at this end. But I doubt if a batsman would notice that. These models won't last for ever, because they're very experimental; the sort of thing that scientists do with some bits and pieces. Every time I come here I look with some anxiety to see if they're still working. They're all right at the moment. They are the result of a sort of evolution. In the beginning we had a radio link which became interfered with, I think, by BBC television transmissions and things like that. But now we've overcome that and they're very reliable.

BRIAN And I think it's terribly good for the public. They can at least see just what is being done to them.

(The light meters continued to function efficiently at least until the end of the 1992 season when the old Wilson Stand was demolished to make way for a new one. They are being rebuilt on the Red Rose and Executive stands, so that they are in line with the pitch. Ed.)

SIR BERNARD I started the light meters off, but then I was asked by the TCCB to investigate the possibility of electronic aids for umpires other than light meters.

BRIAN When I came to see you in your office at Jodrell Bank, you'd just had a meeting with two umpires and you asked them a simple question. How could you best help them?

SIR BERNARD David Constant and Don Oslear. They were very nice and they said that the things that worried them were, on the LBW law, whether the ball really would have hit the wicket if the batsman hadn't been in the way.

BRIAN Which they can't tell.

SIR BERNARD They said, 'Look, we can tell you whether the ball has pitched in the right place or whether it's going to go over the top of the wicket, if you can give us some indication if it would have hit the wicket. Well, this was a fascinating problem – a very difficult one. The TCCB financed a feasibility study with a firm we knew in the south-east of London and this study was presented to the Board last summer and I heard recently that they decided to do nothing about it. It is rather expensive.

BRIAN What does it involve? Is it cameras?

SIR BERNARD You need very sensitive cameras of the type you use on your television and the computational problem is quite difficult.

BRIAN And at each end of the ground you'd have to have two?

SIR BERNARD You'd have to have four cameras to do this and the communication with the umpire would be quite simple. One would show lights on a board, for example.

BRIAN And would that be instant?

SIR BERNARD Absolutely instant.

BRIAN The ball hits the pad; there's a shout of 'How's that?' How long would it be before he could say?

SIR BERNARD This is one of the problems, that the computation would have to be done at very high speed. You can't keep the umpires waiting. But this problem is solved and each installation would cost somewhere between a hundred and two hundred thousand pounds. Incidentally, doing this, one becomes aware of the immense power and accuracy of the human eye. People say that computers can do everything. The umpires are jolly good. You have to do a very expensive design of equipment to give an answer equivalent to what the eye can do.

The other problem that interested the umpires was caught behind. I asked some of the Test Match cricketers and some of them were most unhappy that they had been given out erroneously on many occasions because they hadn't touched the ball. We have also solved that. This means inserting something in the bat and a few weeks ago here at Old Trafford I tested what I thought was going to be the final development model. I tried it in the nets and the first ball the whole thing more or less disintegrated. It's a very sensitive device.

BRIAN Inside the handle of the bat would it be?

SIR BERNARD That's right. And from there you transmit a signal to the umpire. He has an earphone.

BRIAN That does sound good. Are you going to do it again?

SIR BERNARD Oh yes. The TCCB are still interested and the problem is mine and that of the firm who are doing this. We have to produce this final model so that it will withstand the impact of the bat on the ball.

BRIAN What do the bat manufacturers say?

SIR BERNARD Well, we haven't asked them, but it's a very small device – something about as big as your little finger. The miniaturisation of modern electronics is quite astonishing.

BRIAN What about the other controversial one, which shows up on these big screens they have in Australia – the run-outs. They can be very difficult to judge with the human eye.

SIR BERNARD Well, that's very easy. The device which would do the LBW decision could easily do that as well. That would be an easier problem than the LBW decision. This would be an electronic decision from the video responses of the cameras as to where the bat and the crease are in relation to the ball hitting the stumps. But you're quite right, this is another thing that worried the umpires. A lot of things are easy if you're prepared to spend money.

(A straightforward experiment with a third umpire watching video playbacks of run-outs and stumpings was introduced for the South Africa v. India series of 1992/93. Light meters which show the worsening light on a series of illuminated lamps, rather than Sir Bernard's system, have been introduced on most first-class grounds in England, although this system was tried at Old Trafford several years ago and discarded in favour of the more accurate clock-type meter which will continue to operate there. The LBW and caught-behind devices have been shelved because of expense. Ed.)

SIR BERNARD   I think if these devices ever went into use, there would be many more decisions against the batsman, because the umpires always give him the benefit of the doubt.

BRIAN   Which is right.

SIR BERNARD   Which is right, but I think the batsmen would probably be rather annoyed, because they would be given out legitimately but they might not think so. But I do think it would save a lot of these irritating uncertainties. Of course the umpire's decision is always final. There never has been any suggestion of taking the decision away from the umpire. It's a matter of giving him some assistance in the things he really needs.

PETER SCUDAMORE

FOR SOME reason many jockeys seem to be mad about cricket, especially the jumpers, as opposed to the flat. Their season gives them a short break during the summer so that they are able to play or watch cricket and run a very useful jockeys' team, which plays for charity. At Headingley in 1989 I was able to say with *some* truth, 'We are very lucky to have a leg-spinner in the box with us today. He also happens to be quite a useful National Hunt jockey.' In fact Peter, in the season just finished, had ridden 221 winners, breaking the previous record by 72.

We commentators often think that we are busy, but what about this? Peter had flown in from New York that very Saturday morning having ridden at Belmont on Friday. He had only agreed to go to America, provided they guaranteed he would be able to get to Headingley by Saturday lunchtime. After watching the afternoon's play he was due to go down to Cheltenham to ride in two exhibition races against Willie Shoemaker the next day. Although he had a pale complexion, he looked pretty well on it all, and his sparse wiry figure put all of ours in the box to shame.

HEADINGLEY, 10 JUNE 1989

PETER SCUDAMORE I wouldn't have missed this for the world. My father's a great cricketing man and that's influenced me. We used to go and watch Worcester play when I was a child and a lot of cricketers are friendly with the National Hunt jockeys. I think it's because we're on holiday when they're playing and they're on holiday when we're out riding, so they come racing, we go cricketing and so you get to know some of the players.

BRIAN JOHNSTON So how much cricket have you managed to get this summer?

PETER I've played twice this summer. I've been lucky enough to play for the Starlight XI, raising money for terminally ill children. It's the brainchild of Eric Clapton.

BRIAN What sort of chaps do you have playing with you?

PETER Well, the last couple of times I've been out I've been bowled by Ian Bishop, the West Indies fast bowler – one of his leg-spinners, but it came very quickly to me at any rate (that's my story) – and Derek Underwood's first ball of the season absolutely clean` bowled me.

BRIAN You didn't drive it through the covers.

PETER Well, I went to.

BRIAN Where do you bat normally?

PETER Anywhere I can, basically.

BRIAN And you like a bowl; do you give it a bit of a tweak?

PETER I do, yes. Colin Cowdrey called them tweakers. I think they're definite leg-spinners.

BRIAN And how much do you manage to watch. Do you support Worcestershire still?

PETER Yes, I follow Worcestershire very closely. But I get to know a lot of the county cricketers. I know Andy Stovold very well and some of the Gloucestershire boys, so I follow them and I know the Warwickshire boys – Andy Lloyd's a great racing man.

BRIAN Of course, you live in Gloucestershire.

PETER Yes, I've got the three counties all round me, very close.

BRIAN Do you have any particular heroes?

PETER The Scudamore family are great Botham fans. We follow Botham avidly. The editor of the *Sporting Life*, Monty Court, rings up and says, 'Botham should be dropped from the England team,' and we argue the other way for hours on end.

BRIAN Your father, Michael Scudamore, rode a Grand National winner.

PETER He won the National and the Gold Cup. He was second in the championship one year to Fred Winter, so I had a bit to follow.

BRIAN But, remarkably, I can't find that you've ridden the winner of the Grand National or the Gold Cup.

PETER No, that's all to do yet.

(And it was still all to do at the start of the 1992/3 season. Ed.)

BRIAN Did you ever think that 221 winners in the season was going to be possible? I think Jonjo O'Neill's 149 was the previous highest.

PETER I was obviously lucky I was riding for two top stables – Charlie Brooks and Martin Pipe. Martin had two hundred winners himself, which is a record. The season set off very well. It's just like making your runs at cricket, you like to get your first winner, it's like getting your first run – and then hit a few sixes – get a few trebles and four timers – and you can say to yourself, 'If you keep up this average, you're going to ride two hundred winners.' But you don't actually believe it. Then it starts to materialise in mid-winter and people start saying, 'You'll ride two hundred winners.' You tend to get over the bigger races and then, come April time, concentrate on the two hundred.

BRIAN You're making it sound very easy, but that's ten months of hard work – or more. How much time do you have off between the end of one season and the start of another?

PETER We get most of June and most of July off – about ten weeks. But it's like being a cricketer or in the theatre, it's wonderful to get paid for doing something you enjoy.

BRIAN We rather feel that up here, but we don't like to tell our bosses that. You're taller than I expected. How tall are you?

PETER I'm about five foot eight, which is about the right size, as long as I don't eat too much.

BRIAN Well, what's your average weight?

PETER I ride at ten stone, which is the minimum weight that we have to ride at. So I have to get my bodyweight down to about nine stone nine pounds – that's with the saddle and all the equipment.

BRIAN Well, tell us the ghastly routine that you have to get to that. It absolutely terrifies me. Give us a daily diet.

PETER   I wouldn't eat breakfast, because you're either travelling or riding out at that time of the day. If I've got a light weight, I wouldn't eat lunch, so I wouldn't eat till the evening. People say, 'Oh, you're silly not eating till the evening,' but it's my immediate weight loss that I'm worried about.

BRIAN   How hungry are you getting by then? I should be absolutely ravenous.

PETER   By the evening you're getting hungry, but it's the matter of doing things. I couldn't diet without doing something.

BRIAN   Well, Scuders, it's tremendous discipline, undoubtedly. And when you do have your evening meal, is it a good tuck-in? Yorkshire pud and roast beef?

PETER   No. You concentrate, obviously, on not too many chips or white bread. I tend to eat spinach. I find it a great help to me.

BRIAN   Old Popeye found it a good idea.

PETER   He did. I try to eat a lot of fish and lean meat.

BRIAN   It doesn't sound very attractive to me, but now you've got time off, so are you getting a better diet?

PETER   Well, you get used to it and whatever I put on I've got to get off, so I don't like to put too much weight on during the summer. It's not too bad. It's just one of the disciplines that we have and it's just there in the back of your mind all the time. I just don't over-indulge.

BRIAN   Can you give us a typical day in the winter months when you're riding out and racing?

PETER   One of the great things about it is that you don't have a typical day. It's like asking Goochie what his typical day is. What your typical day would like to be is getting up late and going to Cheltenham to ride three winners.

BRIAN It doesn't happen. You get up early to ride out somewhere.

PETER Two or three times a week I'm riding out at Charlie Brooks' or Martin Pipe's. I go and school and it usually means setting off fairly early in the morning – six o'clock-ish. Then I school up until probably breakfast time, usually arriving in the yard at about half past seven. Then I go and ride them over some jumps – usually teaching the young horses.

BRIAN You're teaching them. That's part of the thing, is it?

PETER Yes. The mutual benefit is so that I can trust the horse, I know what he's going to do and he can get used to me a little bit.

BRIAN I asked you before we came on the air what happened in New York and whether you'd ridden the horse before and you said you hadn't. How important is it to know the horse before you ride it?

PETER I got to New York yesterday and I found out all that I could about the horse. It is difficult. The horse I was riding yesterday was held up for a late run. Well, you don't know what your opposition are going to do, so you're guessing a little bit.

BRIAN Do you let it snuffle you? Do you blow up its nose?

PETER Doing a Barbara Woodhouse?

BRIAN Have you ever tried that with a horse?

PETER I always go up and give him a pat. I think if they trust you to start with you're better off. Give them a pat, try and make friends and say, 'Please – let's you and I get round safely here.'

BRIAN Well, you don't always get round safely.

51

You've had quite a lot of body damage. What sort of things have you got which haven't been hurt? You mustn't mention them all.

PETER I've been hurt a few times. But coming back last night on the plane they showed the Centenary Test in Australia when Randall made 174 and they showed Lillee bowling and I think I would definitely rather do what I do than face Lillee or Holding or one of those bowlers.

BRIAN That was a marvellous Test, where Randall rather baited Lillee, didn't he?

PETER It was very funny. The bouncers were coming in and he was falling over backwards and pushing his hat onto the back of his head. You forget actually what a great batsman he was.

BRIAN I emulated something. You remember in 1981/82 you were leading the championship and you fell off and broke your arm and John Francombe drew level with your number of winners a few weeks later and threw away his saddle and said, 'I'm not riding again.'

PETER Yes, that's right.

BRIAN I did that when I was doing *Down Your Way*. I gave it up at the same total as Franklin Engelman. I copied what John Francombe did, because old Jingle up there couldn't do anything about it and you weren't able to do anything in hospital.

PETER It was a marvellous sporting gesture by John and that's what sport's about, isn't it?

BRIAN Well, it is. In cricket on the field it's a bit rough sometimes and off the field it's friendly. What about jockeys? It's a very physical game, isn't it?

PETER It's the same. Early on in a race people try to help each other, but you come to a certain point in the race where it's really business and you don't expect help.

BRIAN But out in the country if you're going along in the lead with someone, do you have a chat with them?

PETER Yes. It's not quite cantering along in the English country sunshine, but you'll help one another, give a little bit of room and manoeuvre not to upset one another. But at a certain point of a race then there's no mercy and if you get done or get hurt, well, that's what you accept before you go out.

BRIAN What's the best horse you've ever ridden?

PETER Probably Celtic Shot, because I won the Champion Hurdle on him and that's the best hurdling race and the best championship race I've won, but I've been lucky to ride some very good horses.

BRIAN The difference between hurdling and the big fences – which do you prefer?

PETER I don't mind as long as I ride a winner over each. It's a great thrill to ride a good steeplechaser. I've ridden Burrough Hill Lad and Corbière – as good jumpers as I've ever sat on.

BRIAN How old were you when you first learnt to ride? Were you taught in an orthodox way? Did you have fairly long stirrups as a boy?

PETER Yes, I learnt the orthodox way. I never really had riding lessons. My father was always the sort of tutor in the background, but never actually gave me a lesson. I just picked it up. As long as I can remember I've ridden and played cricket. One's gone one way and one's gone downhill.

BRIAN You've just said you wouldn't have liked to have played Lillee, but would you have preferred the life of a professional cricketer?

PETER If I could dream about doing anything else, I would be a fast bowler.

BRIAN You've got slight aggression, haven't you? You've got to have to be successful.

PETER It's always appealed to me, the Lillee type, Holding type.

BRIAN What has happened to you in the Grand National? How come you haven't won it?

PETER I always blame the horse. The trainer always blames me.

BRIAN Do you do the Fred Winter thing of staying on the inside?

PETER I've done it all ways. The closest I got was third on Corbière and then I looked like winning one year on a horse called Strands of Gold and I fell at Bechers. I was going on the inside then and everyone said that it was because I was going on the inside that I fell.

BRIAN So next year you went on the outside.

PETER And got beaten. It's one of the goals. I would love to do it.

BRIAN How different is it riding in the Grand National from riding in an ordinary steeplechase at Haydock Park or somewhere like that?

PETER You go slightly slower and horses tend to look at the fences a little bit more, because they're big and they're different and most times horses jump better for it. People say, 'Oh, the Grand National must be frightening,' but sometimes you can have a better ride round there than you can normally.

The man who valets me in the weighing-room – when we're in the weighing-room we have valets who clean all our tack and make sure we go out on time and in the right colours – is John Buckingham. He won the National on Foinavon. He's quite a good cricketer and tells some of the best cricketing stories that I know.

BRIAN Tell us one if you can remember.

PETER The Jockeys' XI were playing in Derbyshire against a local league side, which included Alan Ward, who had broken down and was having a bit of a comeback. And the local side batted first and made 250 or so and then the jockeys went in to bat and Alan Ward bowled early and knocked about three down very cheaply. So they gave the jockeys a bit of a chance. It began to look as if they were going to get the runs. They were about six wickets down and David Nicholson and John Buckingham were nine and ten, sitting there, waiting to go in. Then Alan Ward comes back on, bowling very fast and knocks the next one out. David Nicholson, who's always captain and a very, very keen cricketer, turns to John Buckingham and says, 'Come on, you're in.' John says, 'Hang on, I'm number ten. You're number nine.' 'I'm captain,' he says. 'You're number nine.' In he goes and Alan Ward starts walking back and, as he turns, John walks away. 'Hold on,' he says, 'I don't go that far on my holidays.' I think he lost his sense of humour with that, Alan Ward. He came roaring in and bowled one at John who jumped out of the way. It hit him on his bottom and bounced out for four runs. He was very pleased. And the other great story he tells is when he was umpiring and David Nicholson was bowling. John had broken his leg. David Nicholson comes roaring in and hits this player on the pad and appeals to John and John says, 'Not out.' John, because of his broken leg, is sitting on a shooting stick and David walked back past him, kicked the shooting stick from beneath him and said, 'Rubbish.'

JOHN KETTLEY

THE WEATHER plays a vital part in cricket. Ask Dickie Bird. He knows! So we thought that it was about time that we had someone who could forecast for us whether rain would stop play. We were lucky to find that the youngest of the weather forecasters was also a very keen cricketer, and needless to say it was raining when he joined us in the box at Old Trafford. I think they do a super job with their live, off the cuff, commentaries on local showers, high winds and depressions. I have never heard them make a gaffe as we (occasionally!) do at cricket. But in the days when they used magnetic devices to put letters or logos on the weather board one of them did slip up once. He was sticking letters all over the board showing where there would be RAIN, WIND, SHOWERS or FOG. As he tried to put FOG on to the board, the 'F' came unstuck and fell to the ground, leaving 'OG' over south-east England. He finished up with: 'So the outlook for tomorrow is still unsettled, with some strong winds – and I'm sorry about that "F" in FOG!'

OLD TRAFFORD, 29 JULY 1989

BRIAN JOHNSTON   Well, if you presented this weather, you know what you can do with it. You are from Yorkshire.

JOHN KETTLEY   Born in Halifax.

BRIAN   Are you a committed Yorkshireman?

JOHN   There's no choice – I am a Yorkshireman. I never lived in Halifax, I was just born in hospital there and lived in Todmorden. Many people will know that Todmorden is just about twenty miles from here. It's the border town. Administratively, of course, it's under Lancashire, in some respects, but not others. We're the only Yorkshire team in the Lancashire League. We've always been known as the border team, but there's no doubt about it, anybody who lives there is really a Yorkshireman.

BRIAN   So did you learn your cricket there?

JOHN   I'm still learning my cricket, Brian. It's very difficult to put it together sometimes, but yes. I did start as a very young boy. In fact I was taken round in my pram by my dad when I was a baby – all round the ground at Todmorden.

BRIAN   What sort of cricketer are you? What's your forte?

JOHN   I laughingly call myself an all-rounder, which means to say that if I fail with the bat, I've still got a second chance. So I do a bit of both – a bit of batting and a bit of bowling.

BRIAN You've brought these Lancashire League handbooks along with you. One's for '61 and one's for '56.

JOHN Well, the '56 one you'll see me appearing in – I was only four at the time, but I was taken round by my dad and saw all these really good cricketers. Everton Weekes was playing at Bacup at that time. But 'Lancashire Cricket League', priced ninepence in 1961, is the first one I really remember. I was doing a lot of scoring in those days.

BRIAN Some wonderful pictures of some young people who played in the league there – Hughie Tayfield, Everton Weekes, Harry Halliday.

JOHN I played in the league – mainly second and third team, it must be said. I only ever played in the first team once. It's the story of my life, really. I was selected for the first team in about 1969 or 1970. Peter Marner was the pro., who used to play here and went to Leicestershire.

BRIAN Hit the ball well.

JOHN Certainly did. But that game I was selected for it rained all day long. The game was called off about four o'clock. My card playing improved.

BRIAN It counted as being in the first team, anyhow.

JOHN Oh, I think it did, but nobody remembers, of course.

BRIAN But you still play cricket in charity matches. You're in much demand. Have you got a regular team?

JOHN I play for a village called Ardeley, which is very near Stevenage.

BRIAN My sister married the son of the people who used to live at Ardeleybury. It wasn't a great cricket ground. I played cricket there against the village.

JOHN We've actually lost our ground, now. We

were kicked off it last season. We now use a recreation ground at the next village called Walkern. It's actually a football ground in the winter. Variable bounce is the most accurate way of describing our pitch.

BRIAN How often are you doing the weather?

JOHN We have three shifts. One morning shift, broadcasting domestically and then we have the afternoon shifts, one into Europe and one into BBC1 and BBC2. The broadcast for Europe many people here wouldn't ever have seen, because we're broadcasting to Superchannel on the satellite and we're also broadcasting to the forces in Germany.

BRIAN How long does the preparation take?

JOHN We've got a poky little office and we have a camera in there. We put the whole lot together and we do our own graphics. We sit at the console all day long, that's why we're all blind.

BRIAN Do you make all the marks on the maps?

JOHN Yes, we do everything. We couldn't possibly go in there cold one morning at seven o'clock and do a broadcast at ten past, because we have to get all this information together and put it into graphical form.

BRIAN I watch your hand with fascination because you have a little clicker.

JOHN That's right. We change the picture when we want to. That's the wonderful thing about it – we control our own destiny.

BRIAN So how long did it take you to learn about the weather? Is there a weather school?

JOHN We have a college at Shinfield Park near Reading. We are employed by the Met. Office, of course, and we go down there for refresher courses. I must be due for another one if it's raining on a Saturday at Old Trafford. We go down there for several weeks at a time on courses, just to see what the latest research is doing and whether we can actually still do it properly.

BRIAN And the actual things you say – those are your own words?

JOHN Absolutely, yes. We don't have a script or anything like that. There's no autocue. We don't read anything. We just make it up as we go along. It's got to agree with the forecast coming out of headquarters – the engine room at Bracknell. They're providing us with the latest computer information, which says, for instance, if a band of rain coming across tomorrow is going to reach Manchester at five o'clock in the afternoon and we can't go on and say it's going to arrive in Manchester at three o'clock, otherwise we'd get our backsides kicked. But essentially we present the weather as we wish. We present it in the nicest possible way to explain the situation to the public.

BRIAN Are you allowed to crack any jokes? What's the best joke you've cracked?

JOHN I can't remember jokes, Brian. But I do like to be fairly light-hearted on television. I think if your own personality comes across, that's the main thing. I was told when I did my first audition in BBC Midlands back in 1980, 'Nobody's invited you into their lounge, so you've got to go in there and be pleasant. You mustn't upset anybody. Be yourself and don't try to copy anybody else.' It was a great temptation, when I first started down in London, to copy who I thought was the best – that was Jim Bacon at the time. But, what's the point. You can't be another Jim Bacon. You've got to be your own personality.

BRIAN Is there a Big Brother listening and watching who rings up afterwards and says, 'Not bad, Ketters, but if I'd been you I'd have said a little bit more about those storms coming in from the east'?

JOHN Yes, we've got our people at Bracknell who monitor everything. I think they record every broadcast and it is quite strict, but on the whole they do trust you. They've got to trust you – they're the people who put you on in the first place.

BRIAN I'm sure you get ninety-nine per cent right, but has there been a one per cent where you've made a most terrible bloomer, said it was going to be the most glorious day tomorrow and it's pelted down all day? Don't be afraid of revealing – Big Brother's not listening.

JOHN It does occur and I think the public know that we're not trying to get it wrong.

BRIAN Where were you before the famous 1987 storm? Were you on that night?

JOHN I was on the breakfast time of the storm, travelling in to do it at four o'clock that morning. The A1 was like a chicane. There were trees all across the road and of course there were no traffic lights working in London that morning, so it was a really hairy journey. We were in Lime Grove in those days and everybody was standing outside with candles when I got there and a great cheer went up, 'Here he is. The man who's responsible for all this.' There'd been a power cut inside the studio, so we went up to Television Centre to do the broadcast from a little annexe. I was due to start on the air at five to seven and my shift finished at nine. I was doing updates with no graphics at all about every twenty minutes about how the storm was going. And I was still there at two o'clock in the afternoon, doing little updates.

BRIAN People do tend to blame you, don't they?

JOHN Yes, they do, but it's like expecting the bus to be on time. Everybody knows the bus is always late. It's just an old-fashioned thing that's carried on for ever.

BRIAN We talk of long-distance forecasting. Had I come to you in May, would you have forecast this glorious summer?

JOHN Oh, I did. I'm sure I told you that. I had a hunch, actually, because it was an odd year – '89 – that it was going to be a good one. And we'd had two very mild winters. It was only a hunch and I would not have dared go on television and say so.

BRIAN And I believe you said, if you remember, 'Except on Saturday 29 July, when it may drizzle during lunchtime at Old Trafford.'

JOHN Well, we should have played this Test a week ago.

BRIAN Now, you are one of the few people who've been mentioned in a hit at the top of the pop charts.

JOHN It was a rather boring title called 'John Kettley is a Weatherman', which is open to debate. But it could have been the end of a wonderful career and the start of a new one. But I never really got into the music industry. It was a band called the Tribe of Toffs who wrote to me in about February last year and said they'd got this song together. I questioned whether it was a song at all.

BRIAN Can you remember the words?

JOHN There weren't many. 'John Kettley is a weatherman. John Kettley is a weatherman. And so is Michael Fish.' Since that day Michael Fish thinks the song is about him.

BRIAN Now let's go back to Yorkshire. Who have been your real favourites there?

JOHN He's not here at the moment, but when I was a kid Freddie Trueman was my hero. And then I must admit, even though things were a little unsettled at Yorkshire in recent years, Geoffrey Boycott became a hero as well.

BRIAN Well, he was a marvellous player. You could admire the technique.

JOHN Since then it's been difficult to have heroes, because they're not really performing as we'd like them to perform. But they're a great bunch of lads and nothing would give me greater pleasure than to see Yorkshire a fine side again.

BRIAN Do you go and watch them?

JOHN When they pop down south. I went to Lord's last year for the county match on a Wednesday afternoon. It was a nice day, but there weren't many people on the ground. I was walking towards the pavilion and David Bairstow saw me, so I had to go and join them in the dressing room. That particular day Yorkshire were having a bad time of it and Kevin Sharp was the twelfth man, but he had done something to his back. He really was in a bad state and he was on antibiotics. So that day I almost went out subbing.

BRIAN Would that have been the climax?

JOHN That would have been absolutely wonderful.

BRIAN Walking along the street, do people stop you and say, 'What's it going to be like for our fête next Saturday week?

JOHN Yes. It's nice in a summer like this. People ask about wedding days and they think you know months and months ahead. I think about it first and then I'll say, 'Yes, it looks as if it's going to be OK. I think the temperature – not as high as it is now, of course – about twenty-one degrees – seventy. A bit of cloud, but yes, it should be fine.' Because that stops them worrying about the weather.

BRIAN When you work out the centigrade and Fahrenheit thing, it doesn't quite work out the way I do it, which is to double it and add thirty.

JOHN No, but it's not far away. We do tend to remember all the conversions now, with years of practice.

BRIAN At thirty-three centigrade what is it?

JOHN Ninety-two.

BRIAN Under my method it would be ninety-six.

JOHN The bigger the number, the more out it will get. But sixteen–sixty-one is a good one to remember. You just reverse the numbers: 16–61.

BRIAN What happened then?

JOHN Oh dear. This is the end of a promising interview.

BRIAN 1661?

JOHN Not in 1661, Brian. Sixteen celsius is sixty-one Fahrenheit.

BRIAN I was thinking something might have happened to Charles II then.

JOHN There's another one: 28–82.

BRIAN Oh, I'll be able to do that. What are the finer parts of the British Isles as regards weather?

JOHN Apart from St John's Wood, of course, the south coast of England is probably just about the driest. But the east of Scotland usually does extremely well – surprisingly well. They do get this horrible 'haar' effect off the North Sea. This low cloud and cold wind sometimes, but they actually get very good shelter from the Grampians.

BRIAN Are we too unfair? There's always the joke about rain at Old Trafford.

JOHN Well, they get about thirty-five inches of rain here a year, I think, off the top of my head. It is cloudier up here in the north-west of England, but the rain isn't necessarily all that heavy. The Lake District probably bears the brunt of most of the rain. That's why it's so green. But I thought you were going to ask me about this England team.

BRIAN   Well, do you have a quick solution?

JOHN   It would be nice if there was more pride put back into English cricket by having people wearing caps, like the Australians do.

MAX JAFFA

I WAS ESPECIALLY pleased when Max Jaffa accepted to be our guest at the Oval in 1989. I had known him as a brilliant violinist who entertained holiday-makers at Scarborough for twenty-seven years, and had listened to him and his trio for even longer on their regular BBC broadcasts. What I did not know was his love of cricket. He and his wife, Jean, had lived in Elm Tree Road, St John's Wood, for thirty-two years before he so sadly died in 1991. From his house in the shadow of the Grandstand it was perfectly possible to lob a cricket ball over the wall into Lord's. But strangely I seldom if ever saw him there. For some reason he preferred the Oval and was a strong supporter of Surrey. He also was a regular at the Scarborough Festival and other first-class matches on the famous ground at North Marine Road. He enjoyed meeting all the cricketers – usually in the Mayor's Tent – and was especially fond of Herbert Sutcliffe and Len Hutton. He even played in a charity match with Freddie Trueman but had to retire hurt with an injured achilles tendon – not Fred's fault!

I have given these cricket details because on reading our conversation, I find that I was so intrigued with his life story, that I almost ignored the cricket side of it.

One thing which perhaps did not come out in our broadcast was what a great communicator he was. One of the joys of being at one of his concerts or listening to his broadcasts, was to hear his friendly, amusing and completely relaxed introductions to the various items. He was also a very modest man. Our billing in the *Radio Times* had described him as 'the popular musician'. He said he was delighted just to be called a musician, and he didn't demur when I suggested he should have been called 'the great fiddler'.

What made his visit to us at the Oval so special was that he was accompanied by his dear wife, Jean, who is not only a wonderful singer, but also a fabulous cook. To prove this she brought us a splendid chocolate cake, topped with strawberries and cream.

THE OVAL, 26 AUGUST 1989

BRIAN JOHNSTON   Did you ever play cricket?

MAX JAFFA   Oh, yes. My most memorable match was for the Guildhall School of Music XI, where I was a student, against the Royal Academy. We won by seven runs. I was the last man in, to cat-calls of 'Watch those fingers'. I scored seven not out and we eventually won by seven. I remember it so well, because it's only a hundred years ago.

BRIAN What about this finger business? There you were, a budding violinist, playing cricket.

MAX I didn't play a lot of cricket. I watched a fair amount.

BRIAN Let's go right back to the beginning. Why did you start playing the violin? Were you bullied into it?

MAX I wasn't bullied into it. I had an extraordinary father. He was, I am sure, the original patriarch and on my sixth birthday he came into my bedroom to wish me happy birthday, handed me a fiddle and said, 'You're going to be a violinist'. And nobody ever argued with my father – certainly not at the age of six.

BRIAN So what did you do then?

MAX I sort of looked at it and looked at him and said, 'Well, thanks very much,' and thought if only he'd brought me a bat or a ball or anything.

BRIAN Was he musical?

MAX No, not a bit. There is no music in my family except my offspring and they're not professional. They are just very musical. My father hadn't a note of music in his entire body. But he was keen. He loved to listen and he did do me a very, very great favour. At the time I didn't realise it, but he took me to a concert at the Queen's Hall. We lived round the corner from the Queen's Hall. I was born in Langham Street, just by the BBC. By the way, while I think about it, this is a great day. On 26 August 1929, I did my first broadcast.

BRIAN At what age?

MAX Young.

BRIAN But how long did it actually take you to learn? When could you actually play the violin?

MAX I gave my first concert at the Pier Pavilion in Brighton aged nine. I've got a picture at which the entire family laugh every time they see it – and they ask to see it very often – of myself in a sort of velvet suit, clutching a fiddle.

BRIAN The little genius.

MAX Well, hardly.

BRIAN That's very young and you began conducting orchestras and leading orchestras in your teens.

MAX Yes, in fact in 1929 it was my orchestra from the Piccadilly Hotel and it was from there that I did my first series of broadcasts, which seemed to go on for ever. They broadcast from there once a week at lunchtime from one until two as, indeed, we are doing now.

BRIAN What was it that made you become a leader?

MAX I wouldn't know. I've never thought about it. One doesn't lead. One's called a leader, but I think really and truly that's a misnomer.

BRIAN Well, they've got to have confidence and they've got to like you.

MAX I think you've got to be able to answer silly questions from other musicians like, 'Why do we have to do it up-bow? Why can't we do it down-bow?' And if you're a decent leader you say, 'Do it your way.'

BRIAN So from the Piccadilly in the early thirties, where did you go then?

MAX From there I graduated into the dance band world and I became the only violinist to lead a dance band for a then very, very popular dance band leader, Jack Harris.

BRIAN Did you enjoy that?

MAX Well, it was fun. Of course, I didn't play jazz. I think I was the straight man. I played the odd chorus in the way that the singer might sing it. But we're getting on towards the war, you see, and I felt I really couldn't win the war playing the fiddle. There had to be something I could do to win the war. I wanted to get into the RAF as aircrew, but, unfortunately, I was too old. So I joined the Artillery and I was a bombadier. I was stationed for a while on the heath at Blackheath. There were nine of us there. Seven gunners, one bombadier and a second lieutenant. We had a search light and a Lewis machinegun. The searchlight was to guide the German planes into London and the Lewis machinegun was to shoot them down if they were silly enough to come low enough. I got a bit fed up with that after a while, though. Then I began to answer every Army Council Instruction that came round asking for volunteers for this, that and the other. I volunteered for everything, including the Palestine police – that's one I remember with affection, because I was turned down for that one also. Eventually an Instruction came round asking for volunteers to transfer from the Army into the RAF for aircrew duties. Of course I volunteered and fortunately for me the qualifications asked for were not very high, so I was able to get in. I transferred to the RAF and eventually, after training at various stations, I got my wings in Rhodesia.

BRIAN Did you actually fly a plane?

MAX I flew 32 different types of plane. I'm very proud of that, actually. I got my wings in Rhodesia and did my operational training and went up to the desert and was finally sent home. There they said, 'You're too old to fly operationally.' They gave me the option of either becoming an instructor on Tiger Moths – and flying Tiger Moths was lovely, but the instructing on them I didn't really fancy, because if I'd got hold of any pupils that were as bad as I was, my life would be in danger. The other option was to join the Air Transport Auxiliary, who were ferrying pilots. They ferried aircraft from squadrons to maintenance units and back again. And I said I thought that would be rather nice and, as it turned out, it was better than rather nice. So I was discharged from the RAF and joined the ATA – not to be confused with the ATS.

BRIAN Amy Johnson was on the same job. Now, you haven't played the fiddle all this time. What happened to your fiddle?

MAX I sold it just before the war and the first thing I did with part of my gratuity when I came back was to buy a fiddle. But I hadn't really thought about the fiddle very much except for one very stupid occasion in Rhodesia when I was a bit the worse for drink and somebody said, 'I understand you play the fiddle.' I said, 'I used to.' He said, 'We have a symphony orchestra in Bulawayo. Would you play a concerto with us?' I said, 'Yes, of course,' and thought no more about it until the following morning, when I received a note thanking me for my offer to play the violin at their concert, which was in ten days' time. Not only had I not got a fiddle, I hadn't got my music and I hadn't played for a few years. However, I did it and I still have the programme. 'Acting Sergeant Max Jaffa, by kind permission of Group Captain French, is going to be the soloist at tonight's concert.'

BRIAN How were the old fingers?

MAX Bunch of bananas. Absolutely ghastly. But I did sort of settle down. They found me a fiddle and they were very good about it. At the performance at Bulawayo Town Hall it was great, because the place was full and they were all on my side. I can't remember much about the concert, but, looking back on it, I should think the performance by the solo violinist was pretty dire. The orchestra were jolly good and well behaved.

BRIAN You say you bought a violin after the war. Is it the same one you've used ever since?

MAX No. I've still got it, but in 1947 I raised my sights a bit and thought it was about time I had a decent fiddle. I'd saved £600, but the one that I really liked was £1,200, so I went to my bank manager and he was very kind. That's the one I've used ever since with the odd day when I practise on the old one which is pretty bad, but it's good for practising.

BRIAN What is this – a Stradivarius?

MAX It's a Guarnerius, made in 1704. Somebody asked me if I got it when it was new. In fact most of the great violinists of today who have one of each prefer the Guarneri.

BRIAN I should be terrified of carrying it around and dropping it.

MAX I don't really think too much about it. Jean won't let me leave it in the boot of the car, locked up, if we go into a restaurant. She says, 'I'll carry the fiddle in.' I say, 'Leave the damn thing there, it's quite safe.' But I suppose she's right, of course.

BRIAN Now we've got to deal with two things. The Grand Hotel – I don't know how many years you did that for the BBC – and then Scarborough.

MAX The Grand Hotel, actually, I didn't do for very long, in fact for the shortest time of any leader of the Grand Hotel broadcast.

BRIAN Well, why do we associate you with the Grand Hotel?

MAX I don't know – maybe oranges and palms. But it's stuck.

BRIAN And you played in Scarborough for how long?

MAX Twenty-seven years. I was asked to do it. The Scarborough people got on to me 28 years ago and asked me to do this thing and I said, 'No, thank you very much.' I was rather busy and it was Jean who talked me into it, because she'd been up there as a guest artist. You know she's a jolly good singer. She said, 'You do it for one year and I promise to show you some of the loveliest countryside you've ever seen.' And I said I'd do it for one year and stayed 27. But coming back here to the Oval is boyhood memories, because although I'm a Middlesex man born and bred and still live there, Surrey was always my team and I saw on this beautiful pitch – and it is a beautiful pitch – some of the greatest players of all time. The most wonderful cover point, who could also bat a bit.

BRIAN Hobbs.

MAX Yes. And Sandham and Strudwick.

BRIAN So you came more to the Oval than to Lord's.

MAX Oh, much more, yes. It's been a great joy looking out from this window in your palatial commentary box.

ERIC IDLE

WE HAVE HAD a number of comedians as our guests in 'A View from the Boundary' – Michael Bentine, Brian Rix, Willie Rushton, John Cleese, Leslie Crowther and Max Boyce. They all seem to love cricket and it's often the one thing in life which they take seriously. I am not so sure, however, that our guest at Trent Bridge, Eric Idle, did so. In fact, after meeting him I could not discover what he *did* take seriously, except perhaps for comedy itself, which strangely is a very serious business.

Mind you I am probably wrong in classifying Eric as a comedian. He is so many other things as well – writer, guitarist, composer and film star. At the time he was living in a large house in St John's Wood, not far from me, but only a penalty kick or so from Gary Lineker, one of the Wood's other most distinguished inhabitants.

On reading through the transcript of our conversation I suppose I should also award him the accolade of 'singer'. I also found fascinating his description of how Monty Python was put together. I told you comedy was a serious business.

I began by asking him about the tie which he was wearing.

TRENT BRIDGE, 9 JUNE 1990

ERIC IDLE This is actually a Pembroke College tie – which I borrowed from a garage attendant on the way up.

BRIAN JOHNSTON You were at Cambridge.

ERIC Yes, I put this on to remind you, so you would mention it and people would think I wasn't quite so eccentric.

BRIAN Did you perform at cricket at Cambridge?

ERIC No, I wasn't half good enough for that. I just performed on the stage. I wasn't even good enough to play for Pembroke.

BRIAN But you achieved a certain prowess there, because you were President of the Footlights. There must have been some famous names.

ERIC When I got there Tim Brooke-Taylor was president and I had to audition for him and Bill Oddie. John Cleese was there and Graham Chapman. The Frost had just left.

(David Frost. Ed.)

BRIAN What do you do when you go to an audition?

ERIC We did a very bad sketch. I went with some other people who laughed all the way through and giggled and I didn't laugh. They thought, therefore, th·t I must have been funny.

BRIAN   What has been your cricket connection? What county do you follow?

ERIC   Warwickshire. I lived quite a lot of my early life there. The first game I ever saw was about 1953, Warwickshire against Australia. Freddie Gardner and Norman Horner opened the batting, I think, and I used to have one of those books and used to do all the dots and all that on the Rea Bank.

BRIAN   Oh well, Frindall's getting a bit past it. Would you like to come and do it for us?

So you went and watched. What about actual playing?

ERIC   I was at school at Wolverhampton and we had a cricket pitch and I became a wicket keeper, because I realised fairly early on that you had gloves on. This was obviously much better. Also I tended to go to sleep on the boundary and if you're wicket keeper you know pretty certainly that it's coming in your direction every ball.

BRIAN   It's essential to keep awake.

ERIC   And much easier, because something's always about to happen. I broke my nose keeping wicket, which is why I have this rather handsome and eccentric profile.

BRIAN   I thought it was a very distinguished nose. I was getting rather jealous about it.

ERIC   It depends which side you look at.

BRIAN   Keeping wicket can be quite dangerous. I was standing up to a moderately fast bowler and the batsman snicked it onto my nose. It's painful, isn't it?

ERIC   It's very painful.

BRIAN   What it does reveal is that both you and I stood up at the wicket. They don't nowadays, which is very cowardly. I know you're always travelling all over the world. Do you follow the cricket at all?

ERIC I love watching cricket, yes. Wherever England are losing abroad, I'm usually there.

BRIAN What about the film career? We've all seen you in *Nuns on the Run*. Was that fun to make?

ERIC It was an hysterical film to make. We spent most of the six or seven weeks dressed as nuns, walking round west London.

BRIAN What did you have on underneath?

ERIC We had our trousers and jackets. It was freezing. So you can whip it off and leave for home at once or nip into the pub quickly.

BRIAN Are they quite comfortable with that thing across your forehead?

ERIC They're horrendously uncomfortable. They're tight and only your face protrudes. You can't hear anything and you can't see anybody. If they approach you from behind it makes you jump. You can understand now why nuns take a vow of silence.

BRIAN What about old Robbie Coltrane, is he funny?

ERIC Coltrane is hysterical. And he is huge. He's a very big man.

BRIAN What do you like to be called? Writing is your basic business.

ERIC Well, it was my basic business, but for the last five or six years I seem to have been doing nothing but acting. I like to be called a comedian, really.

BRIAN In Monty Python you started writing, did you? And then you wrote yourself some good stuff I suppose.

ERIC The whole thing about the Footlights is that you write and act. Nobody else is going to write for you, so you're virtually forced into writing for yourself. And we were very lucky. When we came down from Cambridge we got co-opted by Frost who dragged us off to write for him. We were writing his ad-libs for about ten years.

BRIAN Do you mean to say you've written some of Frost's jokes?

ERIC Some of Frost's best jokes. He still uses some of mine.

BRIAN You're the chap I've been wanting to meet for years.

ERIC I can let you have a few after dinner jokes, partially used.

BRIAN What were all these people like, Michael Palin, Terry Jones and the late Graham Chapman?

ERIC Chapman was a mad, pipe-smoking eccentric.

BRIAN John Cleese said you used to sit round the table and discuss the next Monty Python and all go away and write something completely different from what you'd agreed to write. Was that roughly it?

ERIC Usually, yes. You can't really map out comedy. It just has to come and you have to say, 'Well that works and that doesn't work.'

BRIAN How disciplined was it? Because it looked zany and inconsequential.

ERIC It was completely disciplined. We worked from about ten till five solidly and we never ad-libbed a word. It was always completely scripted. We did all the ad-libbing in the writing sessions, so we always knew exactly what we were going to say. The Footlights motto is 'Ars est colare artem'.

BRIAN Oh, quite. You needn't translate for me, but for the sake of the listener, would you mind?

ERIC I will translate. It's 'The art is to conceal the art', which is true, I suppose, of most activities in life.

BRIAN Why do I always think of the sheep in Monty Python?

ERIC Well, we always used to drop sheep on people's heads when things were going a bit slow.

BRIAN Why did you select sheep? Because they're harmless characters?

ERIC Well, they're very boring – sheep. They stand around all day not doing much and then being eaten. It's hard to sympathise with them, isn't it? So being dropped on people's heads on television is relatively a stage up for a sheep.

BRIAN How long ago was Monty Python? It seems so recent.

ERIC It started over 20 years ago.

BRIAN And how many series did you do?

ERIC We did about 45 shows in all and we finished in about 1973, so we're already history.

BRIAN And then you made films.

ERIC We made films until about seven years ago and since then nothing really.

BRIAN And how different was it doing the telly and then films?

ERIC In television everything can go in, because you're going up to the last minute. Filming is so slow and you've got to get the script right. We'd always take two or three years to write the script and re-write it and re-write it. So it's all much more prepared and there's much less room for spontaneity to add things at the last minute.

BRIAN You took the micky out of the establishment always.

ERIC That was our job at the time and now we've become the establishment.

BRIAN Have people taken the micky out of you?

ERIC Oh, absolutely yes.

BRIAN How many people copied Monty Python? It's been copied in various degrees, hasn't it?

ERIC   It's like a cricket team. We were the team at that time and now there's the current team. They remember you when they were kids and they say, 'Oh, that's why we became comedians.' In the same way, I imagine, as cricketers today say, 'We became cricketers because we saw Mr Trueman bowl.'

BRIAN   I always hope that the film you did called *The Life of Brian* was named after me.

ERIC   As a tribute, of course. I think you actually appeared in one of the sketches a long time ago.

BRIAN   Oh, I did – Peter West and myself. You took the micky out of us. Are you a team man, or are you happier performing individually?

ERIC   I am much happier in a team. I think essentially as a comedian I'm a wicket keeper.

BRIAN   But you have floated off into different films and things.

ERIC   Even in a film it's a team activity, really. I would never want to be a stand-up comic or just on my own.

BRIAN   Have you ever done that in cabaret or anywhere?

ERIC   The cabaret was at Cambridge. We used to do that at weekends and make quite a good living out of it.

BRIAN   Are you a good stand-up comic?

ERIC   No, hopeless. I'm terrible. I can write other people's jokes and one-liners, but it doesn't appeal to me. I like to hide behind a character and put on some make-up, or in Peter West's case I had a whole bald head to put on.

BRIAN   You tended often to be in drag.

ERIC   (*with a sigh*) I had the best legs, it has to be said. But with Python we'd just divide up the parts and whatever was going we'd grab. So usually by the time Cleese had taken all the bullying parts and the slapping cars and the hitting people about the head parts and Jones had taken the smaller parts, there were only a few women left, so I used to end up with those.

BRIAN Going back to Warwickshire, Freddie Gardner, who you mentioned, was a great character, although he didn't appear to be one on the field. Did you mingle at all with the players?

ERIC I think I saw them in Stratford once, but the only player I met in the early days was Tom Graveney, who was my great hero.

BRIAN He's the ideal chap to have watched.

ERIC Wonderful batsman.

BRIAN You don't see so many like him.

ERIC Well, I think Gower's in the same mould.

BRIAN He's outstanding.

Now, I believe you play the guitar. The fingernails of course are beautifully manicured. Do you use a pleckers – a plectrum?

ERIC I have a plectrum, yes.

BRIAN Is that cheating, or is it allowed?

ERIC It's totally allowed. Anything is allowed, I think – unless you get caught at it.

BRIAN Do you play for fun or just for yourself? Have you done it professionally?

ERIC I've done it semi-professionally. I came out of a fridge in *The Meaning of Life* and sang a song about the galaxy. I sang a catchy little ditty on the Cross – 'Always Look on the Bright Side of Life', which I wrote. (*In* The Life of Brian. *Ed.*)

BRIAN What about your voice. You've just performed Co-co in *The Mikado*. Did you enjoy doing that?

ERIC I loved doing Co-co. I did it at the English

National Opera and then last November I went to do it in Houston, Texas.

BRIAN The Doctor produced you – Jonathan Miller. Was it very different from the orthodox?

ERIC I said to him, 'What are you going to do with *The Mikado*?' And he said, 'Well, I'm going to get rid of all that Japanese nonsense for a start.' Which is very good, since it's set in Japan. He made it entirely black and white, with dinner jackets and thirties style. A cross between Fred Astaire and the Marx Brothers.

BRIAN Did you do one or two of the traditional twiddling dances which they used to do in Gilbert and Sullivan?

ERIC Well, I had to do quite a lot of dancing. I had seven songs and about four or five dances. You get 'Tit Willow', you get 'A Little List' – I used to re-write the list every day for the performance. I used to put whoever was in the news on the list that night and the chorus used to face me upstage and look at me, so that I'd always try and make them laugh.

BRIAN You were unlucky in a sense in that you missed the great music-hall period.

ERIC There was a bit of that around when I first started. I went to see Norman Evans in Manchester and Morecambe and Wise were just young comics then. Rob Wilton – that wonderful man with 'The Day War Broke Out' – I saw a bit of that. There were still music-hall acts.

BRIAN Have you ever modelled any of your female parts on Norman Evans?

ERIC He was very Python – he was huge.

BRIAN And he did that marvellous act like Les Dawson does today, with no teeth.

ERIC Well, I think Lancashire comedians are probably the best and certainly were the funniest.

BRIAN Oh, yes. If you just go through them from Tommy Handley to Arthur Askey to Ted Ray – they're helped a little by the accent. If you tell a story in a Lancashire accent it sounds a bit funnier than if I tell it. You never saw Max Miller, did you?

ERIC No, but I adored his records. I used to play them regularly. I never saw him live and he wasn't allowed on television, was he?

BRIAN He was the great insinuator. He never quite got to the point and left it to people's imaginations. Nowadays people go a bit further.

ERIC He used to let the audience complete the joke, which is very clever: 'You're the sort of people who will get me into trouble! Now then, is this Cockfosters? No, madam, it's Max Miller's.'

BRIAN Oh, that one he didn't leave to the imagination.

What about alternative comedy, as they call it? Do you think sometimes they go a little too far? Or do you think you can't go too far?

ERIC I think it's the job of comedy to go just that bit too far. It's just to stir people up and make them laugh a bit and I think you have to go a little bit too far to do it. Then the line keeps moving as life continues. Python looks quite staid now – conservative.

BRIAN But the essential bit of your comedy was to shock, I think.

ERIC Well, yes, partially. It's too easy to do that. We tried not to rely on just pure shock. There's a limited return on it. You can't just shock and keep shocking. So we'd always try to provide good laughs.

BRIAN What about *Baron Münchhausen*? That's a good film.

ERIC It's a lovely film. It was one of the most nightmarish experiences of my life. I had to have my head shaved. I was bald for six months. I was in Rome, being hung up in tanks, being blown up and suspended from the ceiling and it was total hell.

BRIAN Can you stay bald for a week, or do little tufts of hair start growing?

ERIC They have to shave it every day, otherwise it becomes like velcro and you can run into the wall and stick to it with your head.

BRIAN And how long did it take to recover from it to the fine head of hair that you've got now?

ERIC I am terribly butch, so it grew back quite quickly.

BRIAN Will you do anything for art, then?

ERIC Anything for a laugh is what I was accused of. Art? Yes, I think you have to. If you're doing something you have to plunge yourself totally into it to get it right.

BRIAN You live in St John's Wood, will you be going round the corner to Lord's this summer?

ERIC Yes. I hope to see Mr Gower occasionally.

BRIAN He is great fun to watch. You probably like him because he's artistic – the touch player.

ERIC That's what the game's about for me. It's what makes the difference between that and baseball and anything like that. It's the class shot. You can't describe it, it's a thing of beauty – the good cover drive.

BRIAN I was delighted to hear that you've written a play about cricket. It's one of my ambitions. You have produced a musical comedy – not for the stage.

ERIC We wrote it originally for the stage and then we thought it would do very nicely on radio. It's called *Behind the Crease* and it's about the three things the English like most – sex, royalty and cricket – not necessarily in that order. I've written it with a friend of mine called John Du Pre and we did it with Gary Wilmott playing a West Indian hotel owner and I play a seedy journalist.

BRIAN A cricket writer? Or one who sits by the pool and takes notes of what goes on that shouldn't.

ERIC Exactly. It's all about entrapment. Which, of course, never happens.

BRIAN No, no. It wasn't, of course, based on any tour in the West Indies.

ERIC No, it just came to me while I was on holiday in the West Indies one year.

BRIAN Is it easy to compose a cricket song?

ERIC We did a lovely song which went:

> Oh jolly good shot
> Oh well played, sir
> Oh well let alone
> Oh he's hit him on the bone
> Did it hit him on the head?
> No it hit him on the leg
> I think the fellow's dead
> No he's getting up again
> Oh it's just a bit of rum
> No it's hit him on the bum
> Is he out? Is he out? . . .

We should have had fifteen people singing this – very tightly.

BRIAN That was very good – quick moving. Is there a wicket keeper's song? Why he missed a stumping, perhaps – a wicket keeper's lament?

ERIC There should be a wicket keeper's lament.

Gary Wilmott is playing this hotel keeper at the Nelson Arms – 'We turn a blind eye to most things.' It's set in 'the Wayward Isles', which I rather like. I play the seedy reporter who's trying to get something on this English cricketer called Brian Steam, who's a fast bowler. There's a seedy journalist's song, 'Strolling Down the Street of Shame':

> I saw judge outside a judge's quarter
> Messing with another judge's daughter.
> I said, 'Hello, hello, me lud,
> I'd keep this secret if I could,
> But I have a moral duty as a reporter.'

BRIAN Very good. It seems to be all sex so far.

ERIC It's mainly sex. There are one or two bits of cricket in there.

(And finally Eric was persuaded to finish with a reprise of, 'Oh jolly good shot'. Ed.)

GEORGE SHEARING

ONE OF THE bonuses of my 47 years of cricket commentary has been the way it has brought me in close touch with the blind. From our letters we know that we have thousands of blind listeners, who rely on the radio cricket commentator to paint the picture of a match for them. Many of them follow the placings and movements of fielders on a braille pattern of a cricket field. Some, like our special friend Mike Howell up at Old Trafford, actually come to the Tests, and listen in to our commentaries. They like to feel that they are part of the crowd and enjoy absorbing the excitement and atmosphere of everything happening at the ground.

Most of you will know that on every Saturday of a Test Match, in addition to 'A View from the Boundary', we make an appeal on behalf of the Primary Club. The qualification to join is simple. Whatever sex or age you are, or in whatever class of cricket, if you have ever been out first ball (except for a run-out) you are qualified to join. All you have to do is to send £10 to: Mike Thomas, P.O. Box 111, Bromley, Kent. He will then send you a tie and membership certificate. If you are a lady there are brooches instead of ties, and if you are feeling extra generous, you can send £15 instead of £10, and you will get *two* ties. The money received goes mostly to the Dorton School for the Blind at Sevenoaks. Originally it went towards their cricket only. But as more and more members joined, the money is now used on a broader basis, especially for sport. As an example, a perfectly equipped gymnasium has been built as the result of the generosity of 'first ballers'.

Some of the money is also distributed to the various blind cricket clubs round the country. I happen to be President of one of these clubs called Metro, a sports and social club for the visually handicapped. They play cricket and have given exhibitions of how to play blind cricket at the Oval and Lord's. They have also been the National Champions.

You can imagine therefore how pleased I was to receive a letter from a lady in Stow-on-the-Wold telling me that the world-famous blind pianist George Shearing came and lived there every summer, which he spent listening to Test Match Special. We immediately contacted him in New York and invited him to the first of the two Lord's Tests in 1990. MCC gave special permission for his wife, Elly, to accompany him up to our box in the pavilion – a privilege only those ladies who *work* in the pavilion enjoy.

I had met him just once, 44 years before during a broadcast from a restaurant off Bond Street. I had forgotten what a wonderful sense of humour he possessed and from the moment he entered the box he had us all laughing. Two years later I went at *his* invitation, to hear him in a concert at the Festival Hall. He gave a marvellous performance and I was fascinated to watch his fingers moving swiftly across the keyboard, hitting all the right notes, none of which, of course, he could see. He is one of the happiest men I have ever met.

LORD'S, 23 JUNE 1990

BRIAN JOHNSTON Are you a jazz pianist, classical pianist, or just a pianist?

GEORGE SHEARING I'm a pianist who happens to play jazz. I have said this quite frequently. I'm also a pianist who happens to be blind, as opposed to a blind pianist. I may get blind when my work is done, but not before.

BRIAN We heard of your enthusiasm for cricket from, I think, a lady down in Stow-on-the-Wold, where you come every summer. You live in America now.

GEORGE Yes, we've lived in New York for almost twelve years and we lived in California before then. What do you think about the retention of my accent? Is there much?

BRIAN There's a little tingle of American, but mostly it's the good old basic English. And it is pretty basic – it's Battersea, isn't it?

GEORGE It is. Until I was sixteen I was very much a Cockney and I think the thing that got me out of being a Cockney was when I was doing some broadcasts for the BBC and the announcer came on and said (very properly), 'For the next fifteen minutes you will be hearing the music of George Shearing.' I played the first medley and said, 'Good mornin' everybody. We just played the medley of commercial popular numbers includin' "Tears on my Pillow", "Let Me Whisper I Love You", "Magyar Melody" and "Jeepers Creepers".' And the announcer came back after the show to say, 'For the last fifteen minutes you have been hearing the music of George Shearing.' Fortunately I had some good ears and I was able to dispense with the largest part of my Cockney accent.

I was in a residential school between the ages of twelve and sixteen – and I'm going to be 71 this August. In this school we played cricket. Now you can imagine blind people playing cricket. First of all we played in the gymnasium. We played with a rather large balloon-type ball with a bell in it and all the bowling was underhand, of course, and this ball would bounce along the gymnasium floor. The wicket was two large blocks of wood, perhaps fifteen or sixteen inches long, bolted together with a heavy nut and bolt on each end. Sandwiched in between was a piece of plywood, so that we could hear this ball when it hit the wicket. You'd know very well you were out if that happened.

BRIAN   No disputing with the umpire.

GEORGE   Dickie Bird would have no problems.

Now, if you hit the side wall it was one run; if you hit the end wall of the gymnasium it was two runs; if you hit the end wall without a bounce it was four; if you hit the ceiling at the other end it was six and if you hit the overmantel it was three weeks' suspension.

BRIAN   Much the same rules for indoor cricket today. But – born blind – how do you picture a cricket ball or a cricket bat?

GEORGE   When I was a kid I used to go out in the street and play cricket with sighted people. And my little nephew would hold the bat with me and he would indicate when he was going to swing it. We actually did make many contacts with the bat on the ball – a regular cricket bat and ball.

BRIAN What was your father? Was he a musician?

GEORGE No, Daddy was a coalman. He would deliver coal.

BRIAN With a horse and cart?

GEORGE Yes. I often wondered if he shouldn't put on his cart: 'COAL A LA CART OR CUL DE SACK'.

BRIAN Not a bad gag. Now, did he start you on music? How did you get into that?

GEORGE I'm the youngest of a family of nine. There were no musicians in the family at all, so I imagine that in a previous life I was Mozart's guide dog. I don't really know how it started.

BRIAN Can we have a look at your fingers? I'm always interested in the fingers of guitarists and pianists. Yours are fairly delicate. They're straight. They haven't been broken by a cricket ball. So when did you first feel the touch of a piano and decide that was what you wanted to do?

GEORGE Before actually trying to make music as a pianist, I would shy bottles out of the second-storey window and hear them hit the street and they would have quite musical sounds. I had quite good taste, because I would use milk bottles for classical music and beer bottles for jazz.

BRIAN I wouldn't talk too loud, because the police have probably got all the records. They've been looking for the chap who did that.

GEORGE I first put my hands on a piano, I think, when I was three years of age. I was listening to the old crystal set. It was stuff like the Roy Fox band. Then I would go over to the piano and pick out the tune that I had just heard.

BRIAN   Is there such a thing as Braille music?

GEORGE   Very much so. In fact I've learnt a number of concertos in Braille and played them with many symphony orchestras in the United States. I have given that up because I'm a little afraid of memory lapse. I had one thirty-bar memory lapse, I remember, when I was playing with the Buffalo Symphony and my wife noticed that I was leaning towards the orchestra. Being, of course, a musician who plays jazz, on hearing the chords of the orchestra, I could immediately improvise in the style of Mozart until my mind decided to behave once again and go back to the score.

BRIAN   So you can do it from Braille, but basically you're an ear pianist.

GEORGE   Yes, very much. You see, if you were to do anything short of sitting on the piano, I could probably hear what you were playing. If you played a ten-note chord, I could probably hear.

BRIAN   If I sat on it it would probably be a twenty-note chord.

GEORGE   Well, I didn't say that.

BRIAN   George, do you remember when we first met?

GEORGE   Yes, it was in Fisher's restaurant in about 1946, when we were with the Frank Weir band.

BRIAN   We did a *Saturday Night Out* when I first joined the BBC. I joined in January and this must have been about April 1946. And I was amazed then as I talked to you and I asked how you were getting home. You said, 'Oh, I've come by tube, I shall be going home by tube.'

GEORGE   And I used to do it without the aid of a

cane or a dog or anything else. We've had a man in the United States who used to do that. His name was Doctor Spanner and you could prove that he did it, because he had all kinds of bruises all over his body where he'd got into various accidents. They used to refer to him as 'the Scar-Spangled Spanner'.

BRIAN But did you tap your way along Bond Street to the tube station?

GEORGE When I started to use a cane I did. One time during World War Two I remember somebody said to me, 'Would you see me across the road?' And I took his arm and saw him across the road. It's the only case I've heard of the blind leading the blind.

BRIAN Do you still walk around on your own if you know the district?

GEORGE Not very much. One tends to lose one's nerve a little bit when you pass 65, I think.

BRIAN Oh, get away! Describe for me what you think you're looking out at here.

GEORGE Well, we are probably at one end of the cricket field and are we looking down the length of the pitch?

BRIAN Yes.

GEORGE I have light and dark, but that's all I have. Sitting in this box, of course, it's an interesting aspect of controlled acoustics and wonderful daylight and fresh air coming in through open windows. As a matter of fact I wouldn't mind buying a lifetime ticket here.

BRIAN Well, you'd be most welcome. When we say that the umpire's wearing a white coat or the batsman plays a stroke, can you figure what that means?

GEORGE No. Two things that a born-blind man would have difficulty with are colour and perspective. When you think about it, you can be satisfied that you're looking at a table on a flat piece of paper, although it obviously has cubic capacity. And I suppose my education and my instruction gives me the information that perhaps you draw two legs shorter than the other two and something about the way the light gets it. I have no conception at all of colours. In fact, once when I got a cab in the mid-town area of Chicago, I was to meet the Count Basie band on the South Side. They were all staying at a hotel mostly frequented by black people at that time and I said to the cab driver, 'Could you take me to the South Central Hotel?' And he said, 'Do you know that's a coloured hotel?' I said, 'Really? What colour is it?' And when we got there I gave him a tip about twice the size one would normally do, to make up for his ignorance, got into the bus with the Basie band and took off and hoped that he was duly embarrassed.

BRIAN   Does green grass mean anything to you?

GEORGE   Oh, yes. What a lovely smell when it's freshly mowed and when it's been watered. It means a great deal to me. But I suppose if you want colour description, I would say that blue would be something peaceful, red would be something perhaps angry and green – I don't know.

BRIAN   Well, it's something very pleasant to look at, if you have a nice green cricket field.

You've lived in America a long time – have you always liked cricket?

GEORGE   I've always been very fond of cricket, but, as you can imagine, being in America, one has had a great many years *in absentia*, which always makes me sad and I can't wait to get over here and render my wife a cricket widow.

BRIAN   How much do you come over now?

GEORGE Three months a year and my aim is to make it six months a year.

BRIAN You go to the Cotswolds and do you sit and listen to the Test Matches?

GEORGE Oh, yes, of course I do. As a matter of fact, we may catch the three-thirty this afternoon, so that by five I can be in my deck chair in the garden listening to the rest of the afternoon's play. And incidentally, I think you're a very logical and wonderful follow-on from Howard Marshall.

BRIAN Did you hear him?

GEORGE Oh, many times.

BRIAN Did you hear him describe Len Hutton's famous innings at the Oval – the 364?

GEORGE Yes. I used to listen to him on the first radios I had in the thirties.

BRIAN He was lovely to listen to. He could take his place here and show us up. In other sports, commentators of that vintage would be old-fashioned, but he would be absolutely perfect.

Are you a good impersonator? Can you pick up people's voices?

GEORGE I used to do Norman Long monologues on my show.

BRIAN 'A song, a smile and a piano' – Norman Long.

GEORGE (*in character*)

> I've saved up all the year for this
> And here it is, no kid.
> This here Irish Sweepstake ticket
> And it cost me half a quid.
> Not much of it to look at,
> Bit expensive like, of course,
> But if I draws a winner,

Gor, lumme, if I even draws a horse,
The quids, just think about them,
Thousands of them, lovely notes
Not greasy – nice and new.
I'll take me wife and family
Down to Margate by the sea.
Cockles, rock and winkles,
Shrimps and strawberries for tea.
A-sitting in your deckchairs,
With your conscience clear and sound,
A-smiling at the bloke and saying,
'Can you change a pound?'
Instead of hopping out of them
Each time the bloke comes round.
Thirty thousand quid!

BRIAN That's marvellous. Did you get all that from memory, or did you used to write it down?

GEORGE No, I never wrote it down. I listened to it enough until I remembered it and I've never forgotten it since 1935 or '36 when I first heard it, any more than I've forgotten the geographical version of the Lord's prayer.

BRIAN Which is what?

GEORGE

How far is the White Hart from Hendon?
Harrow Road be thy name.
Thy Kingston come, Thy Wimbledon
In Erith as it is in Devon.
Give us this Bray our Maidenhead
And forgive us our Westminsters,
As we forgive those who Westminster against us.
And lead us not into Thames Ditton,
But deliver us from Yeovil [or from the Oval if

you prefer]
For Thine is the Kingston and the Purley and
the Crawley
For Iver and Iver,
Crouch End.

BRIAN Have you ever done stand-up comedy?

GEORGE I'm far too lazy to do stand-up comedy.
I sit down at the piano because I have embraced the
philosophy for lo (!) these many years, 'Why should any
man work when he has the health and strength to lie in
bed?'

BRIAN You sit down at the piano. You had a
quintet for many years which was famous. Did you
enjoy playing with people, or do you prefer to be solo?

GEORGE Well, I enjoyed it for 29 years. I've now
pared down to just bass and piano, because I can address
myself to being a more complete pianist with a much
greater degree of freedom every night to create what
comes into mind – obviously restricted by the chords
of the particular tune that I happen to be playing.

BRIAN Now, in addition to playing, you are a
composer. How many hits have you composed?

GEORGE Oh, I can play you a medley of my hit
in two minutes. It's called 'Lullaby of Birdland'. I've
composed about 99 other compositions which have gone
from relative obscurity to total oblivion.

BRIAN But what do people want? When they see
you they say, 'Come on, George, play . . .' What?

GEORGE They still want 'September in the Rain',
which was one of the quintet's most famous numbers.
We did 90,000 copies of that. It was a 78 when it started.

BRIAN Now, 'Lullaby of Birdland' – I always thought
that was a lovely lullaby of a little wood with the birds

twittering, but Birdland wasn't actually that, was it?

GEORGE Birdland actually was a club in New York dedicated to Charlie Parker, who was nicknamed 'the Bird' and I've played Birdland many times. It was a little basement kind of dive.

BRIAN We have thousands of blind listeners. Any word for them about cricket and what it's meant to you?

GEORGE I hope they enjoy cricket as much as I do, because I really love it. Incidentally the Royal National Institute for the Blind put out the cricket fixtures in Braille.

BRIAN If I was to ask you to sing or hum your favourite tune to finish, what would it be?

GEORGE It would be almost anything of Cole Porter or Jerome Kern. One thing that comes to mind is:

> Whenever skies look grey to me
> And trouble begins to brew;
> Whenever the winter wind becomes too strong,
> I concentrate on you – Graham Gooch
> I concentrate on you – Richard Hadlee.

THE RT. HON.
JOHN MAJOR

AT ALMOST every Test Match from 1988 onwards, John Major has been a regular visitor to the *TMS* commentary box. It was always on a Friday and he was usually accompanied by his cricket-loving friend Robert Atkins, who later was to become Sports Minister. He would stay about half an hour and took an interest in all that was going on in the box. He also showed his expert knowledge on all aspects of cricket – tactics, techniques, records and so on. In fact, after our talk together on the air, he said he had hoped that I would have asked him what he thought of the modern game and what changes he would like to make in its laws and playing regulations. (This was in 1990, so perhaps it was a gentle hint that he would like to do another 'View from the Boundary'!)

When he first came to visit us he was Chief Secretary to HM Treasury, then had a brief spell as Foreign Secretary and by the summer of 1990 he was Chancellor of the Exchequer. Since he became Prime Minister at the end of November, 1990, his visits to our box have become rarer. This is partly due to his crowded programme of duties, and also to security, especially at grounds like Old Trafford where he has to walk round the ground to get to our box. In 1992, his duties were particularly arduous as he had a six-month session as President of the European Community. But he did find time to do a short interview at Lord's in which I chided him for allowing European affairs to interfere with cricket, and another by telephone to the Oval while he was at the Barcelona Olympic Games.

Cricket has been lucky to have a number of cricket-loving Prime Ministers – Stanley Baldwin, a member of MCC, Clement Attlee, Alec Douglas-Home (he played twice for Middlesex), Ted Heath (a keen Kent supporter who gave a splendid reception at No. 10 for Ray Illingworth's victorious team on their return from Australia in 1971) and now John Major.

I have one happy memory of John Major off-duty in 1992. Paul Getty opened his lovely cricket ground on his estate of Wormsley on the Buckinghamshire/Oxfordshire border. The opening match was Paul Getty's XI against MCC, which the Queen Mother and John Major attended. He spent a large part of the day bowling to a number of boys aged from four to ten behind the pavilion. If ever a man looked happy he did.

I'm not sure whether he bowled any of them out with his slow medium deliveries, but it did show what a great relaxation cricket can be, away from the stresses and responsibilities of a Prime Minister.

LORD'S, 28 JULY 1990

BRIAN JOHNSTON   When did your interest in cricket start? You were born in Merton, so you were qualified for Surrey.

JOHN MAJOR   I was qualified for Surrey in everything except talent. It really started when my family moved to Brixton and I was about ten. I was within walking distance of the Oval and that was at the time Surrey were beating everyone, generally within two days – that marvellous team that won the championship from '52 to '58 inclusive. It was, I think, probably the best county side I ever expect to see. They were truly magnificent and I watched them whenever I could.

BRIAN   Where did you sit at the Oval, under the gasometer?

JOHN   No, I sat on the other side. I sat at square leg with the batsman at the pavilion end, in the popular seats there and by pure habit I used to go there for years after as well.

BRIAN   What chances did you yourself get of playing cricket? Were you coached?

JOHN   I played a bit at school. We had quite a good cricket team at school. I played for them and I played a bit of cricket after school as well. I played a bit in Nigeria when I first went there at about twenty to do some banking. But my cricketing days came to an end after a motor car accident in Nigeria when I was twenty or so and I haven't played since.

(This interview came before the 1991 meeting of Commonwealth Prime Ministers in Zimbabwe when Mr Major opened the batting with the then Australian Prime Minister, Bob Hawke, in a match to mark the occasion. Ed.)

BRIAN   So we were robbed of – what? A fast bowler,

or what would England have had if you'd been fit?

JOHN You were robbed of an extremely mediocre medium-paced bowler.

BRIAN Banking in Nigeria sounds an interesting job.

JOHN Yes, it was. It was certainly that. The greatest enthusiasm that most of the people had there was for the weekly cricket match. They had their priorities absolutely right.

BRIAN It does happen all round the world. So when you watched that Surrey side, were there any special favourites you picked out? Was it the bowlers you liked – Bedser, Laker or Lock?

JOHN Oh, they were tremendous. It was such a superb team and they were so varied. I always thought Alec Bedser bowling was rather like a galleon in full sail coming up to the wicket. Last evening, Brian Rix said to me that he'd been batting a few years ago against Alec Bedser in a charity match and he'd said to Alec, 'Let me have an easy one to get off the mark.' And he said Alec couldn't do it. He couldn't bowl the bad ball. And I can well believe it. But the rest of the team were superb. I used to time, with an old stopwatch I had, how long it took the ball from leaving Peter May's bat to hitting the boundary. It wasn't long.

BRIAN Ah, those famous on-drives.

JOHN And I think that Tony Lock was the most aggressive-looking bowler I ever saw – and fielder.

BRIAN And a little lesson in leadership, too, because old Stewy Surridge was a tremendous leader. He was a very forceful leader, too.

JOHN He was. I met Stuart Surridge for the first time about six weeks ago. It was a very great thrill. I remember thinking as a boy, when I watched him standing there, round the wicket, where he fielded absolutely magnificently, that he was one of the few men I've ever seen who could scratch his toes while standing upright. He had these amazingly long arms and he just caught everything – truly wonderful.

(Sadly, Stuart Surridge died in 1992 at the age of 74. Ed.)

BRIAN Very brave he was, but then they all were – Micky Stewart and Locky walking in when he was fielding at backward short leg, which not many short legs do.

JOHN Some of Lock's catches are still unbelievable even in retrospect. You just didn't know how he got there and how he held it.

BRIAN But when did you see your first Test Match? Do you remember that?

JOHN Well, I remember the first Test Match I listened to seriously. It was an Indian Test Match and it was in 1952 when India were nought for four in the second innings.

BRIAN We had a certain gentleman – Fred Trueman – in here just now, who was not unconcerned with that.

JOHN He took three of the four wickets. It was an astonishing scorecard.

BRIAN But have you been able to go to Test Matches much?

JOHN I've been to quite a few – a good deal fewer than I would wish to have gone to, but, yes, I've been to quite a few over the years. I saw a bit of the last Test Match in 1953 when the Ashes came back and I saw some of the '56 series.

BRIAN I wonder, when you have all these conferences, are you ever brought in notes with the latest score?

JOHN Certainly in the period I was Chief Secretary and we had great negotiations with colleagues about spending matters, the meetings did used to break up for critical parts of the Test Match, to watch it. My then secretary, who was a Surrey member and a fanatical cricketer, used to send in notes to say the Test Match had reached a critical stage and we used to break up and watch it. Nigel Lawson is also a great cricket supporter – a great Leicestershire fan – and we used to sit there, with Nigel in the chair, his fellow ministers, lots of extremely important mandarins and others at the other side of the table and a piece of paper would come in that would be passed gravely round the table. It was the Test score, it wasn't the markets, I promise you.

BRIAN Did you just nod as though it was important financial news?

JOHN Well, over the last couple of years, some of it was very grave.

BRIAN Are quite a few members of the Cabinet keen followers?

JOHN The best cricket player in the Cabinet is probably Tom King. He is a good cricketer.

BRIAN He also keeps wicket, I think.

JOHN He keeps wicket as well. Peter Brooke is a walking Wisden and knows a great deal about cricket.

BRIAN We could put him against the Bearded Wonder and he'd stump him, d'you think?

(The Bearded Wonder is, of course, Bill Frindall. Ed.)

JOHN Well, I think as a non-gambling man, I might put my money on the Bearded Wonder, but not by much. Peter Brooke knows a great deal about it and there are a number of others.

BRIAN I suppose, because you were injured, you haven't been able to play for the Lords and Commons.

JOHN No, I'm afraid that motor accident ended my

playing days. I wouldn't run too well now, otherwise I would love to play.

BRIAN They play some very good cricket. It mingles up the parties, too. They don't seem to bother about the politics.

JOHN Indeed not. Bob Cryer, the Labour MP for one of the Bradford seats, is a very fine left-arm slow bowler. There are some good cricketers right across the Commons.

BRIAN What's the first thing you read in the papers in the morning?

JOHN I do read the sports pages every day. I tend to read Matthew Engel when he writes cricket. That is the first thing I turn to in that particular newspaper. *(Matthew Engel was appointed editor of Wisden in 1992. Ed.)* I much miss the fact that Jim Swanton doesn't write quite as regularly as once he did. I thought he was supremely good and I much enjoy reading Tony Lewis. But I do turn to the sports pages at an early stage in the morning.

BRIAN Are you great on the literature of cricket? Have you got a big library of cricket books?

JOHN Well, quite big, yes. I do read a lot of cricket. I've been trying to get hold of a book on cricket that Richard Daft wrote a long time ago – way back in the 1870s or 1880s. Richard Daft's great grandson, incidentally, is the Cabinet Secretary, Robin Butler – another fine cricketer. The Civil Service has some extremely good cricketers. But I haven't been able to find that book in old bookshops. Robert Atkins has a copy, which he jealously guards and lends to me occasionally.

(As a result of this broadcast, Mr Major received a copy of the Richard Daft book. Ed.)

BRIAN What other great cricket writers in the newspapers do you remember especially?

JOHN In the evening papers, when one used to go out and see how Surrey were doing and whether the game would go into a third day, I remember reading E. M. Wellings a lot.

BRIAN He wrote a lot of very good sense – and played for Surrey, too.

JOHN And of course, in terms of literature, like everybody, I've read a lot of Cardus.

BRIAN Which is absolutely marvellous stuff. He and Arlott and Swanton – and Robertson Glasgow – did you ever read him?

JOHN I've not read a lot of him.

BRIAN Well, if you can get any of his little vignettes about players, they were absolutely brilliant. He was the chap who said, 'Hammond, like a ship in full sail', which was a perfect description of Hammond going to the wicket.

JOHN I wish I'd seen him bat, too.

BRIAN But I suppose you don't get a lot of time to read, do you?

JOHN Well, I do, actually. Whatever time I go to bed, I tend to pick up a book for half an hour or 45 minutes, just to wash away the rest of the day, and it is often a cricket book.

BRIAN I hope that doesn't send you to sleep.

JOHN Well I go to sleep, but it's not the book.

BRIAN Young James, your son, is he a good cricketer?

JOHN He's a better footballer and for the reason that there isn't as much cricket at schools as there ought to be. The point about cricket in schools is that it takes such a long time-span. That's the real difficulty and whereas I think the staff are willingly prepared to give up an afternoon for a football match to get the pupils there, play the game and get them back, it is a good deal longer for a cricket match.

BRIAN Are you a quick learner? I mean you had to switch suddenly to the Foreign Office. How did you brief yourself in that short time, because you appeared terribly knowledgeable when you went to conferences immediately afterwards.

JOHN Well, you're very kind to say so. You read a lot and hopefully recall. It's really a problem of total immersion. It's the same in cricket in many ways. I'm sorry to name-drop, but I bumped into Arthur Morris today – a very great player – and he remembered hitting Wilf Wooller for four fours off the first four balls of a game down in Glamorgan. And I said, 'That was a bit extravagant.' And he said, 'Not as extravagant as the field that had been set,' which he then described to me. So I think these things just stick in the mind. He, 40 years on, remembers the field placing.

BRIAN If you ask Fred Trueman about any of the wickets he took or the innings he played, he'd tell you exactly. He's got a marvellous memory.

JOHN Yes, it's a great gift.

BRIAN Are you great on music?

JOHN I like music very much and I go whenever I can, which isn't as often as I would wish, with Norma. She's forgotten more about music than I'll ever know.

BRIAN And besides cricket, any particular hobby?

JOHN Well, I read a lot; I'm very fond of the theatre; I go and watch a fair bit of football and athletics if I can – most sport.

BRIAN John Major, thank you very much. You're

a cricket fanatic and a man after our own hearts and I hope you'll continue to listen to us.

JOHN Brian, I will. I wouldn't miss it for the world.

VIC LEWIS

CRICKET ENTHUSIASTS DON'T come much keener than Vic Lewis, band leader, jazz musician and agent for musical stars. He is a regular at Lord's, not just for the big matches, but for all the Middlesex games as well, where he has become the genial host of the Middlesex Club Bar at the back of the Allen Stand.

You will gather from what follows that he had a lifelong passion for the game, not only as a spectator but as a wily captain of his own side for many years, during which he made several million pounds for various charities.

During our conversation he talks about his unique collection of ties, but he did not tell us how he nearly lost the lot. He returned one night to his house to find a number of suitcases stacked one upon the other, and strewn all over the sitting-room floor, hundreds of his ties. He found the back door into the garden open, and he had obviously disturbed a burglar who was searching for something more commercially valuable than mere cricket ties.

Luckily they were all intact but unfortunately many of the tags which had been on each tie had become detached and were scattered all over the place. Each tag had got the name of the club to which the tie belonged. Poor Vic spent the next few months trying to match each tie with its tag, as, somewhat naturally with so many ties, he couldn't recognise every one.

His book *Cricket Ties* is a fascinating mini encyclopaedia of the origins and descriptions of many of the ties, and I was proud to discover that the very first cricket tie ever issued was in 1863 for the Eton Ramblers, of whom I have been a member for over sixty years.

I have always been grateful to Vic for the tremendous support and help which he gave me when Decca kindly recorded the 'Ashes Song', sung by Ray Illingworth's victorious England team which brought back the Ashes in 1971. Vic miraculously pressed his magic button and gathered together for just this one recording a selection of all the top session musicians in London. Their accompaniment to our 'singing' was the highlight of the record. If only our singing had matched their playing we might have had a hit!

OLD TRAFFORD, 11 AUGUST 1990

BRIAN JOHNSTON Before we talk about cricket, how did you get started in music?

VIC LEWIS It was quite simple, I was born into it. I don't remember whether it was when I was two or three when

I first picked up a banjo. My family on my mother's side were all musicians and at a very early age I was hauled off down to Southsea where my uncle, who was a professor of music, lived and I started playing.

BRIAN The banjo. I wish you'd brought it with you. Do you still play it?

VIC Can't stand the banjo any longer.

BRIAN Oh, I love it. Did you play it like old George Formby did?

VIC Oh yes. I played the banjo, but then I changed to guitar within a very short time, because I liked the sound better.

BRIAN Your first love was jazz – what I call old-fashioned jazz?

VIC Yes, Dixieland – Chicago-style really. But then I changed when I joined Django Reinhardt and Stefan Grapelli.

BRIAN So, who did you first play with? Give us some names.

VIC I first played with Django and Stefan. In 1938, before the war, I went to America under my own power. I said to my parents, 'I want to be a professional musician,' and I went to New York. I played over there with Bobby Hackett and Eddie Condon and Peewee Russell and sat in with Tommy Dorsey and Jack Teegarden.

BRIAN Did you have your own little band yourself, or did you play in other people's bands?

VIC In '38 I had my first band with one of your previous guests – George Shearing. He was on piano.

BRIAN Then when did you get into the big band business?

VIC I came back in 1939 and went to play in Belgium and then joined up in the Air Force and they knew that I'd been messing around with music. I was an air gunner in Bomber Command when they said, 'How about organising some music for us?' And for the rest of the war I was running around playing music all over the place.

BRIAN And then the Vic Lewis Orchestra. It was a great band and quite a loud band. I mean you liked it forte.

VIC It was progressive, shall we say. I think it came, surprisingly enough, from my love for classical music. I had a pianist in the band, Ken Thorn – in the Dixieland type of band – and after studying with Ken for a bit of time I fell for the music of Delius and Shostakovich and our big band evolved out of a line that spreads between classical and jazz.

BRIAN What do we mean by big? How many musicians?

VIC In the beginning it was seventeen and then I went up to twenty – five trumpets, five trombones, five saxophones.

BRIAN Did you do a lot of the arranging?

VIC Very little. Ken Thorn did most of the arranging and then I teamed up with Stan Kenton in America and we started swapping arrangements and that was it.

BRIAN Later on you went behind a desk. You were an agent cum impresario for the Beatles and people like that.

VIC Yes, that was another sphere. In '60 I could see the writing on the wall. It seemed as if people weren't going to go and see big bands any more.

BRIAN And they were expensive, I suppose, to run.

VIC Well, we couldn't keep up with it. And I thought, 'I know, I've been backing these people like Nat King Cole and Johnny Ray and Frankie Laine. Why not become an agent? They'll know me and I can say, "I can look after all your wares and welfares." ' And other than dragging them round all the cricket grounds, which I used to do, I became their representative. Mr Ten Per Cent.

BRIAN So that's your musical side, but how, then, did you get into cricket?

VIC Well, as I said, my mother's side were all musicians. My father played for Kent seconds and the Royal Flying Corps in the First War. He was a slow left-armer and I have two or three balls at home which I treasure very much. 'Nine for forty-six' was one particular one and there was one 'eight for twenty-seven', polished and with little plaques on them. Dad would take me into the garden and he just continually bowled and said, 'Look, put your foot to meet the ball,' and all that. And really I went from there into school, from school to college and I always loved cricket. It was born in me.

BRIAN And you became a very subtle slow bowler.

VIC Became a very subtle, long-running bowler that sometimes didn't get the ball down the other end.

BRIAN When did you start your Showbiz XI?

VIC That was in '52. It really came out of a very strange thing. It came out of my love for cricket ties. I started this thing off in Derby through the Derbyshire side.

BRIAN How did you meet them?

VIC We were playing in Taunton, a one-night stand, and my manager came round to see me and said, 'There are some chaps at the door who want to get in – they're the Derbyshire County cricket team.' I said, 'Let them all in!'

BRIAN People like Cliff Gladwin.

VIC Gladwin, Jackson, Dawkes, Derek Morgan, Donald Carr – and I became a devotee of Derbyshire. I said

I'd love one of the Derbyshire county ties and they sent me one and when I got this chocolate and light blue tie, I said, 'This is wonderful. I'll go in for collecting.' I knew a lot of cricketers through my musical business, which was handy, because people used to come up and see me and say, 'I've brought you a tie.' So eventually my wife, who was also in show business in the early days, said, 'You can't keep accepting all these ties. What you'd better do is have a tie.' So I formed my own cricket club tie and had my own purple, green and blue colours.

BRIAN   So you had to get a side.

VIC   A side to fit the tie. And so to everybody who gave me a tie, I gave one back, until in '52 we formed the team. Then we became much stricter. It meant everybody had to play three games to get a tie. They had to qualify.

BRIAN   How many matches a year do you play?

VIC   In the beginning about eight. At the end of '78, when I more or less packed it in, we were doing every Saturday and every Sunday.

BRIAN   Don't be modest, I know you've collected a tremendous amount for charity. Does it run into a million or more?

VIC   Roughly we figured round about four million. We basically started by doing it for cricketers, because cricketers didn't have benefits. They just had their match.

BRIAN   Did you administer it yourself and say, 'So-and-so is down on his luck'?

VIC   The cricketers used to write to me and say, 'Look, I've got a benefit coming up, can your side come and play?' And I'd say, 'Yes, we will.' And, of course, as it went on, we found that apart from cricketers we were getting hospitals ringing and I did some for the

Taverners, because they really weren't doing anything at the time I formed my own cricket side. Then I ran a few matches for them and it just grew out of all proportion.

BRIAN You had a good mix, because you got the top class players. Name one or two who used to play for you.

VIC Well, the greatest: Weekes, Worrell, Walcott, Sobers, Pollock, Glenn Turner, Richard Hadlee – they've all played.

BRIAN And then you went into the musical world and the stage.

VIC I think one of the greatest stories was Andy Williams. Nobody could imagine him being a great cricketer at all, so I dressed him up and took him down to the Oval. The coach was Arthur McIntyre at that time and Micky Stewart. We shoved him out in the middle the day before the game, bowled anything we could and he couldn't hit a ball. So eventually I said, 'I know, Andy. Hold your bat out straight like a baseball bat.' And I said to Micky, 'Let's throw him a couple of full tosses,' and bang! They went straight into the pavilion. So we said, 'That's the way we're going to play it. Full tosses way outside the off peg.' And he just hit it like a baseball.

BRIAN What was it like being captain of all these great players? You used to field at mid-off in the right captain's position.

VIC Usually at mid-off, because I feel you can direct the side better, because we had people like, say, Tommy Steele.

BRIAN What was it like taking, say, Gary Sobers off? 'Gary, would you mind coming off? I don't think you've quite found your length.'

VIC I always used to find them great. I have so many

wonderful stories. For instance about Fred Trueman, because he was playing with me one day and he'd bowled a couple of overs and nothing was happening. And I thought this local side were thinking, 'What an idiot he is.' So I went over to Fred and said, 'Fred, it's about time we got some wickets.' 'Aye,' he said, 'how many do you want out?' So I said, 'Well, just a couple for the time being to be going on with.' So first ball of the next over – bang! Second ball – bang! He said, 'Is that all right?'

BRIAN   A strangely confident Fred. He's not normally as confident as that. Of course now Eric Clapton with his eleven does a lot of the work which you used to do. They play most Saturdays, I think.

VIC   It's much harder to run a charitable side today because there is Sunday cricket.

BRIAN   Well, this is it. After the war I was so lucky and played for about fifteen years and kept wicket to all these great bowlers, because they were free – and the visiting people. You'd get the West Indians or the Australians to come. They loved a nice, pleasant charity match on a Sunday. But now everybody's playing.

VIC   That is the tragedy. I would never have got the opportunity. I did a book on my life, called *Music and Maiden Overs* and I had pictures there of opening the batting with the late Sir Frank Worrell and Manjrekar. It's a dream – a picture of leading my side out at Lord's. Twice we played at Lord's and I had in my side such wonderful players as Wes Hall – Nicholas Parsons, Elton John, Brian Rix – we had a very good side of show people – John Alderton, Michael Parkinson. I think you umpired in a couple of these games.

BRIAN   I've raised the dreaded finger once or twice.

So you've got your own tie and at one period you wrote this book about cricket ties. How many had you collected by then?

VIC I should think up to then about a thousand to fifteen hundred.

BRIAN Have you any idea how many cricket club ties there are?

VIC Well, I have roughly now about 5,600 and I should think I'm not even a quarter of the way.

BRIAN It's unbelievable, isn't it? Do people send them to you?

VIC Yes, sometimes people do. I have said that eventually what I intend to do is to give the whole collection to Lord's, I hope a little while before my demise, but one never knows when that is. But I'm trying to log the collection. Lord's do ring me. Stephen Green (the curator of the Lord's museum) sometimes calls to ask, 'What is a green tie with a bat hanging upside down from a lamp post?'

BRIAN You're good at identifying, are you? And for people listening to you now and cricket clubs, do you want more ties?

VIC Oh, yes. My wife doesn't, but I do.

BRIAN They send it to Vic Lewis, care of Lord's, and presumably you'll have to write another book. How many did you get in this excellent little book?

VIC About 280.

BRIAN With all the little notes about each one and they're beautifully displayed – very colourful.

VIC The people who published it did a wonderful job.

BRIAN The only thing I don't like about it is that you didn't take my suggested title – *The Result is a Tie*. Instead of which they called it very boringly, *Cricket Ties*.

VIC Stupid title.

(Cricket Ties by Vic Lewis was published by Ebury Press in 1984. Ed.)

BRIAN Any particular favourite of all these many ties?

VIC I like quite a few of them. I like stripes as opposed to motifs.

BRIAN I think the most unusual one is Bertie Joel's, where they have stripes, but they go down vertically.

VIC Well, if Bertie's listening, I don't wear that one.

BRIAN Now, what about your role as administrator? How do you get to represent America on the ICC, which is the premier council of world cricket?

VIC Well, I played in Hollywood for the Hollywood Cricket Club, because my business used to take me out there, both musically and as an agent.

BRIAN Were there any film actors we would know who you played with there?

VIC The major side of C. Aubrey Smith and Errol Flynn has finished. It's a largely West Indian and Pakistan side now. We did get Olivia Newton-John's manager, who's an Australian.

BRIAN Oh, I thought you'd got her. That would have been a coup.

VIC She would have drawn a large attendance. But I used to go out there and I knew the American captain who led them in the first ICC Trophy quite well. He originally came from Lancashire and had been in America for about twenty years. He was retiring and there'd been a bit of fall-out with the previous US representative, who shall remain nameless. A new president was coming in and the captain said, 'I'm going to recommend you to take over the USA at the ICC. Would you like to do it?' So I said, 'Yes, I think I would.' So I went to Philadelphia, met the new president and he grilled me. Then he wrote to Lord's and said, 'This is my new representative.'

BRIAN And you attend all the ICC meetings representing them.

VIC Oh, yes. I've been to twelve meetings.

BRIAN You are also on the Middlesex committee and actually do a lot of work for them.

VIC Yes, I enjoy it. I've been on twelve years, actually. And we now have the Allen Stand, which has been open two years.

BRIAN For people who don't know, this is the one on the left of the pavilion as you look at it. It's the old 'Q' Stand and Middlesex have had a glass enclosure made. You've got a very attractive bar and you can have a meal.

So, your love of Middlesex – which are the great cricketers you've followed and liked?

VIC From the early days, of course, Denis Compton and Bill Edrich were absolutely magnificent – and Jack Robertson.

BRIAN You were too young for my particular hero – Patsy Hendren.

VIC No, no. I saw Patsy play – this as a young boy. I also saw Don Bradman play.

BRIAN Now, we must come back to something to finish with that you and I were concerned in. In 1970/71 Ray Illingworth toured Australia. And on a certain occasion in Sydney we won the Ashes. We won the series by two to nil and every now and then I get brainwaves and I thought, 'We must celebrate this.' I'd heard some of these awful football songs they sing and I thought, 'We must get a really good song for the team to sing.' And I thought, 'Who should write the lyrics?' And I could think of no one better than myself, so I sat down and wrote them. Then I thought, 'What about the music?' And Don Wilson and myself had done a little cabaret turn to a marvellous tune called 'Show Me Your Winkle Tonight' and this has got a great lilt. Then we thought, 'We've got to have a band,' and I think I called you from Australia.

VIC You did. I remember the call and you sent me the lyric.

BRIAN But I came to see you in your office and you had Ken Thorn taking down me singing it.

VIC That's right. And we scored the whole thing out from your voice.

BRIAN And you got together famous session players.

VIC Oh, yes. They were the best musicians that we had in London. In those days I'd stopped being a band leader and all you do is ring a fixer and say, 'I want so-and-so and so-and-so,' and I thought the team did well as a choir.

BRIAN Well, let's hear how the first verse went, with my little bit of commentary at the start.

(The record was played as recorded by Ray Illingworth's team in 1971, following Brian's commentary on the moment when Derek Underwood had Terry Jenner caught by Keith Fletcher to win the Sydney Test and the Ashes for England. Ed.)

> We brought the Ashes back home,
> We've got them here in the urn.
> The Aussies had had them twelve years,
> So it was about our turn.
> Oh, what a tough fight
> It's been in the dazzling sunlight.
> In spite of the boos from the mob on the Hill,
> We won by two matches to nil.

VIC I think it was a shame it wasn't a number one.

BRIAN It was rather a long way down the list. I think we made 55 quid from it.

VIC No, it was 118. It was a smash hit.

BRIAN Oh, I always thought it was 55. That is a smash, isn't it?

VIC We thought, 'What are we going to do with this cheque? We can't split it between twenty.'

BRIAN Well, we had a draw for it, didn't we? And Ray Illingworth drew it and won the money himself!

HAROLD PINTER

I HAD NEVER met Harold Pinter before he joined us at the Oval for the third Test against India in 1990. I had always heard how keen he was on cricket. Indeed his sole recreation recorded in *Who's Who is* cricket. Funnily enough I never came across him in any of the many charity matches in which I have played.

At the Oval he was accompanied by his lovely biographer wife, Lady Antonia Fraser, who was wearing what I think I remember calling 'a smashing hat'. Incidentally it is now perfectly easy for a lady to visit our box at the Oval because ladies are allowed in the pavilion even for Test Matches.

It was not always so. On one occasion some twenty-five years ago a high-up at the BBC had had a very good lunch with a lady friend, and decided to go down to the Oval to watch a Test Match during the afternoon. He paid at the gate for both of them, and then asked where was the BBC commentary position. He was told that it was on the roof at the top of the pavilion, but that ladies were not allowed into the pavilion. Nothing daunted he noticed some BBC engineers climbing a ladder up the side of the pavilion and decided to follow them. Precariously he started to climb, he in his black Homburg hat, his lady friend in a picturesque Ascot hat, and wearing a rather short, flimsy summer dress.

The members in the stand below watched fascinated. There was a stiff breeze blowing and the higher they climbed, the higher was the lady's skirt blown up over her thighs. All eyes were on her; no one was bothering with the cricket.

There were gales of laughter and loud applause as they finally reached the roof. How much she had revealed I'm not sure, but I think it was lucky that she was not wearing a kilt! The Surrey Secretary, Brian Castor, was not too pleased and there was a lot of apologising to be done by the hierarchy of the BBC. It wouldn't happen today. Ladies can come up to us in the orthodox way.

But to get back to Harold. I am ashamed that I have never seen any of his twenty or more plays which he has written for the theatre, not even his most famous – *The Caretaker*. I have of course seen plays he has written or directed for films, TV and radio. He does, and is, so many things these days that I am amazed that he finds any time at all for cricket. But he does, and as you will gather from some of his observations, he has a surprisingly deep knowledge of the game.

THE OVAL, 25 AUGUST 1990

BRIAN JOHNSTON You were brought up in Hackney in the thirties. Not the sort of playground, I would imagine, for someone who enjoys cricket.

HAROLD PINTER Oh, we had cricket. When I finally went to Hackney Downs Grammar School during the war there was lots of cricket. We played as much cricket as possible and I also went to Lord's a great deal during the war. I started to go to Lord's in about 1944, but really in 1945, when the Victory Tests were taking place and I saw Keith Miller and Wally Hammond and Hutton and Washbrook. Compton was still in India, but it was a very exciting period.

BRIAN But you were also evacuated during the war. Did you get any cricket in the country?

HAROLD Oh, yes. I was evacuated to Cornwall, right down in the South – Carheays Castle, in fact, with about 26 other boys. We played cricket there. Cricket was very much part of my life from the day I was born.

BRIAN Were your parents keen on cricket?

HAROLD No, no, there was a general feeling about cricket. In the thirties the whole of England loved cricket, I think, at all levels. That was my impression as a child, anyway.

BRIAN And your skills as a boy – what were you – a batsman?

HAROLD Yes, a batsman. I'm 60 next month, but I still regard myself as a promising batsman.

BRIAN Who have you played for?

HAROLD Well, I've really only been associated with a wandering side called Gaieties for the last twenty years. That was originally a theatrical club started by Lupino

Lane. I started to play in about 1969 for Gaieties. It was called Gaieties because Lupino Lane was working at the Gaiety theatre – nothing to do with other kinds of Gaieties.

BRIAN The theatre is, alas, no more – on the corner there in the Strand.

HAROLD It was originally a stage side, but now it's still very active and we have a strong fixture list. I'm the chairman now. I skippered the side for about five years in the seventies. I'm still very, very involved in it. In fact, I'm also the match manager, I have to tell you.

BRIAN You stand a good chance of going in first and getting the opening over, don't you?

HAROLD No, they wouldn't let me do that any more. We don't have a theatrical thing any more. Our last few games of the season are Oxted, Ashtead and Roehampton and we're going to play a club in South Wales.

BRIAN That's getting serious – Roehampton.

You're a member of MCC. Did you get in as a playing member?

HAROLD No, no. I don't know how I got in, but I became a member in the sixties. The changes at Lord's are very interesting. I remember very well I happened to be in front of the pavilion when Freddie Titmus was playing and before the game he walked in front of the committee room and looked inside and there was Freddie Brown and Gubby Allen and he said, 'Good morning, sir.' And Freddie Brown said, 'Morning, Titmus.' That doesn't happen any more.

BRIAN There was the business of initials, too. An announcement was made at Lord's once. It said, 'On your scorecard, for "F. J. Titmus", read "Titmus F.

J." ' Because they'd put him down as an amateur.

HAROLD   Wouldn't do at all.

BRIAN   Do you support Middlesex? Are they your side?

HAROLD   No, I've always supported Yorkshire. I don't know why – actually I do know why, because Len Hutton was my hero from 1946.

BRIAN   A good man to pick.

HAROLD   He still is, really, though I've never met him. I could watch him bat for ever. I thought he was the most wonderful batsman and I did as much of that as I could – following him all over the place. So Yorkshire became my side.

BRIAN   I thought you had associations somehow with Somerset.

HAROLD   No. I was lucky enough to play with Arthur Wellard. He actually played for Gaieties. He played in the seventies when he was in his late sixties. He was a wonderful man, a great cricketer.

BRIAN   Was he still hitting sixes?

HAROLD   Oh, yes. He could really give it a tremendous whack. He was my teacher, actually. He was very rigorous with me. I produced the odd six.

BRIAN   Now, Jeffrey Archer told me he read an article by you about Wellard. He said it was one of the best articles he'd ever read.

HAROLD   Well, that's very kind. What always impressed me about Arthur was that his life really was cricket. He would hold a cricket ball as if it was a golf ball, his hands were so big, but the point really was that he'd lived a life that was really happy, playing cricket.

BRIAN   I was lucky I saw him playing in the Lord's 1938 Test Match.

HAROLD   Where he got 38.

BRIAN Well done – and Denis Compton helped save us in the second innings.

HAROLD Arthur bowled Badcock, you know, and he gave me the stump.

BRIAN Big hands. Alec Bedser's got huge hands and Alan Davidson had big hands, but Arthur Wellard's were real Palethorpe sausages, weren't they? The fingers and the huge palms.

HAROLD But he was an inspiration to the club side, you see. And then he umpired when he couldn't get the arm over.

BRIAN He took a few wickets for you umpiring, did he?

HAROLD No, never. He wouldn't do a thing like that at all. 'Not out,' he'd say and that was it. And 'You're joking,' he'd say.

BRIAN I know he played on fairly small grounds – Frome and ones like that, but he did hit I don't know how many sixes.

HAROLD Well he twice hit five sixes off successive balls.

(Arthur Wellard died at the end of 1980, aged 78. Until Ian Botham's 80 sixes in the 1985 season, Wellard held the top four places in the record list of sixes hit in a season: 66 in 1935, 57 in both 1936 and 1938 and 51 in 1933. Ed.)

BRIAN What had he got? He was very strong. He must have had a super eye.

HAROLD He had a wonderful eye and he told a wonderful story of when he was on the Lionel Tennyson tour of India in 1936. He hit the biggest six off Amar Singh. He said it was going into the Ganges, but something stopped it at the top of a stand. He said, 'I really got hold of that ball.' And on that tour was Joe Hardstaff, who I thought was a wonderful batsman. In fact, watching Azharuddin the other day – I'm not old enough to remember Ranji or Duleep – but I thought Hardstaff had that grace.

BRIAN Well he was like Cyril Walters or Tom Graveney, it didn't matter if he was defending or not – rather like David Gower. When you see him just stroking one through the covers, it's lovely to watch.

You go to Lord's; do you come to the Oval a bit?

HAROLD Yes, I'm a member here, too. It's a great ground.

BRIAN Now you don't play, you watch, do you?

HAROLD I don't play much. Oddly enough, it's the fielding. The eye's gone. I used to be really able to catch. I had quite a good eye, but that's become very blurry now.

BRIAN How do you mix it with your writing? Could you write a play sitting in the dressing room? Or did you have to take time off to do the writing and play cricket another time?

HAROLD You find it's like a good old stew, you throw a few things in. I've always enjoyed the range of life that I've been lucky enough to experience.

BRIAN Have you written a play about cricket?

HAROLD No, but in a number of films I wrote I managed to get a cricket scene in, like *The Go Between*. There was a very important cricket scene in that.

BRIAN Oh, that was lovely.

HAROLD And another film I wrote – *Accident* – I got a cricket scene in.

BRIAN Are you tempted now to sit down and write a nice cricket play, because there's room for one.

HAROLD It's not an easy thing to do. I've thought about it a bit. I think the real cricket action goes on in the dressing rooms, you know. All the real aggro.

This is amateur, of course, I've never been in a professional dressing room, I don't know what it's like. People – particularly foreigners – tend to say cricket is a peaceful game – like a ballet. Obviously it's not. It's a very, very violent activity, I think. A lot of people are bowling very hard and trying to hit the ball hard and the feeling is incredibly intense. The thing that always continues to amaze me about cricket is that every game possesses tremendous tension and drama.

BRIAN It's the team drama; it's the individual drama. Imagine the scene now when Gower goes back. Is he left alone to sit and mope? Knowing him, he'll probably be smiling.

(David Gower, after missing the previous winter's tour to the West Indies, had only returned to the England side for the second half of the season. He had not had notable success and now, with his selection for the forthcoming tour of Australia very much in the balance, he had been out for eight. On the final day of this Test, though, he was to add to the drama with a superlative 157 not out to save the Test against India and secure his tour place. Ed.)

HAROLD That phrase, 'Bad luck', covers an awful lot, doesn't it?

BRIAN With the pat on the back from the skipper, 'Bad luck.'

HAROLD That's it. But I think the aggravation and the disappointments are so profound, aren't they?

BRIAN Do you enjoy captaining? There's something about it. I used to enjoy captaining teams. I think it adds tremendous fun working things out.

HAROLD Oh, I found it very tough, because everyone knows if it goes right you're fine. When it goes wrong there's only one person that's to blame and that's you. I actually resigned my Gaieties captaincy on the spot one day on the field.

BRIAN   Oh no!

HAROLD   Yes, I did. Because I took a bowler off and said, 'Thank you very much, Mac, that's it.' And my vice-captain, who was one of my greatest friends and still is, said to me, 'You're taking him off, are you?' I said, 'That's right,' and he called me a short, sharp word, so I said, 'That's it!'

BRIAN   Talk about tension in cricket.

HAROLD   So I then said, 'OK, Chris, you're the captain.' This wasn't a democratic election. 'You're taking over.' And the next game I played under him – it was at Ashtead – they were 174 for two and he came to me and said, 'What do you think I should do?' And I said, 'I haven't the faintest idea.'

BRIAN   No more responsibility.

HAROLD   Absolutely. 'Sort it out for yourself.' It was a wonderful moment of relief, I must say.

BRIAN   Is there anything about the modern game you'd like to see changed?

HAROLD   Someone was saying, I think, this morning in one of the newspapers – and I entirely agree – this is a detail, but it's rather important – with the helmet situation, you can't actually discern the batsmen. My world was the world of Hutton, Bradman and Miller and they were all absolutely individual.

BRIAN   They were people you could see. We have asked Micky Stewart, in fact, to ask his players to come out holding their helmets, so people could at least see who these zombies are before they put their helmets on. They say it's difficult to fit it on. It's a pity for the game, but then you and I don't have to go out and face the bouncers.

HAROLD No, that's right, but when Griffith and Hall were bowling – they were pretty quick too – people weren't wearing helmets. Brian Close didn't wear a helmet; Dexter didn't.

BRIAN I once asked Bradman if he came back now if he'd wear a helmet and he said he would, but I reckon he was being polite. He didn't wear one against Larwood.

HAROLD I was very lucky to see Bradman. I saw him in 1948.

BRIAN Were you here for the famous dismissal?

HAROLD I certainly was.

(Don Bradman was out second ball for nought at the Oval in his last Test innings. Ed.)

I was here for Hutton's 30 when he was caught by Tallon off Lindwall.

BRIAN Down the leg side. I think he was the only chap who got to double figures. We made 52.

HAROLD That's right, 52 all out.

BRIAN You've got a retentive memory for these things.

HAROLD Yes. I was thrilled to meet Keith Miller and Denis Compton a couple of weeks ago and I asked both of them a question I've been meaning to ask for many, many years and I've never had the opportunity. Was Bradman caught by Ikin for 28 at Brisbane in 1946?

BRIAN Was he out? Well, Wally Hammond thought he was.

HAROLD Well, Miller and Compton also thought he was. Miller was the next man in. He was just reaching for his gloves and suddenly he saw that Bradman wasn't walking.

BRIAN This was one in the gully and it was a question of whether it touched the ground or didn't.

HAROLD   And of course Bradman went on to get 187 and 234 in the next match.

BRIAN   And if he'd failed in that match he might have given up, because he wasn't a very fit man.

HAROLD   Yes, but he didn't.

BRIAN   To go back to the war, when you went to Lord's, the matches involved teams like the Home Guard and that sort of thing.

HAROLD   Absolutely, but at the end of the war – I was a boy of fourteen at the time – I heard a report that the Americans were going to play baseball at Lord's. And I rang Lord's and asked to speak to the Secretary of the MCC. I said, 'I'm ringing you as a schoolboy and I feel that this report that the Americans are going to play baseball at Lord's is the most disgraceful thing I've ever heard.' And he said, 'Don't worry, my dear fellow, I don't think you should take these reports too seriously. I don't think we're actually going to allow it to happen.'

BRIAN   Let's just talk about your acting. Do you enjoy that?

HAROLD   Oh, yes, I enjoy acting. But the trouble with acting was that I couldn't play cricket when I was young, because I was moving about so much in rep. And I was in Ireland, but I took my cricket bat there with me and we played a bit on the meadows over there.

BRIAN   But you've now gone to the other side of things, directing. Do you enjoy that?

HAROLD   Oh, yes, I enjoy the activity, but there's nothing I enjoy more than being at the Oval today. That's the truth.

THE RT. REV.
AND RT. HON.
LORD RUNCIE
OF CUDDESDON

I HAD ALWAYS heard that the Archbishop of Canterbury liked pigs and bred them with great success. This was confirmed when I interviewed him at Lambeth Palace for *Down Your Way* shortly after he had become the Archbishop in 1980. I was met at the Palace by none other than Terry Waite who took me to meet the Archbishop. During the interview which followed I also learnt of his love of cricket, and subsequently met him several times in various boxes at Lord's. He, somewhat naturally, was always asked to the President's tent during the Canterbury week. This probably led to the apocryphal story told on page 133.

There is also another story which I did not dare to tell the Archbishop. It's of two visitors to Canterbury having coffee in a café. One of them spotted a grey-haired man with horn-rimmed glasses sitting at a corner table. He said, 'I swear that's the Archbishop of Canterbury sitting over there.' His companion replied, 'Don't be ridiculous. Of course it isn't.' 'Right,' said his friend, 'I bet you a quid that it is. I shall go and ask him.'

He went over to the corner table and after a brief conversation returned looking very red in the face. 'Well, what did he say?' his friend asked. 'He told me to mind my own —— business and to —— off!' He handed over his one pound to his friend who said, 'Thanks. But what a pity. Now we shall never know whether or not it *was* the Archbishop.'

After a session in the commentary box in his company, it was much easier to understand how, in the Second World War, the Archbishop had been a successful tank commander in the Scots Guards. He came over as a very strong character with a delightful sense of humour, neither of which could perhaps be sensed during his many TV appearances on state or ceremonial occasions.

LORD'S, 22 JUNE 1991

BRIAN JOHNSTON How long was your reign as Archbishop of Canterbury?

LORD RUNCIE Ten and a half years.

BRIAN That's quite a long innings.

LORD RUNCIE It's enough – for me.

BRIAN Well, you're looking very well on it now in retirement. What are you doing?

LORD RUNCIE I'm settling down and watching a bit of cricket occasionally. I've been in America, delivering some uncontroversial lectures. I hope I didn't undermine my successor. And I've been opening things and launching things and I've got a variety of occupations, some ceremonial and some on which I want to focus. I'm going to be President of the Classical Association, which is quite formidable, but there is an old association between the classics and cricket, I think, as a civilising element in national life.

BRIAN You've got some rather grand title – the High something.

LORD RUNCIE Yes, I'm the High Steward of Cambridge.

BRIAN What on earth does that involve?

LORD RUNCIE Well, it doesn't involve a great deal. It doesn't carry any emoluments, but it's a very ancient title and ceremonial figure in the university and it was once held by people like Thomas More. Now I walk in processions and actually last week I made my debut as High Steward and walked behind Prince Philip as Chancellor. One of the people who was getting an honorary degree, an East European mathematician of great distinction, turned to me as we were robing and said, 'Vot does ze High Steward do?' And I said, 'Well, he's rather a ceremonial figure, you know.' And then, trying to make it more exciting, I said, 'I walk behind the Chancellor and of course I suppose, if anything happened to the Chancellor . . .' 'Oh,' he said, 'I see you are a kind of Dan Quayle.'

BRIAN Well, how did the kind of Dan Quayle start? You were born in Liverpool. Did you go to school in Liverpool?

LORD RUNCIE Yes, I went to Merchant Taylors, which is in Crosby, between Liverpool and Southport, and learnt to love cricket there.

BRIAN Did you play cricket a lot?

LORD RUNCIE Yes, I was very keen on cricket. It was my first love, I think, in sports. I was not a great cricketer, but I captained the school in a lean year.

BRIAN Look, we're not modest in the box. What did you do well? Did you bat?

LORD RUNCIE Yes, I was an opening batsman – pretty steady – and a poor bowler. I've always been a poor bowler. I played what I suppose may be my last game last year, the Archbishop of Canterbury's XI v. the Governor of the Bank of England's XI and, in order to jazz up this charity match, they persuaded me to bowl an over. Of course, even in my heyday, I've never been a bowler and it was a rather disastrous moment, particularly as the television cameras happened to be there at that moment. And for weeks and indeed months afterwards people would say to me, 'That was a spectacular wide you bowled on television.' That was the first ball.

BRIAN You got through the over all right?

LORD RUNCIE I managed to get through the over. I actually bowled against Colin Cowdrey and one ball scarcely reached the stumps at the other end.

BRIAN So you had the powers of leadership as a boy – you were selected as captain.

LORD RUNCIE I don't know who selected me, but I was actually captain and we used to play around the various schools. Our most distant one was playing in the Isle of Man against King William's College. I think that's where I made my best total. I think I scored a century.

BRIAN You made a hundred! I never did.

LORD RUNCIE I've got this in the back of my mind. The unfortunate thing is that, although I've been parading this story and I did have very happy memories of the Isle of Man, I've got to go there to present the prizes at their Speech Day in the autumn. I'm not sure if they've invited me because of my great century in the past or whether they're going to disabuse me of this illusion by showing me the scorebook.

BRIAN I'm sure you wouldn't say you'd scored one if you hadn't. So, living in Lancashire, did you support Lancashire as a cricket side?

LORD RUNCIE Liverpool had two games a year.

BRIAN At Aigburth.

LORD RUNCIE Wonderful Liverpool name that – Aigburth – Saxon name. They were interesting games, because you had the tourists once and a county match the other. I used to set off with my sandwiches and I saw Wally Hammond, playing for Gloucestershire, and Cyril Washbrook and also saw Bradman and saw George Headley. So before the war, when I was at school, Aigburth was a place of pilgrimage.

BRIAN Were Hallows and Makepeace around?

LORD RUNCIE Yes, they were playing and the Tyldesleys.

BRIAN Ernest Tyldesley and Richard Tyldesley – a rather rotund character who bowled slow leg-breaks.

LORD RUNCIE And a very gentlemanly captain, P. T. Eckersley.

BRIAN He was killed in the war, wasn't he?

LORD RUNCIE Yes, a fine man. And there was a lot of cricket around Liverpool. The Liverpool Competition brings together Bootle and the Wirral, or did in my day.

BRIAN So, what did you do before the war?

LORD RUNCIE I just went up for a year to Oxford at the beginning of the war and then I went away to the Army and came back in 1945.

BRIAN We were both in the Brigade of Guards. You were in the Scots Guards; I was in the Grenadiers. I got in because we decided before the war started we might try to get into the best regiment. We went and drilled in the summer in our black Homburg hats and city suits at Wellington Barracks. How did you get in?

LORD RUNCIE   Well, it's a long story. I got in because the Scots Guards had lost a lot of officers in the Western desert.

BRIAN   This was in '42?

LORD RUNCIE   Yes. I was going into a Scottish regiment. My father was Scottish and we came of a Scottish family and I was at Oxford in the Officer Training Corps and they put into my mind the idea of becoming a Scots Guardsman. And I said, 'But I haven't got a private income.' And the adjutant said across the room, 'I think in wartime, you know, it wouldn't matter greatly. It's more important that we have soldiers these days.'

BRIAN   As long as you've got a few polo ponies. And you were a tank commander. We were tanks, too. So, you commanded a troop?

LORD RUNCIE   A troop of tanks, under the command of people like Willie Whitelaw.

BRIAN   You're a splendid couple, you and Willie Whitelaw. No wonder we won the war!

LORD RUNCIE   We soldiered together. The Scots Guards weren't mad keen on cricket. I couldn't persuade the tank crews much. I always remember a day when we were in Normandy and it was a very fine day. We'd cleaned the tanks and so on and I suggested to the sergeant, 'What about a game of cricket?' And this Glaswegian looked at me witheringly and said, 'Crucket? Yon's a daft wee girlie's game!' So I didn't get much cricket in the Army.

BRIAN   So when you came out of the Brigade of Guards, what did you decide to do?

LORD RUNCIE   Well, I wasn't too sure. I had at the back of my mind, but not very much at the front of my mind, that I might one day be ordained, but I went back to Oxford, where I'd started, in the early years of the war, to read classics. I went back and read ancient history and philosophy and finished off my course until 1948, when I went – it sounds rather unadventurous – across to Cambridge.

BRIAN   Yes, two universities. A bit greedy.

LORD RUNCIE   Yes, and I stayed there a bit, although I was ordained after two years and went up to Newcastle. I then came back and taught in Cambridge for a time. Then I married a wife who was the daughter of a real cricketer. He was the Senior Fellow of a college of which I was at that time the Junior Fellow, which was rather a crafty move, I think. It's called endogamy – marriage within the tribe. He was a man called Turner – and this is the only bit of homework I've done for this conversation, I've looked him up in *Who's Who* - he played for Worcestershire 40 times between 1909 and 1921. I went to a Worcester diocesan festival shortly after I became Archbishop of Canterbury in 1981 and it was held on that marvellous cricket ground beneath the cathedral. It was an open air service and I wasn't sure then about my father-in-law's cricketing past, but I risked saying at an early stage in the sermon, 'My unbelieving father-in-law would have felt that at last I had been preaching on a sacred spot.' And by the time I'd finished the service, the cricket officials, who'd been watching and suddenly leapt into action when I mentioned this, produced for me his average over the years. His bowling average and his batting average. I thought that was a good example of dedication.

BRIAN   Can you remember what they were?

LORD RUNCIE   Modest.

BRIAN   How long did you have a parish for?

LORD RUNCIE   Well, first of all I was in Newcastle and only for a short time was I in a parish, because I came back to teach. But when I'd left teaching in Cambridge I went to be principal of a college just outside Oxford for ten years, between '60 and '70 and during that time I was also vicar of the parish of Cuddesdon, a place to which I'm devoted. And for me being in charge of that parish, though it was tiny but full of character, was, perhaps, more significant than running a college. I learnt more and was rather a Pooh-Bah in those days, because I was chairman of the parish council and chairman of the sports committee.

BRIAN Were you selected to play for the village, though?

LORD RUNCIE I played cricket for the village against the college and I played cricket quite a bit during those years, because there was, for example, in the neighbouring village of Garsington a famous manor house. The squire of Garsington was somebody called John Wheeler-Bennett and every year he had a tremendous occasion when the squire's XI played the village at Garsington. And the squire's XI was a mixture of real cricketers, local characters and royal equerries. It was free drink for everybody and the village really turned out. It was a weekend, so he had a house party. Then there was always a service on the Sunday and I remember that if you were recruited to preach before the village and before this cricketing house party, it was traditional to get up some striking text appropriate to the occasion, like 'Ruth came down with a full pitcher.' The man who won, having regard to the sociability of the previous afternoon, was the man who ultimately became the Dean of Lincoln and rejoiced in the name of Oliver Twisleton-Wykeham-Fiennes. He discovered a text in 'Chronicles' which was 'The lords of the Assyrians were drinking themselves drunk in the pavilion.'

BRIAN What was your text, do you remember?

LORD RUNCIE I think mine was fairly unadventurous.

It was, I think, in 'Kings' – Saul: 'Give me a man that can play well.'

BRIAN Well, I think Gooch would say that.

Are you in favour of cricket-playing vicars? I have a friend, John Woodcock, who has the gift of giving the local vicar his job and he sets a great importance on the religious side, but he does always ask him, 'Do you play cricket?'

LORD RUNCIE Well, I think it's a good qualification. Obviously I think the spiritual qualifications are the ones that really matter, but it's a symbol of something rather good. It's the same with the classics. I remember, in years gone by, meeting once Isaiah Berlin, the great Oxford savant, and I had a cricket bag in one hand and a copy of Plato under my arm and he was delighted. I was an undergraduate at the time and he stood in the middle of the pavement and said, 'Ah! What we all stand for, what we all stand for!' In my experience, I have to say that the cricketers form a very good ingredient in the clergy in any diocese. There was in the diocese of St. Albans in my days a very old-fashioned, rather eccentric clergyman who I remember once saying that until clergy give up their modish obsession with synods and return to their traditional activities of cricket, bee-keeping and siring Nelsons, we shall have no improvement in the morals of this country.

BRIAN You talk about bee-keeping, what about pig-keeping, which is your big hobby?

LORD RUNCIE I've got, perhaps, too much attention over that. My pigs are looked after by a splendid farm for mentally handicapped people and I'm interested in that. It's Oast Farm Trust and I have a few black Berkshire pigs.

BRIAN They win prizes, though.

LORD RUNCIE We've got a secret weapon in a man who lives near the community, who is an international

141

expert on pigs. He gives advice and the pigs win prizes and I get this notoriety and indeed a spurious reputation of being a distinguished pig-keeper. We've got a very fine sow called Portia, who won the Kent Show two years ago, then she had a year off for motherhood last year.

BRIAN Would she rival the Empress of Blandings? Do you go and poke her with a stick? Pig owners generally do, don't they?

LORD RUNCIE My Portia is a black Berkshire pig, which the Empress of Blandings was, although it's sometimes depicted as a pink pig. I could prove to you from the texts of Wodehouse that she was a black Berkshire pig.

BRIAN To come back to cricket, when you were in Canterbury, did you go to the county ground to watch?

LORD RUNCIE I wish I could say that I did. I only really was able during the last ten years to have two days that I kept particularly and that was to have a day at the Lord's Test and a day at Canterbury cricket week. I think Canterbury cricket week is something that nobody can match.

BRIAN There was an occasion there – I don't know if you know – when you were sitting on the right hand of Mr Swanton when he was president. On his left was the Duke of Kent and do you know what the chap walking past said? 'Who are those two people sitting with Jim Swanton?'

LORD RUNCIE I can well believe that. I've had some wonderful conversations with people there who were my boyhood and young manhood heroes. Like Leslie Ames – I miss him a great deal – we always used to have a little talk about George Duckworth, his old rival at Lancashire, and he was always so generous.

BRIAN Who else were your heroes in the cricket world?

LORD RUNCIE The first real bat I had, had 'Len Hutton' on it and it's been a great thrill in these last few years to be able to see him and talk with him here. And yesterday I was with Clyde Walcott and he reminded me that there's a marvellous story of my predecessor, Michael Ramsey, who was in Barbados. He was a wonderful, lovely, saintly man, looking patriarchal and he had this rather sing-song voice and he gave out his theme. He said, 'I'm going to speak to you about the three Ws.' And there was a great sigh and all the congregation looked eager. Then he said, 'Worship, witness and work,' and a great groan went up.

BRIAN We're both of us cricket nuts. Do we exaggerate the importance of cricket in character-building? Do you think it's got something that other games haven't got?

LORD RUNCIE Well, I hope it can preserve some of the sort of decencies that surround the way in which the game is conducted. And I think the need for patience and sticking with things is very important in character-formation when we live in a society where short-termism and immediate satisfaction is so dominant, partly from the communications explosion and also the huge variety of options for people about what they should believe and how they should behave and the way in which they can change so quickly from one thing to another. I think the stabilities and the need for patience, cooperation and team-work and, yes, something of the romance that attaches to cricket has within it the seeds of idealism without which no society will ever be well nourished.

BRIAN And it's a very good mix, because it's essentially a team game, but when it comes to the crunch, you're out there alone against Curtly Ambrose, aren't you?

LORD RUNCIE It's all up to you, but you in company with others. You can't be unaware of the other people with whom you're working. And I do think the need for decisions – I remember this as a captain, but it goes for anybody in the side, you do have to make quite a lot of decisions over quite a period of time and they're decisions which are sometimes immediate and sometimes call for reflection – I think that's character-building, too.

BRIAN You've had some great cricketing people in the Church – the present Bishop of Liverpool, a Test player, Canon Parsons, Canon Gillingham . . .

LORD RUNCIE Yes, and E. T. Killick, who died at the crease in a diocesan match. He is someone who is very well remembered in Hertfordshire even today. The influence of a cricketing parson.

MAX BOYCE

IT WAS DAFFODIL and leek time in the commentary box at Trent Bridge on the Saturday of the third Test against the West Indies in 1991. The start had been delayed after a violent thunderstorm had flooded the ground, and the luncheon interval had been brought forward. This gave Ron Allsopp and his ground staff team time to carry out a magnificent mopping up operation, using machines called 'whales'. They did so well, that allowing for an extra hour at the end, only thirty minutes' actual play was lost altogether.

Anyhow there was no gloom in the box as our guest Max Boyce regaled us with stories in his lilting Welsh accent – stories of rugby matches when 'I was there', or tales of strange events in the valleys. Max has an infectious chuckle and as he reminisced he reminded me so much of my old friend, the late Wynford Vaughan-Thomas. Wherever he was, at a party or in a bar, there was always a crowd around him enjoying his non-stop flow describing things that had happened to him. There was always a strong element of truth in all that he said, but he embellished each story with a few additons of his own which made it sound funnier than it probably was.

So it was with Max, who like so many of our guests had made a long journey, just to be with us for our lunchtime spot. We were especially grateful to him, as he had to rush back to Wales for an engagement that evening.

TRENT BRIDGE, 6 JULY 1991

MAX BOYCE I was listening this morning on my way here and I heard David Lloyd say something about Wales had done terribly well. I thought, 'Oh good, Wales have done well in Australia.' But he meant the whales – the water-sucking machines drying the ground.

BRIAN JOHNSTON Have you ever seen Wales play in Australia?

MAX Yes, I was out there thirteen years ago. I went on the 1978 tour and I followed them. It was a wonderful tour, because it was the grand slam side, but of course they didn't do terribly well out there. There was a wonderful woman from Llanelli out there and she asked me where the Welsh team were staying, because, she said, 'I've made 30 warm Welsh faggots for the team.' She went round to the hotel with these and Clive Rowlands, who was the team manager, accepted them and said, 'The boys will have them for breakfast.' Well, Wales played the Test and they lost and the next morning the first person I saw was this woman in a Welsh costume with tears running down her cheeks. 'Don't be upset,' I said, 'It's only a game.' 'Oh, Max,' she said, 'Do you think it was the faggots?' I was telling the story on Australian television and of course a faggot in Australia has got a totally different connotation. They were falling about in the studio when I said that Wales had lost because someone had given them 30 warm Welsh faggots.

BRIAN What about the cricket side of your life?

MAX It was my great love when I was younger and I played from about sixteen in school and then in the South Wales League. Every side had a pro., so it was a good standard of cricket.

BRIAN What sort of a cricketer were you?

MAX Alan Jones, the former Glamorgan opening bat, described me as having the finest temperament of any fast bowler he'd ever seen. My line and length lacked a bit, but I had a fine temperament. I was a fiery opening bowler. I liked it very much.

BRIAN Did you base yourself on Fred Trueman?

MAX Yes, I used to pretend to be Fred.

BRIAN You are Welsh through-and-through. Where were you born?

MAX I was born in a little mining village called Glyn Neath in the Glyn Neath valley, which is about sixteen miles from Swansea.

BRIAN Was that a mining area?

MAX We had six pits there and there aren't any at all now. The last one closed during the last miners' strike. Very much a pit village – a very pretty village now.

BRIAN Was your father a miner?

MAX Yes. My father was killed in a mine explosion a month before I was born, in fact.

BRIAN But that didn't put you off, because you went into the mines.

MAX I suppose, coming from an area like that, you didn't think of it as being dangerous and hazardous, because all your friends did it and all your family did it. People who've never lived in a mining area would say, 'Why did you go down the pit?' exactly as you've just said. But you didn't think of it, because it was part of the lifestyle of that particular community. There was nowhere else to work. There were no factories. Everyone worked underground.

BRIAN But did you gradually find that you were able to make people laugh?

MAX I never intended to be an entertainer. I started out as a sort of folk singer. I spent ten years underground and five years in engineering and then I bought a guitar and started singing in the local folk clubs. Just upstairs in a pub and you'd invite professional folk singers down and then the local people would get up and sing a couple of songs. I wasn't doing terribly well and then I started writing my own things. It was the time when Julie Felix was singing about Vietnam. Well, I couldn't sing about Vietnam with any credence, so I sang about the things I knew about, like shift work and the fact that the colliery was being closed. And it struck a chord with people. People could identify with the things I wrote about. Then gradually the introductions became longer and it became a bit of story-telling. The songs became more infrequent and now I'll sing maybe only 20 per cent of the time in a performance of an hour and a half.

BRIAN When did your career really take off? In the early seventies?

MAX I was known in Wales from about 1970/71 but in Britain nationally in about 1973. I cut an album in Treorchy Rugby Club. We couldn't sell the tickets – it was fifty pence – because I was completely unknown. So people went into the streets and said, 'There's a lad cutting a record, will you come in, because without an audience it will be impossible.' And they formed the audience and that record went on to sell over half a million.

BRIAN That was your first big hit.

MAX First national success.

BRIAN I remember all these marvellous descriptions of rugby matches: 'I was there'.

MAX That 'I was there' came about actually in a cricket dinner in St Helen's where I was asked to perform for Glamorgan and I'd never performed in an after-dinner context before. And I thought, 'How can I put these stories together?' And the thing that linked them all was the fact that I was there. From there it became a bit of a catchphrase, so I incorporated it in the stage act. I heard someone talking about Botham's match at Headingley in 1981 and he said, 'As Max Boyce would say, "I was there." '

BRIAN Having mentioned him, what about Ian Botham, the famous pantomime king? He performed with you in Bradford – a very successful pantomime season. He's a big figure off stage, what's he like on stage?

MAX He was wonderful. I think he'd say himself he struggled for the first week.

BRIAN Well, he would do.

MAX I think if I had to open the batting or come in at number six I'd struggle as well. What I will say about him he was tremendously disciplined. We'd been friends a long time and I said, 'No, I won't have you,' because I was afraid it might destroy our friendship. I

149

thought he'd be terribly bored, but he absolutely loved it. He was never late and he went round all the local hospitals and signed autographs.

BRIAN   Did he sing?

MAX   No he didn't sing. It's not a big part, but the main fact was that it was him.

BRIAN   A few mentions of cricket.

MAX   England were in Australia and whenever Gower was mentioned we'd have the sound effect of an aeroplane. He'd go, 'Hello, David'. What I was most concerned about was I didn't want to ridicule him. I didn't want him to go with some arty director in another show, who'd make him do stupid things and decry him as a person. So, because I have great admiration for him as a man and as one of the greatest players the world has ever seen, I protected him in that way and I didn't give him any line that would have made him look silly. And he became this very strong king and people could relate to him.

BRIAN   Well, I've never known there was a king in *Jack and the Beanstalk*. Was he up with the ogre?

MAX   Some people thought he was the giant.

I saw the nasty side of the press – 'the fibre-tipped assassins'. I think somebody wrote after the opening night, which went sensationally well, 'The only thing more wooden than Ian Botham was the beanstalk.' But he himself stuck it on the dressing room door to remind himself. He was measurably better by the end.

BRIAN   What about Glamorgan cricket? Have you followed that always?

MAX   All my life.

BRIAN   Who were your special heroes?

MAX   Well, at the moment Hugh Morris is on everybody's lips. I wonder if he'd come from Essex or Middlesex, would he have played more?

BRIAN   There's the old Welsh thing – but you've got some very influential people there, Tony Lewis and Ossie Wheatley, for instance. What about the others? Do you ever see Don Shepherd?

MAX   Yes, I play a lot of golf with Don. I used to pretend to be Don. Owen Phillips' garage became the pavilion end and we used to draw white lines on the wall with chalk and I remember Owen Phillips was the best opening bat in all West Glamorgan. He was in once for 23 weeks. And when I finally got him out, he'd say, 'Not out!' 'Why's that?' 'There's no chalk on the ball.' So when I see the action replays and cameras in stumps I think it was a far better day when the reason why you were out or not out depended on whether there was chalk on the ball.

BRIAN   Twenty-three weeks! I think that's one for Bill Frindall's record books. You go round the world literally, don't you?

MAX   I can only really go where there is huge British involvement, like Canada, New Zealand, Australia or Hong Kong. It's not just Welsh. When people are away from home they flock to see you. If the truth be told, you don't have to be terribly good in Australia, because people go there and they drag their Australian friends along and they laugh at everything. So I've had some great tours of Australia.

BRIAN   Can you give us one of your poems? I've been asked to ask you for 'The Incredible Plan'.

MAX   I'd never be able to remember it and it's about twelve minutes long. But this is a similar poem I wrote about when Llanelli beat the All Blacks in 1973. Again an occasion when I'm glad to say that I was there.

'Twas on a dark and dismal day
In a week that had seen rain,
When all roads led to Stradey Park
With the All Blacks there again.
They poured down from the valleys,
They came from far and wide.
There were twenty thousand in the ground –
And me and Dai outside.
The shops were closed like Sunday
And the streets were silent still
And those who chose to stay away
Were either dead or ill.
But those who went to Stradey
Will remember till they die
How New Zealand were defeated
And how the pubs ran dry.
Aye, the beer flowed at Stradey,
Piped down from Felinfoel
And the hands that held the glasses high
Were strong from steel and coal
And the air was filled with singing
And I saw a grown man cry
Not because they beat the All Blacks,
But because the pubs ran dry.
Then dawned the morning after
On empty factories,
For we were shtill at Shtradey,
Bloodshot absentees.
But we all had doctor's papers,
Not one of us in pain
And Harry Morgan buried
His Granny once again.
And when I'm old

And my hair turns grey
And they put me in a chair,
I'll tell my great grandchildren
That their grandfather was there.

BRIAN That is great – well done! And these just
flow out from you, do they?

MAX I've always been an avid listener to the ball-
by-ball. We used to set out on concert tours, with
my friend Philip Whitehead, who plays up in the
Saddleworth League, when there were Test Matches
on, leaving at ten to eleven, before the ball-by-ball
started and we used to look at maps, because we'd hate
to miss a ball and the great problem was – tunnels. In
the Dartford Tunnel especially you'd miss maybe three
overs. So you'd draw out a route plan where there were
no tunnels and you'd listen to Brian Johnston. It took us
one day five hours to go from Bournemouth to Bath or
somewhere! We went the no-tunnel route.

BRIAN You sing and then talk – a mixture?

MAX Yes, a sort of pot pourri of story-telling with
a few songs wedged in between, but they're all true
stories that I've embroidered and coloured and added
to and they've become routines as such. But they're
all born of truth. Some of the most amazing stories are
absolutely true. For instance, I was coming back from
recording an album in London and I went to find a seat
on the train on my own, because I was shattered. I'd been
up all night. And who gets on but Stuart Burrows, the
tenor. And I said, 'Oh, Stuart, I've had too much red
wine last night. Do you mind if we don't chat till we get
to Newport?' And he said, 'I've just finished a week of
opera myself. I feel the same way.' The train pulls out
of Paddington and when we get to Royal Oak a soldier

comes into the carriage. The Royal Welsh Fusiliers have just come home from Belfast. 'Max! How's it going, Max? Hey, Max, give us a song! Sospan Fach! Hang on, I'll go and get the boys.' Fifteen soldiers come in now. 'Max, Max, we've brought you some Newcastle Brown!' And they've got a big crate. 'Max, give us a song!' 'We're on a train, it's first class, come on, lads.' He takes off his hat, with the three Welsh feathers. 'If you won't sing for the beer, sing for this.' So I'm under pressure now. 'Oh, lads, I can't sing.' And then Stuart Burrows, arguably the greatest lyrical tenor in the world, says, 'He is not singing.' This soldier says, 'Who are you? His manager, is it?' Stuart says, 'Yes, I'm his manager and he's not singing.' 'Come on, Max, give us a song.' Stuart says, 'He's not singing, but I'll sing instead.' 'We don't want you to sing, we want Max to sing.' Finally they relented and said to Stuart, 'OK, you sing.' Stuart Burrows got up on that 125 train from Paddington and sang 'Waft of Angels Through the Skies'. This wonderful voice ringing through this compartment. And all these commuters were waking up and saying, 'I say, the sandwiches are stale, but the cabaret is awfully good.' And this soldier turns to Stuart at the end and he says, 'Listen, pal, I don't know much about singing, but as far as I'm concerned you're wasting your time managing him.' True story. You couldn't invent that.

BRIAN   If you'd been feeling fine, what song would you have chosen?

MAX   Strangely enough, when anyone's asked for a party piece, mine has always been 'The Road and the Miles to Dundee', a Scottish folk song. I don't know why, I suppose I can remember it.

BRIAN   (*with studied innocence*) How does it go, Max?

(And Max – after a chuckle – sang a verse of the haunting song. Ed.)

BRIAN   Do you like all sorts of music?

MAX   Yes. I like lyrics perhaps more than music and I was thinking of a cricket link for today and I thought of Dylan Thomas and his wonderful gift of painting pictures with words. The only thing that I know of Dylan Thomas writing of cricket was so vivid a picture that he painted of young kids playing on the beach by St Helen's and another kid who's got nobody to play with and he's stuck, hoping that the family who are playing cricket will ask him to join in. And Dylan Thomas called it 'The Friendless Fielder'.

> The loneliness of the friendless fielder
> Standing on the edge of family cricket
> Uninvited to tea or bat.

I wish I'd written that.

BRIAN   I didn't know he was into cricket.

MAX   He just wrote about anything. He went to St Helen's and he lived near there. He just looked at things and wrote of them. This wonderful descriptive ability. The fattest woman in Neath Fair was described as 'Her eyes like blackcurrants in blancmange'. It's a wonderful vision. And his grandfather was so wild he was 'Like a buffalo in an airing cupboard'.

BRIAN   I wish he'd written about cricket, he could have described some cricketers too. Have you written about a Test Match?

MAX   No, the only cricket I've written about is when I played for a side called Ponteddfechan in the South Wales League and unfortunately, back in about 1970, they drove the extension on the Heads of the Valleys motorway right through our cricket ground and that was the end. It was village cricket at its best and about five years ago we had a reunion match and all the people who ever played for this little village played again. We cut the wicket with a tractor and a five-gang mower and all the old lads came back. Of course you couldn't bowl fast, because it was really wild and, because of the motorway, one boundary was about 75 feet. And there were houses, so you could be 'out in gardens'. This guy, Alan Wicks, played and the next day he was playing for a fairly good side at Arundel. And his captain said, 'Tell me, Wicks, are you playing much these days?' 'Yes,' he said. 'I don't know where to put you in. Are you playing well? Did you play yesterday?' 'Yes, I did.' 'How many runs did you get?' 'I got 70.' 'How did you get out?' 'I was "out in gardens".' So he stuck him in number eleven.

BRIAN We'll have to make that the eleventh way of getting out.

MAX But it was a sad occasion.

BRIAN Yes, awful losing the cricket ground.

MAX And they'd played there for a hundred years. So I wrote a parody of Tom Jones's 'Green, Green Grass of Home' and it got to the speaking bit:

> And as I bat and look around me
> At the four short legs that surround me,
> I realise that surveyor wasn't joking.
> 'Cause they'll bring that ugly concrete highway
> And take away what once was my way.
> I can't believe my green, green field of home.

BRIAN Do you still play a bit of charity cricket?

MAX Yes, I play for the Taverners whenever I can.

BRIAN What length run nowadays?

MAX Oh, it's just as long. But I have a packed lunch half way, now.

BRIAN What's your favourite ground?

MAX Well, obviously St Helen's. I used to go to watch touring sides and my mother used to make me banana sandwiches. And I remember the days when we used to beat Essex before the bananas went black.

BRIAN What about your rugby? Who were the greatest rugby players you enjoyed in Wales?

MAX Probably Gerald Davies and then Gareth Edwards and Barry John was probably the finest outside half. And there's a wonderful story about when we played golf in a big tournament at the Royal Glyn Neath Golf Club and there was the greatest rainfall for 87 years. After twelve holes it was abandoned because the greens were completely under water. We only had three showers and because everybody came off the course together, there was chaos in the changing rooms. So this lad said, 'I only live a hundred yards from here. Come down to my house for a bath, Mr John.' 'Call me Barry,' he said. So they go down to his house and Barry's in the bath, having a glass of home-made ale and this lad's on the phone to his father. 'You'll never guess who I've got in the bath! I've got Barry John!' 'Good God!' he said, 'Whatever you do, don't let the water out. We'll bottle it!'

BRIAN Now, when you leave here, I hope you've mapped out your course so that there are no tunnels on the way, because I hope you'll be listening to us.

MAX I've checked the tunnel route and there's only one in Monmouth, so I'm going to wait until the end of the over and then hurtle through the tunnel at Monmouth so I won't miss a ball.

GRAHAM TAYLOR

I HAVE BEEN lucky for the most part of my life in having a job which I have enjoyed. I expect there are others too, which I would also have liked to have done – such as acting. But there are two jobs which I would definitely *not* want to do – a cricket selector or the manager of the England football team. I am all for a quiet life without pressures, and undue criticism. Both of these jobs get plenty of both, with the football manager having the worst of it. The cricket selector does at least have his fellow selectors to share the criticism and abuse. (At least he should have, but nowadays the selection of the England team does seem to be largely in the hands of the Captain.)

In football, however, the England manager is the supremo with sole responsibility for selection of the side. It must be a tremendous burden but you would not have guessed it had you seen Graham Taylor in our box at Edgbaston. It was admittedly his brief 'off season', but he appeared completely relaxed, and we enjoyed a lot of laughs.

EDGBASTON, 27 JULY 1991

GRAHAM TAYLOR Because I was in a minor county, my cricketing heroes were national ones – May and Barrington. When I heard that Ken Barrington had passed away, it's one of the moments that will always remain with me. The fact that he'd died was very upsetting to a relatively young man, as I was at that time. I'd never met the man, but he was a throwback to my boyhood, when these people meant a lot to me.

BRIAN JOHNSTON He was a very intense character, who took things tremendously to heart. I took him back to London after a Test here when he'd played a very slow innings. I think he was about an hour between 89 and 100 and then, when he got to 100, he hit five fours running or something like that and he got tremendously criticised for that. And I took him back and he was so depressed then, it meant so much to him and he was actually dropped for one Test Match. He came back and made a couple more hundreds. And on the West Indies tour when he died, he'd taken all the problems very badly. He fought for England. It was like seeing the Union Jack walk out when Barrington went out to bat. He'd be the sort of character you'd love to have in any football team.

GRAHAM Well, I think in anything, when you're up against it, you want the fighters. You've got to have the fighters, you've got to have the people who show some stickability.

BRIAN   Are you a batsman or a bowler?

GRAHAM   I'm not really a bowler. I like the batting. My father has always said to me that one of the worst things he ever did was to send me for coaching. He said that before that, when I saw the ball I used to try to hit it. And when I came back from coaching I used to try to play everything technically correctly. I think he would have very much liked me to develop not only my footballing, which, fortunately, I got a career in, but my cricketing ability as well. I always remember as a young lad anything down my leg side as a left-hander, I loved. But then, after coaching, I seemed to have to play every ball 'correctly'.

BRIAN   I think your coaches weren't right. You get someone like Denis Compton, who was a natural. He went to a chap called Archie Fowler at Lord's in the thirties. He said, 'Right, I won't tell you anything.' But he did just teach him the basic forward defensive stroke, because Denis, in the end, was one of the best defensive batsmen if necessary. But they let him do all the unorthodox strokes.

GRAHAM   I'm sure that's right. I think that no coaching in many respects is better than bad coaching. I've always believed that. One thing I remember about my coaching is this business that you must play yourself in. Prior to that if the first ball had been bowled to me and it was there for hitting, I always used to think that you should hit that one. And I tended, when I played cricket, to be quite boring. But the worst thing about trying to play yourself in is if you get out. Because then you've lost it anyway.

BRIAN   Basically, a bad ball is a bad ball, whenever it comes.

GRAHAM   Not that I would ever have made any real level as a cricketer, but I enjoyed it.

BRIAN I know you were manager at Lincoln, Watford and Aston Villa. How much coaching have you done yourself?

GRAHAM I've done a reasonable amount of coaching, but I'm a great believer in playing to people's strengths. In other words, I don't believe in taking people out and coaching on a real weakness that they have. I believe in coaching people to their strengths, because I think that something that a person is good at he's interested in getting better at and I think it gives him a tremendous amount of confidence and consequently any weaknesses – and we all have weaknesses – improve through having a greater confidence. The strengths come through and they over-ride the weaknesses. So I like to think both collectively and individually that my coaching's based on getting people to believe in themselves.

BRIAN You've got to be a tremendous psychologist, though, haven't you? You've got to treat every single person differently, because everyone is different.

GRAHAM Well, everyone *is* different. I don't like it when people say, 'Treat everybody the same.' I'll treat you the same if you are the same, but you're not, so you treat everybody differently.

BRIAN How do you get to know people? Do you wait till an individual comes to join the team?

GRAHAM Well, I was 20 years a manager, because I had to finish the game at a relatively young age.

BRIAN You had hip trouble.

GRAHAM I had a hip injury, yes, so I finished when I was 28 and I became manager of Lincoln basically because there was a boardroom difference, as there tends to be in football, and somebody supported me. And my first nine games as manager we drew seven and lost two and I remember people at Sincil Bank at Lincoln shouting,

'Taylor out! Taylor out!' Now, when you're 28 years of age and you're married and you've two girls under four and you've got a mortgage, that's pressure. Pressure's not the top of the first division and pressure, in many respects, is not being the manager of the England side. Pressure, really, is if you get out of a job and you don't know where your next job is going to come from.

BRIAN I tell you what I would have done, if I'd been a manager. Before I signed a contract I'd have said, 'I cannot be sacked in the middle of a season. I'm prepared to be sacked at the end of a season.'

GRAHAM It's give and take. I think if you can't be sacked, then neither should you walk out.

BRIAN No, you abide by your contract.

GRAHAM Contracts now seem to be just a word and, when it suits either party, they're very easily terminated and that doesn't help the status or standing of any of the professional games.

BRIAN How are you influenced by the press? You get a bad press, poor Micky Stewart gets a bad press. When things go right, it's OK. Do you read it a lot? Do you try to meet the people and talk to them about it?

GRAHAM What I try to do is to be very open in terms of answering questions. You know that you're going to be abused. The disappointing aspect is that so many things that you say are abused and misused to create headlines. But I don't think I'm going to alter that. So one of the things that I've decided – and I don't mean to be offensive to anyone – is that basically I read as little as I can. Far more people know about the things that have been written about me than I do. And it's the best way to go.

BRIAN Now, another thing. We are slightly critical

nowadays about the training methods used by cricket. We think they overdo it and if you play enough cricket you don't need to do all these extraordinary exercises. We look back at the past when they didn't have all these pulled hamstrings and achilles tendons and now they tend to and yet they run round the ground for 40 minutes. What is your view of the training?

GRAHAM   Well, I don't know too much about the cricket training. But what I do know is, you have to be fit to play it. You have to be fit in this day and age to play any sport at the top level. There are specific fitnesses. As a professional footballer, before I became a manager, I was fit to play football and I'm perfectly certain I wouldn't have been fit to play cricket. There's a complete difference between getting fit to play football and being fit sometimes to stand and field for a day and a half and also bat with concentration. So I think there are specific ways of being fit.

BRIAN   No doubt football these days is so much faster because they're so much fitter. I used to go and watch Alex James and he had all the time in the world to sell four dummies and pass the ball three times and he wouldn't get away with it today.

GRAHAM   I think cricket must be the same, Brian. I see the pace these fellows are bowling at! So many people talk about the England football side and the interesting thing is that I consider myself an expert in that field. I don't consider myself an expert in either cricket or athletics, which are my next loves. So I can spectate at cricket and I can spectate at athletics far better than I can at football. I have been listening to Freddie Trueman when he sits here. There's a top class professional cricketer and he's watching cricket with a very critical eye. Now, I watch football like that. When I'm watching cricket I'm spectating.

BRIAN There is this difference with cricket, the captain on the field is in charge and it's very difficult to see what your relationship is in soccer with the captain, as the manager. You're sitting there on the bench. How much does the captain have to say out on the field?

GRAHAM Well, one of the biggest things that you find is that there tend to be fewer and fewer leaders. We all tend to want to follow a little bit. I think it's the way of society more than anything else, but we don't have so many characters in terms of leadership. But the role of captain on a cricket side has always seemed to me almost like a player-manager. He's in charge and a lot more decisions have got to be made in a cricket match by the captain than the decisions made in 90 minutes by the captain in football. Interestingly one of the last few people to combine the two sports was Phil Neale and I signed Phil Neale as a footballer at Lincoln City. He's done so well. As a young boy I couldn't see captaincy material basically in Phil – certainly not in football. But how well he's done in cricket.

(Phil Neale was captain of Worcestershire for nine years and was appointed cricket manager of Northamptonshire for 1993. Ed.)

PETER O'TOOLE

MENTION PETER O'TOOLE, and in spite of the many different parts he has played since, on stage or in films, most people probably picture a white Arab figure in the desert as Lawrence of Arabia. An unlikely sort of cricketer you might think.

On 14 June 1992, Peter played for Paul Getty's XI on his beautiful cricket ground at Wormsley. The opposition was Tim Rice's Heartaches. At his own request Peter went in first and scored a stylish 5, including a fine stroke for 4 through the covers. When Getty's XI fielded Peter bowled five tidy overs of leg-breaks at a cost of only 14 runs.

I had first met him in 1991 in Paul Getty's box at Lord's, where I learnt of his passion for cricket. During the winter – when not working – he goes every Monday night to the Indoor Cricket School at Lord's, where he and Don Wilson became firm friends. In the summer, whenever he is free, he coaches young boys on Friday nights at the Brondesbury Cricket Club.

So he is not just a celebrity who turns out in

occasional charity matches. He plays and practises whenever he can, and is a completely dedicated devotee of the game. With his tall languid frame, his handsome craggy face, and immediately recognisable, somewhat husky voice, he does not look like the average cricketer. But he *is* one, and it's a real joy to meet someone who is so famous in their chosen profession, but who would probably much prefer to be thought of as a cricketer.

On the Saturday when he was with us, we had had a riveting morning's play, in which the West Indies, after looking comfortable enough at 158 for 3, had suddenly declined to 164 for 6.

THE OVAL, 10 AUGUST 1991

PETER O'TOOLE I'm often asked why cricket means so much to me. And it's this high drama. Tufnell comes on – takes a wicket. Botham returns – takes a wicket. Viv Richards, the great king, delays his entrance. Delays and delays and delays. Finally comes on with a couple of balls to play before lunch to a standing ovation. And of course he could have been out first ball.

BRIAN JOHNSTON Have you ever had an ovation like that? That lasted the time it took him to get to the wicket.

PETER And I believe he was deeply moved – and who wouldn't be?

BRIAN Well, Bradman says he wouldn't be, because when I asked him whether he had tears in his eyes when there were three cheers when he went out in his last Test, he said, 'No, no,' but I bet there were really.

PETER I saw Bradman play at Headingley in 1948 and he scored 33, having threatened to score a century in the evening before, and as he walked back to the pavilion there were no tears. He looked extraordinarily grumpy and very, very thoughtful, in a huge cap and walking very slowly indeed.

(Bradman did make a century – a match-winning 173 not out – in the second innings of that Test Match. Ed.)

BRIAN Before we go on with the cricket, I'm colour blind, but I gather those are green socks.

PETER They are green socks.

BRIAN Now, why do you always wear green socks?

PETER Because my daddy was very, very superstitious and wouldn't allow me to wear anything green on a racetrack, so my way of being disobedient was to wear something green which he couldn't see.

BRIAN He was not unconnected with the bookmaking business.

PETER He was a bookie.

BRIAN Were you a runner?

PETER I was a runner, but not exactly an official one.

BRIAN When did you first start playing cricket?

PETER I was reared in the north of England, so cricket for me began in Yorkshire – where else? I remember the first real turn-on for cricket for me was being taken to the news cinema over and over again to watch Hutton's 364, here at the Oval in 1938, when I was six. And the great joy and cheers in the cinema are very clear to me. Then, towards the end of the war, I remember in Roundhay Park Sir Learie Constantine and Arthur Wood.

BRIAN Great wicket keeper.

PETER They put together Sunday sides and there was an Australian team and we little boys could be chosen as ball boys to stand on the boundary and one of my great moments, in fact my greatest moment still in cricket – even though I wasn't playing – was when I was standing at long-off. Constantine scored 50 in eighteen deliveries and he whacked the ball over the ropes and it fell into my hands. I remember this huge man just beaming and waving his bat. It was a lovely moment.

BRIAN Now, what about the talent? We're never modest.

PETER Well, I think this is about my mark, the blind cricket we're watching here.

(A demonstration of the game more or less as described by George Shearing was taking place at the Oval during this interval. Ed.)

BRIAN Come on, now, you're better than that. If one goes to the Lord's indoor school during the winter you can be seen there.

PETER True. I love to turn up and play. I love to be with cricketers. I'm not any good any more. My hope – wish – nowadays is to be involved in a stand. If I can plug up one end and let somebody else do the scoring and occasionally pop in a little single and charge up and down the wicket.

BRIAN Have you got the Trevor Bailey forward defensive?

PETER Yes, I've got that, much to the amusement of all my chums. When I say 'play' it's an overstatement. What I do is creak out to the square and hope to plonk a little timber on the ball. I hope to turn my arm over and get a maiden or perhaps a wicket.

BRIAN Leg tweakers or anything?

PETER I have a delivery which is really, really special. It does absolutely nothing.

BRIAN That's very good.

PETER From leaving the hand to pitching – nothing at all. This confuses many batsmen.

BRIAN But you do go into the indoor school. Who do you play with there? You go once a week, roughly.

PETER Well, I usually go with young chums whose delight is to try to knock my head off. They love it. They see this silly old fool turning up and padding up and they love to fling down the leather and try to take my head off.

BRIAN I saw someone I know who is a member at Brondesbury and he says that every Friday night you go and coach the boys there.

PETER Well, that's a delight for me. Again I'm with my standard – under nines. I love to . . . less coach than encourage.

BRIAN Do you give them a demonstration of your strokes?

PETER No, I'm the bowling machine and the umpire.

BRIAN This is great, because we've got to get at the young, haven't we?

PETER This is why Brondesbury is such an extraordinary club. If you go there on a Friday night it's one of the most delightful sights in cricket. The entire field is filled with little boys. The nets are filled. There are something like a hundred little things in white there and it's a lovely sight.

BRIAN It's a great credit to the club that they get them there.

PETER My job is not to coach. I don't want to say, 'Look, get your foot to the ball.' I like just to cheer them up and encourage them. Cricket is in the hands of the young.

BRIAN   Do you play with odd actors and people still?

PETER   I play for a club called Lazarusians.

BRIAN   I don't really know that one.

PETER   Well, you may. We're not doing too badly.

BRIAN   What sort of people do you play?

PETER   We play some high class stuff. We've played Northamptonshire professional coaches and drew with them and we won against Sandbach.

BRIAN   And where does O'Toole bat?

PETER   He opens.

BRIAN   Against all the hostile fast bowling. What do you look like in a helmet?

PETER   Well, we were playing in Northamptonshire and a distinguished pro., who was in the other side, insisted that we all wear helmets because the pitch was bouncing. So I went into the pavilion and was given a helmet and I couldn't find my way out of the pavilion. I stumbled around and I couldn't see where the door was. I'm sure I looked like a Dalek. So I took it off.

BRIAN   And you can't hear, either. What about the bowling, then? Do you get any wickets?

PETER   Sometimes I get a wicket or two. I get a few maidens. For me one run is now what six runs meant when I was a boy. One wicket now means a five-wicket haul. If I do a piece of decent fielding I'm very happy. If I take a catch I'm delirious and as long as I don't become a passenger with the team I'll keep on playing.

BRIAN   Are you good at sprinting round the boundary?

PETER   Oh, that's a great sight. I'm greatly encouraged by my team who say, 'Go on! Go on! Off he goes!' and I puff and pant.

BRIAN   I think we last met in the box at Lord's, watching a Test Match. Do you go quite a bit?

PETER I always do watch as much cricket as I possibly can wherever I go in the world, be it the West Indies or Australia. I was in Australia for Christmas, watching. Which brings me to the subject of David Gower. I have the solution. David will go to live in the West Indies until he qualifies as a resident and then he will play for the West Indies and come back here at the age of 37 and tonk everybody round the park.

BRIAN I think he'd have to live there a bit longer after having played for another country. He's obviously a hero of yours. Who are the past heroes you've had?

PETER Well, Hutton was my god until along came a tall, handsome man called Flying Officer Miller and to this day he's my cricketing god. I met him in Sydney about a decade ago and we had a long, long chat about the old days. I remember watching him play a long innings. I don't know where or when, but I remember his back foot like a stanchion. He was moving out to everything. He was everything I wanted to be when I was a boy.

BRIAN When he played slow bowling sometimes, he nearly did the splits because his back foot was static at the crease and he stretched forward.

Can we talk a little bit about yourself, because you don't appear to have come from an acting family. How did you get into acting?

PETER Looking back on it now, there seems to have been an inevitable logic to it all, but there wasn't. I really stumbled into it from one thing to another. Somebody got ill in an amateur production and I took over. And then someone said, 'You ought to do it professionally.' Then I thought, 'Well, shall I try this?' Then I got a scholarship to the RADA and it went from there.

BRIAN And you got the scholarship, so I'm told,

for rather sort of bargeing in and making a nuisance of yourself.

PETER It's not quite true, but what is true is that I'd spent the night in Stratford-on-Avon, watching Michael Redgrave play King Lear. Then, looking for somewhere to sleep – I had no money – I slept in a field with a chum and we'd covered ourselves with what we thought was straw, but it was indeed merely the cosy to a dung pile. So when we'd thumbed a lift into London, we weren't exactly fragrant, but the lorry driver dropped us at Euston Station.

BRIAN Very quickly, I should think.

PETER Even that was a bit terrifying. It was a lorry carrying beer barrels and we were standing on the barrels. We got off at Euston, aiming for a men's hostel, where we had booked a bed, and I passed the RADA. I popped in and started talking to the commissionaire at the door. We were looking at a bust of Bernard Shaw and the commissionaire and I were telling stories about Bernard Shaw when Sir Kenneth Barnes came along and joined in the story-telling and one of my stories may have intrigued him.

BRIAN I should think the smell did.

PETER Well, my companion said, 'You will be removed from there, O'Toole, by a person with a clothes peg on his nose.'

BRIAN They tell me your bagpipes played a big part in the first film part you ever got, in *Kidnapped*. Is that right?

PETER That's right.

BRIAN Did you actually have to play them in the film?

PETER I did. It was my friend Peter Finch who was in it. There was a part for Rob Roy MacGregor's son, who had a bagpipe competition with the part that

Peter was playing. And Finchy had said, 'There's only one actor I know who plays the —— bagpipes.'

BRIAN Well, this is useful. For promising people who want to go on the stage, go and learn the bagpipes, you might get a part from it. Now – *Lawrence of Arabia*. One or two others turned the part down.

PETER Did they?

BRIAN Weren't you told? You snapped it up as soon as it came along.

PETER I felt I was in the slips and the ball came my way. I thought, 'I'll have that one.'

BRIAN You were on a pretty sandy wicket for a long time.

PETER Very – and with Omar Sharif, another good cricketer.

BRIAN Did you have any games of cricket?

PETER We did. In the middle of the desert in 120 degrees, to the astonishment of the Bedouin, who hadn't got the foggiest what was going on.

BRIAN Did they field for you?

PETER No, they didn't, but they looked at the ball with great suspicion. Then one of them picked it up and thought this was a wonderful weapon and they were flinging it about.

BRIAN Did it take an awful long time to do?

PETER It took a couple of years. It became my life. It was more than just a film, it was a huge adventure. It was everything that a young 28-year-old man could wish for. I was out in the desert in the Holy Land, working with a genius – David Lean – with a superb company of actors.

BRIAN Quite a few in the cast, to say the least – thousands.

PETER I need a scoresheet, or I'll leave someone out.

I was like a young matador – another bull would come in.
'Who's this morning?' – 'Anthony Quinn.' 'Who's today?'
– 'Alec Guinness.' 'Who's today?' – 'Anthony Quayle.'
'Who's today?' – 'Donald Wolfitt.' 'Who's today?' –
'Claude Raines.' 'Who's today?' – 'Arthur Kennedy.'
'Who's today?' – 'Jose Ferrer.' It was astonishing.

BRIAN Not a bad team, that.

Isn't it extraordinary how many actors love playing
cricket?

PETER Yes, there is an affinity between this game and
ours. Well, think of C. Aubrey Smith, who captained his
country.

BRIAN That's right, only one Test Match he played
and he captained England. Did you ever play in
Hollywood?

PETER No, but Hollywood, as you know, has a
cricket team. And lots and lots of West Indians are going
to live in California. Down in the Valley they're setting
up cricket matches. So it may take on. In America, you
know, they call cricket 'baseball on Valium'.

BRIAN Jonathan Agnew and I disgraced ourselves
yesterday by corpsing. Are you a corpser?

*(This was the day after the infamous 'leg over' incident,
which is described by Brian in the final chapter. Ed.)*

PETER Hopeless – pathological.

BRIAN Have you had any experiences on the stage
or in a film where you simply couldn't go on?

PETER Oh, yes. Twice I've been in productions
where the curtain has been pulled slowly down. One of
my favourite moments was in Brighton in a play which
was not very successful and was not going to have a long
life. It was a complicated play, set on a strand, with the
corner of a little beach-side cottage and the back of the
set was the sea. Lots and lots of gauzes and lights and

174

complicated things to make it look like the sea and, indeed, I entered from the sea with Sylvia Simms, in our bathing costumes. On the beach was a lovely man called Nicholas Meredith – no longer with us – a great giggler – and his first line was, 'Good morning, Roger.' I was Roger. Then he had to erect a deckchair, which is never easy. It's a tricky old business. Your fingers get trapped. And I remember the line very clearly, because I heard it for seven or eight weeks. 'Good morning, Roger. There's something about a deckchair – austerity, poise and comfort. The austerity is an illusion, the comfort is achieved only with difficulty and the poise we leave to Pamela.' Well, he would do that line erecting a deckchair and not once did he get the deckchair up. Nick had a habit of twisting his hair into little spikes. This meant, 'I am not giggling.' Then when he coughed, this meant, 'I am certainly not giggling.' So there was Nick, twisting these huge spikes on his head and coughing away. And after an agonisingly long time of not getting the deckchair up he left behind this crumpled mass of timber and canvas and said, 'I am going to post a letter,' and walked into the sea. The only thing I could think of was 'I did not do this. This is not me.' So I hid behind a palm tree. Nick was floundering round looking for a letter-box in the sea amongst the gauze and electricity at which point everything went potty – sparks and flashes. And onto the beach came a fireman in a brass helmet with an axe. And of course the curtain came down very, very slowly. The producer immediately looked at me and wagged his finger. But it wasn't me.

BRIAN You've done a fair bit of Shakespeare. Hamlet, for instance.

PETER That was funny, too. I came on stage at the Old Vic to play Hamlet and I'd been down below with a stage hand, trying to pick a winner. I walked onto the stage and I knew that Noël Coward was out front and he was sitting in the front row with his friends. And I said, 'To be or not to be, that is the question.' I heard a snigger. 'Whether it is nobler in the mind . . .' – snigger – '. . . to suffer the slings and arrows . . .' – snigger – I thought, 'What am I doing?' And I had a quick glance down to see if my fly was open. Finally there was real proper laughter throughout the entire audience and I didn't know why. At which point Rosemary Harris came on as Ophelia and I put my hand to my forehead and realised I was wearing twentieth-century horn-rimmed spectacles. How should I get rid of them? So I said to Rosemary, 'There should be no more marriages!' And I flung the specs at her.

BRIAN   That's great. And your Macbeth got a few laughs. Was it meant to?

PETER   Not really. Again the chief cause was this awful sense of the ridiculous. As Banquo appeared, drenched from head to foot with blood, down the Waterloo Road came an ambulance and you could hear the siren clearly. I caught Brian Blessed's eye and I'm afraid we were both giggling.

BRIAN   The great thing is, you've had fun all the time.

PETER   All the time. And I hope it continues.

JAMES JUDD

I MUST ADMIT that I am not too knowledge-able about the world of classical music, and its orchestras and conductors. Until Radio 3 suggested the name of the conductor James Judd as a possible for 'View from the Boundary', I had honestly never heard of him. So I took special care to research all I could about him, but was still not satisfied that I knew enough to enable me to carry on a conversation with him for 25 minutes. I was also slightly mystified that he appeared to be an older man than I had thought he would be, my information giving his birth as 1919.

By the start of the Edgbaston Test I was getting a bit worried, so asked Peter Baxter whether the Radio Three music experts could fax me some more facts about him. This was duly waiting for me in the commentary box when I arrived there on Saturday morning. It said that James Judd kept ferrets and was nicknamed 'Ratty'. He was sponsored by Weetabix to conduct the Reykjavik Male Voice Choir, and was also an ardent supporter of Aldershot Football Club.

I hastily added all this fascinating information to

the notes which I had already made, and was trying to work out in my mind how I would weave it into my questions. I was feeling much more confident than I had been, and began rehearsing one or two ferret jokes which I knew. Whilst we were waiting for him to arrive, I noticed a fair amount of giggling in the box, especially when I revealed to my colleagues that James's nickname was 'Ratty' because he kept ferrets.

Thankfully Peter Baxter had mercy on me, and decided to reveal to me that the fax had been sent by that arch leg-puller David Lloyd, and that it had all been made up. I had been well and truly done. It served me right. I have done the same sort of thing to so many other people.

James arrived soon afterwards and I immediately thought that he was a remarkably young looking 73 years of age. I simply had to ask him, and it became apparent that my official notes about him had mistakenly put 1919 instead of 1949 as his birth date. He took it all extremely well and we even let him into the ferrets and 'Ratty' joke. I am not sure, though, how amused he would have been had I started our conversation with 'May I call you "Ratty"?'

EDGBASTON, 6 JUNE 1992

BRIAN JOHNSTON You are based basically in America.

JAMES JUDD That's right. The orchestra of which I am Music Director is in Miami. The Florida Philharmonic plays concerts from Miami up to Palm Beach. There's not much cricketing country round there. It used to be called the Philharmonic Orchestra of Florida and I suggested since it started to record and wanted to have an international career and perhaps tour England, that they should change and perhaps POOF wasn't a particularly attractive title.

BRIAN People could say, 'Are you going to listen to the POOF tonight?'

JAMES That's right. I got quite a few congratulatory cards when I took over this orchestra.

BRIAN And you are also connected with the New Queen's Hall Orchestra.

JAMES That was a lovely experience.

BRIAN But this is an old orchestra.

JAMES It's sort of been resurrected by a man called John Boyd, who got hold of a lot of the instruments that they played on originally, which arc quite different, especially the wind instruments and the timpani. They make quite a different sound from the bigger instruments of today and we play with gut strings on the violins, which create quite a different sound. If you listen to the old Elgar recordings of him conducting his own music, you'll hear that type of sonority. It's very beautiful.

BRIAN Is this the same orchestra that Sir Henry Wood started, though?

JAMES Yes, I think so. And there are recordings of him conducting as well. The balance of an orchestra was quite different in those days.

BRIAN They tell me you're a great starter of orchestras.

JAMES   I've been fortunate in that when I was at music college in London, back at the end of the sixties, beginning of the seventies, we started an orchestra called the Young Musicians Symphony Orchestra, which Barbirolli was the patron of.

BRIAN   Another cricket buff.

JAMES   Yes, absolutely. And then I was part of the team that started the European Community Youth Orchestra of which Claudio Abbado is the music director. And I still work with them. We started that in 1978. And really the orchestra in Florida is another kind of start, because it's an amalgamation of a number of different orchestras.

BRIAN   Someone told me that you've started as many orchestras as Sir Thomas Beecham.

JAMES   I don't know about that, but I enjoy building orchestras. It's quite a different thing from taking over as music director an orchestra that's already great.

BRIAN   Have you got the temperament of Sir Thomas Beecham?

JAMES   I don't know about that. I don't think anybody has the temperament of Beecham. He used to get away with murder. A great conductor.

BRIAN   There's a wonderful story about him in St John's Wood, where he used to live, on the corner of Elm Tree Road. His doctor was summoned. 'Will you come at once, Dr Hunt. It's very urgent. Come at once!' So he got into his car, with his bag, and rushed round and there was Sir Thomas Beecham on the pavement outside his house, with his black Homburg and the big scarf and he said, 'Drive me at once to the Albert Hall! I can't get a taxi and I'm late for a concert.' And the poor doctor had to drive him all the way to the Albert Hall. Would you risk doing that with your doctor?

JAMES There's a lovely interview story when he was in Australia. It was a radio interview, when he had just got off the boat. He was asked a question and he just apparently reached for his cigar. So the interviewer got a bit panicky and asked another question. He lit the cigar and nothing happened for the entire interview. He was really a devil sometimes.

BRIAN We can't offer you a cigar, I'm afraid.

Now, last year you were staying at Langar Hall, that delightful country house hotel we stay at for Trent Bridge, and you were going to see the Trent Bridge Test Match, so we got on to the fact that you rather like cricket. Do you play or have you played?

JAMES Well, I've played very little. I played at school. The last match I played was on the beach at Bermuda with the English Chamber Orchestra, with wine bottles in the sea. It was lovely. They have a good team. A lot of orchestras have good cricket teams. The Hallé Orchestra, who I'm conducting today, is reforming its team, which is a very serious one. We played a marvellous game on the beach with the English Chamber Orchestra, with one cellist, I remember, taking seven wickets in nine balls, which wasn't bad.

BRIAN Very good for a cellist. Do they have a sort of league between the orchestras?

JAMES Not really. The problem is the orchestras are playing so much. The life, for instance, of the orchestras in London is so busy – three sessions a day quite often. But they do have teams and the Opera House has a team and so on.

BRIAN We were quite surprised when Julian Bream came on this programme that he actually played cricket all the time while he was doing his professional concerts. Think of the fingers! The danger! You wouldn't risk your bowling arm, because it's the one you conduct with, I suppose.

JAMES Well, as long as you've got one limb you can use, you can conduct, I think.

BRIAN What was your particular skill at cricket?

JAMES I started when I was practising the piano and we had a little lawn and I remember trying to hit a tree ten times in a row, trying to outdo Jim Laker and never making that. But I was always pointed at the piano when I wanted to be playing cricket. I went through school playing a bit of cricket, but then taking up tennis. But really the problem I have now, living in the States for a lot of the year, through cricket time, is actually to get news of the cricket.

BRIAN There's nothing in the papers if you go to America. It's dreadful. I don't know how you keep up with it.

JAMES During the Test Matches occasionally there is a tiny bit on the World Service. There is a league of sorts in Miami.

BRIAN But no county news. What county do you support?

JAMES Yorkshire always, because when I was growing up my hero was Fred Trueman. I've always followed them, although I lived a long way away. I was born in Hertford.

BRIAN And do you approve of the Yorkshire policy now of having someone from outside?

JAMES I think it had to happen, actually, and I think if you look at the plight of the Yorkshire team over the last year, this is going to give a little bit more spirit in the team. It's hugely controversial and one dares not pronounce on it, not being a Yorkshireman, really.

BRIAN Well, maybe if you're a supporter like that. Any particular hero other than Trueman?

JAMES Boycott was the batsman I admired. I think just that tenacity and that single-mindedness. That's something that's so impressive.

BRIAN When you were at Trent Bridge, it was rather a wet day and David Lloyd was rather amused that you said that you didn't have an umbrella, you had plastic bags. What do you do with a plastic bag when you go to cricket and it's raining? Do you put it on your head?

JAMES Yes. It's very convenient. One loses umbrellas all over the place. It doesn't really matter about plastic bags. It was a very rainy day, but we got a little bit of play.

BRIAN I love Trent Bridge. Do you have any favourite ground?

JAMES It's a beautiful ground. I think Trent Bridge as a Test ground is the nicest to look at.

BRIAN One's in on the cricket, really. It's not so remote.

JAMES It's very intimate, isn't it? It has a very cosy feeling to it. This is the first time I've been to Edgbaston. It also seems to be rather an intimate setting.

BRIAN I suppose you literally don't have enough time to watch now.

JAMES No, that's the position, really, but I'm going to get a day in at Lord's. I've got a ticket for that. So that'll be my next visit to cricket.

BRIAN Well, now, conducting. How do you become a conductor? Do you just say, 'I'm going to conduct,' and pick up a baton?

JAMES You can. It doesn't work too well that way. I think you really need to get a good background in various instruments. You have to build your own kind of knowledge.

BRIAN What have you played?

JAMES Piano I started with and then flute and then some timpani in various local orchestras. In this country we're very lucky, because every town has an orchestra; every school has an orchestra; there are choruses. We get a terrific background in music, which is what a conductor needs, really, so you get a good start. Then you can go to music college and you can study conducting amongst other things.

BRIAN Where did you go?

JAMES To Trinity College of Music in London and then I went on an opera course at what was then the London Opera Centre and then I was lucky – I got a break. I got a bit of professional experience with the Liverpool Orchestra. They used to have a two-week period when they invited four young conductors to work with Sir Charles Groves.

BRIAN That was a good person to work with.

JAMES Yes, a marvellous man.

BRIAN It's rather like trying to get put on to bowl if you're a batsman. You say, 'I can bowl.' You say, 'I can conduct.' But who gives you the first go?

JAMES Yes, it's a terrifying experience when you're standing up in front of those professional musicians for the first time. I was very lucky because I got invited to be assistant conductor in Cleveland in the States to the Cleveland Orchestra, which is one of the world's great orchestras. I remember the first experience of that, just going out and conducting on a children's concert, just one little piece of music.

BRIAN That's quite something, to be invited to go to America. Who asked you?

184

JAMES   It was Lorin Maazel. He was the conductor of the Cleveland Orchestra at that time and now he conducts the Pittsburgh Orchestra. He was the conductor of the Vienna State Opera for a period of time. He's a wonderful conductor.

BRIAN   And he let you conduct under him, did he?

JAMES   Yes. It's a very good thing in the States, you have these assistant conductor jobs, which means you're there, listening to the orchestra the whole time. You get to conduct a lot of children's concerts which they do. Usually in the States the orchestras play to about a hundred thousand kids a year. That's a very serious part of the work. You get to conduct one piece here and there gradually and if you're good at it they invite you to do a little bit more and that's how the career kind of starts, really.

BRIAN   Now, facing a whole lot of musicians who all think they're very good and probably are and there you are, do you do what Mike Brearley used to do – the psychology? Do you get to know their weaknesses and their strengths and treat some a little bit tougher than others and so on?

JAMES   It's true the psychology is a huge part of the sport of conducting, I must say, because every orchestra is different. It's fine when you have your own orchestra, because you get to know them, they get to know you and one builds a sort of intimate relationship, really, to make music together. What's difficult as a conductor is going as a guest and perhaps to an orchestra that you've never met before – especially if they're foreign and you're battling with foreign languages – and to try to get the confidence of the musicians in the first few minutes is terribly important, because, if you don't have it in those first few minutes, you're lost.

BRIAN   But you must have been very young when you first started conducting and you had some veterans scraping away at the violins.

JAMES   I think that musicians are very sympathetic. They know that it's a problem as a young conductor. Musicians are wonderfully educated. A conductor these days is no longer a dictator. He's one musician amongst a hundred very well-trained musicians and the best music-making is really chamber music – making music together.

BRIAN   But how do you impose your style on them? Do you have a conference with them: 'What I want you to do is this, boys. Will you do it?' Or do you say, 'You will do this'?

JAMES   Well, if things are going well – and orchestras will tell you that – they can feel a confidence or they know what a conductor wants just really by gesture, rather than words and that's something we train to do – talk as little as possible, although we're not very good at it sometimes – and try just to show an orchestra what you need, almost with the eyes. You notice a lot of great older conductors no longer moving particularly fluently when they conduct, but it's all done with this hypnotism – telepathy. It's quite extraordinary. I don't know what the answer is really, but you do feel that occasionally there's a kind of circle of music through the orchestra, through the audience and back through your head when you're conducting.

BRIAN   Now, if I was to put on six different records of the same piece conducted by six different conductors, could you cross your heart and say you would recognise which conductor was conducting which?

JAMES   Sometimes. I could with the really great conductors. If you put on a record of Beethoven's

Symphony with Toscanini or Klemperer or Roger Norrington, one would know immediately which one it was. Also the sounds of orchestras you can tell fairly quickly. Although the sounds of orchestras have to some extent been evening out as conductors travel more.

BRIAN But presumably they're all operating from the same score, so the same instruments are going to come in at the same time. So how can you, as a conductor, make it sound different for those instruments?

JAMES Well, you see, orchestras in different countries sound different. In Vienna they use slightly different instruments – some of the wind instruments – and they produce a different sound. As a conductor you have a sound in your head of what you want and that's something that you work on. An orchestra will sound different if, let's say, the strings produce a sound using more bow or if they produce a sound by using a more intense and shorter bow. The sound might be the same volume, but it will be a different character.

BRIAN You impose your thing, but can you choose your own instruments for an orchestra? Can you say, 'I will have three strings there, instead of four'?

JAMES Well, you can do a little of that. Most symphony orchestras are an established size, but if you're doing a work, let's say, by Haydn or Mozart, or a baroque piece, you need a smaller group of instruments. Then it's up to the conductor. The size of the orchestra that he chooses is part of the interpretation in a way.

BRIAN Are you an all-round music man? Do you like jazz as much as you like the classics?

JAMES Well, I love jazz. There's a very good radio station in Miami, which is the classical music station. At midnight they switch to jazz. And there's a wonderful man there called China Verlez, who broadcasts this jazz. I've been on his show a couple of times. I don't know much about jazz. I would love to have learned to improvise, but that's a very special talent and I don't have it, unfortunately.

BRIAN   So, what is your particular favourite?

JAMES   It's a very difficult question. If I was really landed with one composer, in the end it would be Bach, but as a conductor I don't conduct much Bach. I love conducting Mahler – all the romantic literature – as well as Beethoven and Mozart, but Bach would be the composer I would finally come back to if I had only one to choose, I think.

BRIAN   I must ask you one personal question, because I heard from someone that you have to be very careful when you're a conductor to see that your hair is in the right style, because you've got your back to the audience.

JAMES   It's got to be flowing.

BRIAN   Yours is sort of on the neck. Is that deliberate?

JAMES   Well, it's recently been cut, otherwise it would have been well below the collar line. A friend of mine, a very fine Swiss conductor, has a theory about interpretation and length of hair amongst conductors. He has a theory that bald conductors conduct quite differently from those with longer hair, but I've not really seen much evidence of that.

BRIAN   Great bald conductors – Adrian Boult, he was very bald.

JAMES   Yes, he was a very elegant conductor.

BRIAN   Didn't seem to move much. He was very static.

JAMES   Well, I saw him in his later years, but he had fantastic control over an orchestra. Sir George Solti is another great, great conductor who doesn't have that

much hair. He does have one wonderful gesture sometimes. He moves his hand up to his forehead and sweeps
the imaginary locks back.

BRIAN   Well, you could genuinely do that.

Now, you're conducting the Hallé this evening in
Leicester. If you had a good rehearsal and I then took
over the baton and started them off on the same thing,
would they go on without you?

JAMES   Oh yes, they would. If you'd like to come
along, we'll try it this evening. We'll invite you as guest
conductor. The thing about conducting is, if you give an
up-beat in one tempo, the orchestra will continue in that
tempo until you disturb things. So if you were to come
along and conduct you'd get them started and they'd
probably go on pretty well until you gave a gesture
which suggested a change of tempo. Then there might
be chaos.

BRIAN   What's your gesture for stopping?

JAMES   Well normally just shouting at them. No,
I think just a final cut-off gesture.

BRIAN   Under all the noise, are the conductors saying
things: 'Don't scrape away there. Get it louder'? Do you
whisper to them?

JAMES   I was with an orchestra in Switzerland about
three weeks ago and they told me of a conductor they'd
recently had, who was swearing at them during the concert, he got so angry. That doesn't usually happen. He
won't be invited again.

BRIAN   Does that have a good effect on people?
Like when Mike Brearley made Willis bowl uphill at
Headingley and when Willis asked why, he said, 'To
make you angry.' Is it good to get an orchestra angry
before a performance?

JAMES   I don't think so. I've never tried it. I expect

there are some conductors who do. Probably I do without knowing it.

BRIAN Now we've got this slightly delicate situation where *Test Match Special* has robbed – in the nicest possible way – the music lovers of some days of music. And yet I talk to a lot of the music-lovers who say they like listening to the cricket. Do you think it's fair?

JAMES Personally I think it's fair. And it's true what you say. There are so many musicians I know who dearly love cricket and they dearly love this programme, as I do, because for us it's often the only chance we get to be in touch with cricket. And I'm sure there'll be some people during my rehearsal this afternoon with their earpieces in.

BRIAN Ah! Is it possible to play some symphony listening to the commentary?

JAMES I'm not so sure. There was an orchestra in Italy who were watching football on their little screens during a concert – a radio orchestra. There was a big case about it. They said they had a right to do that. It didn't affect their playing. But they're not allowed to do it any more.

BRIAN Do musicians tend to be cross-eyed, because they've got to look at the music and they've also got to look at you? How does that happen?

JAMES People often think that players are not looking at the conductor, but it's all corner of the eye. If there's a gesture they really need to see, they see it.

BRIAN And conductors live to a great old age. It's obviously very good for the chest muscles, the lungs and everything.

JAMES That's my exercise, I think. So I'm pretty healthy above the waist. Below it I'm not so sure.

BRIAN Well, I've learnt an awful lot about conducting. I'm afraid we can't ask you to stay the afternoon because you've got to get in a fast car now and go to rehearse with the Hallé.

JAMES I wish I could stay, but I'm off to work.

IAN RICHTER

ONE OF THE rewards of being a commentator on *Test Match Special* is the number of letters we receive, not just from this country, but from all over the world. They come from many different sorts of people of both sexes and of all ages. It may sound presumptuous but it does give us the feeling of being the centre point of a vast cricket-loving family. It still gives me a special thrill when Peter Baxter puts a small card in front of me which reads 'Welcome World Service'. The thought of speaking to people thousands of miles away in so many countries and different environments, creates a little extra drop of adrenalin.

You can imagine, therefore, how pleased we were when Geoff Parker of BBC World Service Sport told us that he had received the following letter which read: 'As you know I'm confined out here and have been for some time. One of my great comforts is listening to the ball-by-ball commentary, and I have been delighted to hear England's win at Headingley, after a long twenty-two-year wait.'

The letter was headed 'Baghdad' and signed by Ian

Richter, who had been arrested by the Iraqi police in 1986. He was held for five and a half years in gaol just outside Baghdad until his release in November 1991.

He was right on the ball about England's win against the West Indies at Headingley in June 1991. It was England's first *home* victory against West Indies since 1969, when Ray Illingworth's team also won at Headingley.

I'm afraid the weather was not too good when he joined us in our commentary box high up on the stand at the Stretford end.

OLD TRAFFORD, 2 JULY 1992

BRIAN JOHNSTON   It's marvellous to see you and congratulate you on the way you got out of that predicament. It must have been dreadful.

IAN RICHTER   It's wonderful to be here, even in this weather. I've had enough sun in the last few years. I could do with a bit of rain, but I don't like it interfering with my cricket.

BRIAN   I've had a report from the Naval and Air Force Attaché from Baghdad.

(He had rung the BBC that morning, when he heard Ian Richter was going to be our guest. Ed.)

A chap called John Marriott, who said you were a very fine cricketer, that you were a wicket keeper who went in first. So you're a sort of Alec Stewart. He said you were also a fine squash and hockey player. Is all that right?

IAN Yes. In my younger years I did play hockey for South Africa and played cricket for South African Universities and Western Province once. I have two first-class matches to my credit. Not a lot, but I've always had a deep love for the game and it did help me enormously during my early days of solitary confinement – getting into little exercises like picking world cricket teams.

BRIAN That was mental exercise. What about when you were playing out there before you were arrested? What sort of cricket did you have?

IAN Very little in Baghdad – but fun cricket. We used to play for the Embassy side against various nationals. We played an Indian side or a Pakistan side every now and then and occasionally we'd come across a side from a company with a very large contract, one that had enough players to put together a team. The Indians and Pakistanis used to bring on one or two surprises from time to time and it was a variable pitch.

BRIAN What sort of pitches were they? Matting?

IAN No, we had a grass pitch. The British Embassy in Baghdad is delightfully set right on the River Tigris and I think the Iraqis have been trying to move them out for several years now, but been resisted. It's a glorious setting, with many trees and it's a grass wicket of variable bounce.

BRIAN Did you ever hit a six into the River Tigris?

IAN Yes, I did manage one for which I had to forfeit several beers.

BRIAN Since coming back here have you had any cricket?

IAN Yes, I was kindly invited by the Free Foresters to play against my son's school at Ampleforth, so it was a wonderful arrangement and we had a glorious day

194

during the festival weekend. It was quite glorious to be playing cricket again. I was so impressed with the way Don Wilson looks after all the boys there. He doesn't push them too hard, doesn't destroy their natural talent and at the same time he guides and keeps them going.

BRIAN Can you remember what your final World XI was that you selected over the five and a half years?

IAN Well, I found it so difficult defining periods. Originally I started with the post-war period, then narrowed it down to people I'd either seen or heard of. There were two or three sides, I could never actually settle on one, but I guess it would be something like: Greenidge and Barry Richards opening the batting. At three we could have had Kanhai or Greg Chappell or Vivian Richards. I would have looked at Graeme Pollock possibly at four, having a slight South African background. Clive Lloyd at five, maybe. I had great difficulty in choosing the all-rounder – Procter, Botham.

BRIAN What about your bowlers?

IAN So many – Wes Hall, Griffith, Lindwall, Miller – four wonderful bowlers – Fred Trueman.

BRIAN You have to include him, although he's not in the box.

IAN And Geoff Boycott was first reserve, if Richards and Greenidge hadn't got a hundred by lunch.

BRIAN So you're going to get him to bring out the drinks. He wouldn't like that.

IAN Wicket keepers too was a difficult choice. Knotty possibly.

BRIAN You say you received the ball-by-ball. How did you actually get it?

IAN For the first three years I was in solitary, so I had virtually nothing. But eventually I got a radio and I started playing with it and I managed to get a copy of *London Calling*, which announced that they were having a ball-by-ball service and I tuned in quite fruitlessly one morning. I then, quite by chance, discovered that if I listened to a certain frequency, once it finished, shortly after lunch UK time, if I twiddled the knob a little further to the left I would pick up the South Eastern wavelength where it was being beamed to. It was rather faint, but if I cocked an ear to one side and told everyone to shut up – I was quite fierce about that – I would have four or five hours' cricket. So it was wonderful.

BRIAN Let's just work back a bit. How did you get a set?

IAN Well, it took a lot of pushing. As you can imagine, it was not something the Iraqis were terribly keen on doing. I think my wife got hold of three. The third one got to me after various people had intervened along the way and that made a huge difference to my quality of life.

BRIAN And did your Iraqi guard put on the headphones and listen to the commentary?

IAN Er – no. They're not the keenest of cricketers.

BRIAN Let's go back to the beginning. First of all you are South African.

IAN Yes, born there and came over to Britain in '72 after I got my MSc in chemical engineering and I've been here ever since.

BRIAN So why did you go out to Iraq?

IAN We had sold a large water-treatment plant to them – drinking water – and the requirement was that we had to set up an office out there within twelve months of signing the contract. So it was a career move, really. I wasn't an expatriate as such. It seemed a good step forward to move out of engineering into management and so I accepted the chance and went out for three years. I was asked to stay another year and was asked to stay another year and then, actually on my departure to come back, the grey faces arrived.

BRIAN Were you on your way to the airport?

IAN I was at the airport.

BRIAN With the plane outside waiting to take you back to the old country. What did they do?

IAN It was frightening, really. They came up to me and they said, 'Your passport's out of order.' So I said, 'I don't think it is.' And they said, 'Well, come with us to the old airport.' And I thought something was wrong when five goons jumped into a Mercedes with me, because not many people have Mercedes in Baghdad, apart from privileged people. We drove well past the old airport and I was refused access to my wife and I said, 'Where are we going?' They drove me to a piece of wasteland and said, 'Lie down on the floor.' That was terrifying. I thought I was going to be executed then. You hear these stories. In fact all they were doing was preventing me seeing where they were taking me, but I didn't know that. Then I arrived at the great Majabrat headquarters. I guess it's like the KGB headquarters in Moscow. It's a sort of dark place.

BRIAN And were you then questioned?

IAN I was questioned for three days. They tried to associate me with one person, failed to and then a second, then a third.

BRIAN What were they accusing you of?

IAN Various things. One was bribery, second was espionage and as they kept on trying, the more desperate they got.

BRIAN Without offending any of them, I should have thought that bribery was rather a normal thing.

IAN Well, no, it's strictly forbidden out there. As I was not a director, I had no ability to sign foreign currency cheques so it was fairly far-fetched.

BRIAN Who were you accused of bribing?

IAN The mayor of Baghdad, who was not our client at the time. Our client was something to do with the Ministry of Housing, which was nothing to do with him. They quickly found out that he was nothing to do with me and I think all in all I had been held as a hostage for this chap who's over here who had assassinated an Iraqi Prime Minister some years ago.

BRIAN Did you have a sort of trial?

IAN They left me alone after the three days for roughly nine months. That was a challenging period, too. Day after day in the darkness.

BRIAN Were you in solitary?

IAN Yes. That was a difficult period.

BRIAN In the dark. Take us through a day. One just can't imagine it. Do they shove food through at you?

IAN A cup of tea in the morning; a cup of tea in the evening. I went on hunger strike for the first two weeks and refused to eat what they were giving me. I'll never know, if I'd had the courage to keep going, whether they'd have let me go on. But eventually they called me in and they were very upset. They said, 'You've got to eat something. We're going to bring you a roll from outside. Will you eat that?' I said, 'Well, I'll see what the roll is.' And eventually hunger got the better of me and I started eating the roll. But the first two or three months were difficult, because I didn't know what was happening. I kept thinking that help was at hand any moment. But then I just realised that you had to get on with life by yourself.

BRIAN   Were you visited at all? Did the Ambassador come and see you?

IAN   They were trying desperately to get access to me, but it wasn't permitted. I had the pillar of using my mind and that was either developing a mathematical equation for a shadow on the wall or picking a cricket team.

BRIAN   What things did you have? Pencil and paper?

IAN   No, absolutely nothing. No light. It was just a blank cell. I slept on the floor.

BRIAN   Absolutely unbelievable. What do you think of all day? Choosing your World XI?

IAN   Yes. You invent a business. You see how it would do in Britain or how it would do in Saudi Arabia. It was very important to keep the mind going.

BRIAN   Did you get any sense of time?

IAN   I had no watch and couldn't detect time through the light. The only way I kept track of the days was through the tea in the morning and the tea in the evening. I had a passion to keep track of the days. It was a real thing with me.

BRIAN   And no news from outside whatever?

IAN   No. After about three months I was shown to the British Chargé d'Affaires, but I wasn't allowed to speak to him and he wasn't allowed to speak to me. It wasn't easy for a year and a half to two years, but then things got slightly better.

BRIAN   You're throwing that away – it wouldn't be easy for a week or a day. What were the Iraqi guards like?

IAN   Well, at first they were fierce. It was a difficult situation. I don't think they have much regard for human life and they were desperate to extract information from people they held, so they used various techniques in so doing. After that, when I was transferred to the main gaol, I think I was discriminated against for some while, but eventually my discipline and daily routine appealed to them, I think, and we gradually made friends. They weren't the people who had arrested me, they were just normal prison guards.

BRIAN Did they talk to you?

IAN At first they were terrified, because Iraqis are really discouraged from speaking to foreigners, but gradually they plucked up courage and saw that I had two arms and two legs and two eyes and went running every now and then: 'The mad Englishman who likes this, but he doesn't like that.'

BRIAN Where were you allowed to run, though?

IAN Well, that again took about three years, but eventually I persevered and I said, 'I want to run round that dusty football pitch you've got out there.' And they said, 'But no one runs here.' So I said, 'Well, I want to.' It was wonderful, running, because it took me away from the maelstrom of Egyptians and Sudanese and the cigarettes and the spitting and it was just a bit of peace.

BRIAN But how were you physically? Your legs must have been completely weak to start with.

IAN They weren't too bad, because in solitary after two months I realised no one was going to get me out of this and I had to survive myself and I got stuck into the exercises then. So I used to leap about doing star jumps and press-ups and occasionally I'd get a knock on the door saying, 'What the hell are you doing in there?' But generally that kept me going and I did find physical exercise important mentally, too. The two seemed to go together.

BRIAN Now, what about the Gulf War? Did you know when it had started?

IAN Yes.

BRIAN Did their attitude change?

IAN It didn't. They were surprisingly good to me during the war. Whether that was because I'd built up a relationship and a respect before that, or whether they were just hedging their bets on how the war was going to go, I don't know, but they were very good to me during the war. The war itself was difficult to handle, because there was a desperate shortage of food and water, so we really had to struggle to survive.

BRIAN Were you bombed at any time by our planes?

IAN Yes. Funnily enough there was a strike of lightning and thunder the night before the war started and we all thought, 'Oh, God, this is it.' But they came the next night and there was an army camp round us which got plastered. But for the first day or two you get frightened of bombs and then you get used to the noise. You get a bit blasé about it and get this feeling that it's not going to happen to you.

BRIAN Did they try the propaganda and say how great Saddam Hussein was? Presumably they worshipped him.

IAN Well, they had to worship him, but gradually, after the war, when there was this insurrection, I was amazed how many people came to me and said, 'This man has ruined our country.' That took a lot of saying to a foreigner. It could never have happened before the war.

BRIAN And you were made more comfortable, were you? Did you have a better cell with other people?

IAN It was very crowded when I first left solitary and was brought to the main prison. I was in a hall about 40 metres by 60 metres with about 60 people in it, so it was very crowded – a bit like a goldfish bowl.

After five years, yes, I was given a cell of my own and that was marvellous. I put up a big sign, saying, 'ENGLISHMEN ONLY. PICCADILLY CIRCUS. KEEP OUT.'

BRIAN What a relief. And your wife went out to visit you regularly?

IAN Yes. Shirley had come back to Britain after six or nine months, having been refused permission for a while and then led this marvellous campaign. She was absolutely wonderful. She came regularly until the invasion of Kuwait, when, of course, we didn't see each other for a year. Then she came out with ITV and there was this most extraordinary interview. I thought she was coming out, but I'd no idea of the time and I walked into this room and there were all these cameras and Jeffrey Archer was there. So it was a sign that things were going well, but I'd been through so many disappointments I didn't take it as a sign at the time. But the fact that they did allow a TV crew in was good.

BRIAN And how did you actually hear the news that you were going to be released?

IAN The Russian Ambassador came to see me three days before I was released and he said, 'Ian, I'm terribly sorry relations between Britain and Iraq are particularly bad at the moment. Sadruddin Aga Khan's coming out, but I really wouldn't bank on him. He's going to try, but things are just terribly bad at the moment.' So I said, 'Oh, well, thanks for that.' He was a super chap. The Russians were marvellous to me after the war. They found me and helped me.

BRIAN Did you interest them in cricket? One day they're going to play, aren't they?

IAN They got into rugby in quite a big way. So then three days passed and nothing happened and I went out and ran a half-marathon to get rid of my pent-up fury at not being released and I had a shower, which was a bucket of water and a ladle. And a guy came to me and said, 'You've got five minutes to leave.' And I said, 'As I've spent five years as your guest, you can give me a bit longer.' He said, 'No, there is a press conference. We've got to be there.' I think Saddam Hussein would have killed him if he hadn't got me there in five minutes. So I grabbed a shirt, borrowed a tie and unfortunately lost all my letters, but I preserved my books – particularly the cricketing books which people had sent me. Towards the end I got most of the Wisdens.

BRIAN I suppose you had to catch up, didn't you? Those years when you were in solitary you didn't get the cricket scores.

IAN I missed '86 to '89, basically. So I missed a period when we lost a few.

BRIAN And you read of the successes of various new people. That must have been fascinating – a new breed of cricketers.

IAN It was. Lamb had come and gone and come back again and gone again and come back again and, yes, a whole new breed had come through.

BRIAN And as soon as you were released, where did you go?

IAN I went to a hotel and I had 24 hours with Prince Sadruddin and his team and then flew back with his plane.

BRIAN He did a good job, did he?

IAN Marvellous guy. Shirley met him during her visit to Iraq three or four months before I was released. She went to see him and he promised to help and many people who said that helped in their own ways, but

Prince Sadruddin kept in telephone and fax contact with her weekly thereafter.

BRIAN   Would you ever go back there?

IAN   I don't think so. I think I've probably donated enough of my life.

BRIAN   So are you working for a firm here?

IAN   I've come back to my old group company. Not the firm itself I worked for, they were sold off to Thames Water when the water industry was privatised, but I'm in the same group.

BRIAN   And now you're starting a cricket tour. You said you were playing for the Free Foresters. How many did you make? How many stumpings?

IAN   Twenty-six. One stumping and two catches – and the next match I got one and dropped two catches.

BRIAN   That's roughly the way cricket goes. So who are you going to be playing for now?

IAN   Well, I have Emeriti in a week's time.

BRIAN   This is the club formed by the Catholic schools, roughly – Downside, Ampleforth?

IAN   And they had to include St Aidan's in Grahamstown, where I was brought up – a Jesuit school. I'll be playing for a number of sides and Don Wilson wants me to play one or two over the bank holiday.

BRIAN   It would be nice keeping wicket to him. You'd get a few stumpings.

IAN   When I came back I spent the winter up in Yorkshire and he allowed me to play with the first team squad at their indoor nets and he bowled to me and he's a wonderful bowler. He just twiddled it over and stretched me forward and a little bit more forward each ball – lovely to see.

BRIAN   It sounds to me that if we were all put into solitary confinement we'd all become better cricketers.

How did you pick it all up, after five or six years, picking up a bat again or putting on the gauntlets?

IAN   I think a moving-ball game is instinct – squash or tennis, that's all come back to me, too. But I can't hit a bloody golf ball.

BRIAN   But did it affect your eyes? There you were in darkness. What happened when you suddenly saw the light?

IAN   I was worried about that, but it seems fine.

BRIAN   So you can still see the ball. The other thing, having trained running round that football field, you've now run in the London Marathon here. You must be mad. What was your time?

IAN   Four hours thirty minutes, less ten minutes to get to the start, so I claim four hours twenty. When we came back we were interviewed by a lot of people and after one day we said, 'Right, that's it.' Somebody from a running magazine rang up and said she wanted to do an interview. I said, 'Sorry, those times have passed now.' And she said, 'But I'll get you into the London Marathon and I'll get you kit.' The kit disappeared towards my children rapidly, but she got me into the London Marathon and the Red Cross, who'd helped Shirley a lot while I was away, asked me to run for them.

BRIAN   So you got some money for the Red Cross. How did you feel when you crossed the line?

IAN   I felt pretty grim at about 23 miles, when we got to Tower Bridge for the second time, but, as luck would have it, I bumped into Shirley, who'd spent three hours looking for me and that sort of raised me for the last three miles. Yes, it was fun to finish.

ALAN
AYCKBOURN CBE

I FIRST MET Alan a few years ago when I went to interview him at the National Theatre. He was there in his role as a director, the play being *Tons of Money*. I knew, of course, that he lived and worked in what is generally known as the 'Cricket Town' – Scarborough. It was natural therefore that, as soon as the interview was over, we should start to talk about cricket. It soon became obvious that he would be an ideal candidate for 'View from the Boundary', especially when he revealed that he used to keep wicket! I had heard that he used to live in Sussex and had been at school at Haileybury in Hertfordshire, so I started by asking him which first-class county he supported.

HEADINGLEY, 25 JULY 1992

ALAN AYCKBOURN I'm a member of Yorkshire. I think you can't live in Yorkshire for 35 years and support someone else. I've certainly seen them through some lean times and now I think better times are coming. So I've clung to Yorkshire. I think I was temporarily a Sussex supporter, when I was ten.

BRIAN JOHNSTON Slight contrast, really – the Seasiders and the rather dourer Tykes. And I'm told, which pleases me, that you are either a wicket keeper/batsman or a batsman/wicket keeper. Which do you like to call yourself?

ALAN I think my wicket keeping was fractionally better than my batting, which isn't saying a lot. I used to keep wicket, but in the last few years I've become a sort of non-playing manager. I still put a team together – of actors, mainly. I still challenge people, when I've got enough actors in the company to make up a team.

BRIAN We always talk about this association between cricket and the stage. It's remarkable that so many actors seem to enjoy cricket.

ALAN Well, of course cricket's a huge theatre spectacle. Entering a cricket ground like Headingley here is very like going on stage at Drury Lane, I suppose. There is this enormous walk out, with you in the solo spotlight. The only difference is that you are surrounded by total hostility out there – by people who mean you ill. They mean to send you back as fast as possible. It's also a very great game for teamwork. Although you do sparkle as individuals as batsmen, a fielding team is very much a team and actors respond to this. They like a feeling of clear roles, whether you're a wicket keeper or a slip fielder or whatever. I think it has tremendous relationship with theatre, so I'm not surprised.

BRIAN You tell me that you are now 45 not out – not in age, but in number of plays written, which puts you top of the averages for all English playwrights. You even go ahead of Bill Shakespeare.

ALAN Yes, I wouldn't say in quality, but in quantity, certainly. I've shot ahead of him now. I'm hoping to make 50. You get depressed when you read that Goldoni apparently wrote over a hundred plays, so I think the Italians still lead.

BRIAN I think *Mr What-Not* was your first play. At what age did you start?

ALAN *Mr What-Not* was my first London play. I wrote that in my early twenties. I had my first big hit when I was about 25. It was some years ago.

BRIAN Michael Hordern in *Relatively Speaking*.

ALAN Absolutely right.

BRIAN With Celia Johnson.

ALAN That's right – and Richard Briers.

BRIAN But what theatrical experience had you had? Did you do any acting before you started writing?

ALAN Yes, I've worked my way through all parts of theatre, really. I started as an assistant stage manager, which is the humblest form of life. I didn't get formally trained, because we couldn't actually afford it. After being an ASM I then went on to become a stage manager, an electrician and at one stage I got involved with sound, which I'm still involved with. Then I became an actor and a director and finally, oddly enough, I became a playwright. All of that experience has helped me.

BRIAN You learned the business. Did anyone particularly help you early on?

ALAN Yes, a lot of people. I've been very lucky. I always say that if in your life you have one or two guardian uncles and aunts – not necessarily related by blood – you're very lucky. I met this incredible man, Stephen Joseph, whose name the theatre in Scarborough actually bears.

BRIAN It was called something else. The Library Theatre?

ALAN It was at one stage, but when he died in '67, we renamed it the Stephen Joseph Theatre. He was amazing. He encouraged young talent, as I was then, and he encouraged particularly the young playwrights. He had this extraordinary idea that a playwright belonged within a theatre and they weren't sort of mysterious men and women who sent in plays from the Orkney Islands and were never seen. They were actually part of the process of play-making, which was incredibly rewarding and also instructive. If you actually saw your work being done and you saw actors having trouble with it, at least you learnt better next time.

BRIAN Did he do the directing to start with that you do now?

ALAN Yes, he directed the company, but, fortunately for me, he was so busy doing everything – he was a great man of theatre – he often left areas which he couldn't cover and he would just grab the nearest person. In my case he said, 'Go and direct the next play.'

BRIAN Is that as easy as it sounds?

ALAN Well, I said, 'Look here, I've never directed. I've been directed. I think I know what not to do, because I've met some pretty bad directors – not yourself, sir, of course.' And he said, 'Just create an atmosphere in which actors can create,' and walked away. And of course that is exactly what one has to do as a director, but how you do it, of course, takes about 50 years to learn.

BRIAN What is your relationship with the actors?

Do you leave them a lot to themselves, or do you sort of pop in with ideas?

ALAN Oh, yes, I try to pick up on their ideas. I like it if they initiate ideas and then I hope I bounce things back off them. I think actors like a firm framework in which to work. They like to think that somebody's organising it, if only deciding when the tea breaks happen. Somebody needs to be in overall charge and you have to have someone making group decisions like the style you've got to do it in and the way it's going to be set. That has to be the director's decision. But, obviously, the actor is in pole position when it comes to theatre work and it's very important that they're allowed to motor at full throttle, if you like. You don't want people like me standing in their way. I think I've got to get behind and shove them to get them going.

BRIAN You've got this remarkable way of writing a play. Am I right in saying you sit down five weeks away – it's already been advertised, the title has been done, the bookings have been made and you haven't even written it? How long does it take you from the moment the pen hits the paper to production?

ALAN Well, no more than ten days, probably less, actually.

BRIAN This is terrifying.

ALAN There's a lot of preparation that goes on up top in my head. I don't make copious notes. I think with writing plays it's very important to get it all down. If you think about a play, it's a group of people all inter-relying and responding and following emotional lines and plot lines and it's very hard to keep in the air, as it were. I feel like a juggler with a lot of coloured balls, throwing them up and if I actually take too many breaks from it, I drop the lot.

BRIAN One can understand the plot going round, but you've got to put the dialogue down, too. You've got to put yourself in the place of the characters and invent some conversations.

ALAN That's the easy bit. It's the framework, the structure, to try to hold an audience whose attention span these days is getting shorter and shorter. In television now they give them about 44 seconds before they cut to another shot and we're asking them to look at the same shot for probably two and a quarter hours. So it's a very important narrative structure and that's the toughest thing to achieve, to keep their eyes on the play for that length of time.

BRIAN But aren't the actors and actresses there with their hands out, waiting for the script? The first night coming up and you get the script how many days before?

ALAN Well, nowadays I am a little better. I turned 50 not long ago and I thought, 'I think it's about time I stopped this.' Because it wasn't doing my heart any good, either. My best story is of an actor who was really dyslexic and he was terrified of having to sit in front of his peers reading a script he'd never seen before and he said, 'Please, please give it to me, even if it's only the night before. I must read it.' When I finished it it was four o'clock in the morning and I said, 'I don't think I can give it to him now. He must be in bed.' And the lady typing it said, 'I'll take it round to him. He was most insistent.' And she drove round in the car. There was this house all in darkness, his digs in Scarborough, and she slid the script through the letterbox and as it was half way through, somebody grabbed it from the other side. He'd been sitting in the hall till four in the morning.

BRIAN But you don't make things easy for yourself, because I've seen one of your plays where you had four different sets and each one is lit up in turn with different things happening and different families and you have different time-scales. One play, I think, one could choose the finish. What was that one and how many endings were there?

ALAN There was one play I wrote called *Intimate Exchanges* which actually has sixteen endings, which is rather a lot.

BRIAN Who chose which one it was going to be on each night?

ALAN It was generally the actors. I think the audience would have fallen into disarray with sixteen choices. The idea behind that was to try and remind people – and they do tend to forget – that theatre is live. When we think about theatre and we're always contemplating its demise and it never quite dies, it comes back, we're always talking about what is unique about it. The only thing that is unique about theatre is its 'liveness' – the fact that you get, in a sense, an individual performance every time you go. They don't necessarily change the scripts or even the moves, but the performance subtly alters to an audience and I thought I wanted to emphasise this by saying, 'Look, folks, big things can happen in front of your very eyes. The play can take off in another direction.'

Two lots of people came to see a play of mine in Scarborough called *Sisterly Feelings*. One came on one night and saw one version and recommended it to the people in the hotel, who went to see it and saw a different version. When they got back neither realised that there were variations and the most terrible row broke out and we finished up with the man saying, 'Are you calling my wife a liar?' But I think that emphasised the spontaneity of things.

BRIAN   One of the nice things is that you use local talent on the whole up in Scarborough, don't you? Most of your plays have started there with the local talent.

ALAN   It's imported local talent. There are very few native Scarborough actors, but, having said that, not just the actors, but the technicians, the backstage crew and indeed a lot of the people working there have sort of fallen in love with it. A lot of Scarborough residents seem to be people who arrived there, like myself, with no idea that it existed and have then fallen in love with it. I think the people who appreciate Scarborough best are probably people from Basildon and Bedford rather than the Scarborians who are rather dismissive about it.

BRIAN   You've been described, I think, as writing middle-class comedies of anguish in people's lives. Do you regard yourself as a sort of comedy writer or is there an undercurrent? There appears to be, in one or two of your plays, an undercurrent of social trouble, family strife or whatever it is, which is very true to real life.

ALAN   I think I regard myself as a writer, really. I think the category of comedy or tragedian is something that's rather invidious. I don't think William Shakespeare ever thought of himself as a comedy or a serious writer. He was both and I would like to think most of us are. It's a tendency these days to try and put people into one little box and say this is a particular type of writer. What's fascinated me – and increasingly so over the last few years – is to try and get at that balance between the tragedy and the comic. And it seems to me that people's emotional enjoyment can be increased – and of course theatre is a largely emotional experience – if you can get them reacting on two or three levels, it's both exciting and stimulating for them and for the actors.

BRIAN Do the characters come from your head, or are you watching us now and thinking of ideas of characters? Are they based on real people, in other words?

ALAN Bits. I think in the end most characters come from within oneself. It's very hard to say where you get characters. I think of myself as a sort of large reel-to-reel tape recorder that's always whirring. I'm sure that having spent a very enjoyable morning here in the box I've picked up quite a lot of things, but I'm not going to write a play about *Test Match Special*.

BRIAN Why not?

ALAN Because I think I'd get six libel writs.

BRIAN I was going to come to this. Have you ever been tempted to do a cricket play, or have I missed one?

ALAN There was one called *Time and Time Again* in which one character was fielding on the boundary at sort of deep extra cover and at one point dropped a rather important catch. But I haven't gone further onto the field. Richard Harris wrote a rather good play.

BRIAN Very good – *Outside Edge*.

ALAN I used to think that sport and theatre were not very good bedfellows, that maybe the people who liked watching sport didn't necessarily go to the theatre and vice versa, but I've come to the conclusion that may not be true, because we did a play about rowing the other year and that went terribly well.

BRIAN Can we tempt you to write one on cricket? Go off and in five days will you send me the script?

ALAN I've got somehow to get round not writing it with 22 men, because that's rather a large cast.

BRIAN I think it would be in a dressing room, or it could be in a commentary box. There's a lot of drama goes on here – you wouldn't think it. You may have noticed it this morning.

What's going through your head at the moment? Are you broody?

ALAN I'm mid-way through rehearsals for what is a bit of a departure for me really. It's a musical, which I wrote with my resident musical director in Scarborough, John Patterson. It's rather fun. Musicals are always tempting to do and they're always full of pitfalls, but I think we're having fun with it.

BRIAN Are you just the librettist, or have you written some of the music?

ALAN I wrote the book and I wrote the libretto and I'm directing it, but the music is John's. So it's rather nice because for once – and it's quite rare – you have a fellow creative initiator alongside you who's able to share the agonies and the excitements.

BRIAN How long did this one take you to write?

ALAN Well, we're a bit short. We went off for a fortnight to Majorca, because we'd read that's what Andrew Lloyd-Webber does. He goes to his villa in the South of France and writes successful musicals. So we thought, 'We haven't got a villa, so we'll go to Majorca.' We went to a hotel in the north and it was lovely. I wrote the book and most of the lyrics and John cracked the music.

BRIAN In the fortnight!

ALAN Yes. I spoke to Stephen Sondheim on the phone and he said, 'How long did it take you?' I said, 'Two weeks.' He said, 'Two weeks!'

BRIAN Of course Noël Coward used to do this. He even wrote *Private Lives* in a couple of days.

ALAN I don't think speed is necessarily a bad thing. It's not that you have to do it that way, it's just that that's how I paint the picture. I want to get all the ingredients into the frame and the longer you wait the more picky you get.

BRIAN But some of those complicated things you have must take a lot of working out. Do you wait till you actually go into rehearsals and make sure they work?

ALAN No, not at all. It's planned in general broad detail. There's a play of mine that's running in repertory at the moment called *Time of My Life* and this has three time-spans. There is one time going forward quite normally, there's one racing forward two months at a time and there's one going backwards. It sounds complicated, but once I'd got the pattern in my head it wasn't difficult to do.

BRIAN I saw you last when you were directing *Tons of Money* at the National Theatre. How did you like going to the National Theatre away from Scarborough?

ALAN It was nice, as somebody once said, playing with the big boys' toys. There was a lot more money and a lot more space to work in and I worked in all three theatres. We did *Tons of Money* in the Lyttelton and then we did my own play *Small Family Business* in the Olivier, the big one. Then I finished up having great fun with *View From the Bridge* in the tiny theatre and it was very rewarding. I think I love regional theatre and I like running it and I wouldn't be drawn away from it permanently, but I think you have to test yourself in the big arena and I think it was important to go to the National and say, 'Well, I think I'm quite good in Scarborough, but how am I up against the heavy men in London?'

BRIAN Well, how good are you in Oxford? Because you're a Professor of Contemporary Theatre.

ALAN Yes, the Cameron Mackintosh Professor.

BRIAN That's tremendous, but what does that involve?

ALAN Well, I was a little nervous, because I'm very badly educated. I left school at seventeen and went straight into the theatre, so I missed university. So here I come back as a prof., feeling a bit of a phoney. It's a mixture of some splendid dinners at various high tables. I'm trying to go round them all. I was 'buzzed' on the port the other night. I managed to finish up the bottle at Magdalen. I don't know if that's good or bad form, but anyway I got another free glass. The rest of it is very enjoyable. I've been working with a small group who are directly working to me in a series of tutorials, learning playwriting. I've been doing a lot of lectures which were a bit frightening, but I think the feeling is very good there at the moment. The students are bright, questioning, but not bolshy.

BRIAN Do you have time to go up to the Parks and see the cricket?

ALAN Yes. And we played a charity game the other day. I put a team together which thoroughly beat a local XI, though I did cheat a little, because our wicket keeper looked suspiciously like Deryck Murray. He came out of retirement. We played on the St Catherine's ground. I stood on the boundary and encouraged the team and kept the morale up.

BRIAN Who were your cricket heroes? In Sussex in those days did you have any special favourites down there?

ALAN Jim Parks, of course, the wicket keeper there was wonderful. I'm a great wicket keeper watcher. I'd like to meet Jack Russell, because I think he's a wonderful wicket keeper.

BRIAN   And I suppose you now have to have some Yorkshire heroes.

ALAN   Well, I'm very encouraged by the way the team's turned round and I'm a great admirer of Martyn Moxon.

BRIAN   I think he's had bad luck.

ALAN   There are some very exciting players in that team now and I do applaud the inclusion of Tendulkar.

BRIAN   You were in favour.

ALAN   Yes, I was on that side. I did think that we were being ridiculously dog-in-the-manger about it all. There are certain innovations, like that big screen, which I have to shout with everybody else my disapproval of, because it does seem to me that if you're going to have a screen like that up, you might as well dispense with the umpires and just have two cameras. It seems to me just awful. If I thought that my life was run by replays, every time I made a decision it was run back on me, one would become hopelessly inhibited.

One Test Match I saw here, I left the ground with England 500 to one against Australia and as we went home I tore my ticket up for the next day and threw it out of the window. And we all said, 'That's the last time we ever watch England.' And we went back to rehearsals and as we were rehearsing people kept sticking their heads round the door and saying, 'You'll never guess what's happened.' Of course it was the famous Botham match (in 1981) and we missed a sunny day's play and, more important, we missed winning thousands of pounds.

DAVID
SHEPHERD OBE

DAVID IS ONE of those lucky people who leads a happy life because he enjoys his job. Not only that. He is versatile and highly successful. He is best known as an artist of African wildlife, specialising in tigers and elephants. But in fact he started as an aviation artist, and is also a portrait painter of renown. Among his portraits is one of the Queen Mother. His hobbies are driving steam engines and making money for the World Wide Fund for Nature. By selling prints of his paintings he has made hundreds of thousands of pounds for the Fund. He was justly awarded the romantic sounding 'Order of the Golden Ark' by the Netherlands, for services to wildlife conservation. An elephant from one of his prints stares down on me as I write, and for some reason only has one tusk. So it is not surprising that David is often referred to as the elephant man.

Elephants and cricket don't go naturally together, though I did once see some elephants playing cricket in Bertram Mills Circus. So I had never associated David with cricket until we sat together in a box at Lord's watching the Rothman's Village Cricket Championship

Final. It soon became obvious, that, as with everything else with which he is associated, he was an enthusiast, and he leaped at the idea of being our guest in the commentary box the following season. He brought with him a magnificent chocolate cake baked by his lovely wife Avril. On the top was the figure of an elephant, holding a cricket bat in its trunk.

I started by asking David how often he was confused with David Sheppard, the Bishop of Liverpool, and David Shepherd, the umpire.

THE OVAL, 8 AUGUST 1992

BRIAN JOHNSTON How many times have you been asked to come and preach a sermon or umpire in a Test Match?

DAVID SHEPHERD Twice, actually. There's a lovely girl from the BBC who I have yet to meet who, although I live in Godalming, keeps asking me to go on Radio 4 and talk about the Bible. And I was asked to umpire, too. Terribly confusing with all these Shepherds around.

BRIAN Of course Sheppard the Bishop is with two Ps and an A R D.

DAVID He was staying with us last night, actually. He helped to make your chocolate cake.

BRIAN You told me just now that this is the first day you've ever been to a Test Match.

DAVID Does that surprise you?

BRIAN Well, it does. I know you love cricket. Is

it just that you haven't been able to get to it, or what?

DAVID I do love cricket and I love Test Matches. I listen all the time, especially while I'm painting. But I have to say that I never have watched serious cricket.

BRIAN How does it affect your brushwork when you hear, 'He's out!'?

DAVID It's like when I'm listening to a Mahler symphony; I just can't paint at all.

BRIAN You were at school at Stowe. Did you play cricket there?

DAVID No, I was too frightened. I was a snotty-nosed, rather terror-struck little boy, who fled into the art school because I was too frightened to do anything dangerous. I think it's terrifying.

BRIAN It is a hard ball, yes. So what did you do instead of playing cricket?

DAVID I painted in the art school. I was asked to captain – non-playing captain – with Denis Compton about four years ago at the Aldershot Officers' Club, when we were raising money jointly for my conservation foundation and the Parachute Regiment regimental museum. It was one of those drunken afternoons, where by four o'clock we were all paralytic and instead of being a non-playing captain, I was playing. I was absolutely scared stiff. I hit the ball and I was so excited I knocked the bails off and that's apparently not done, is it?

BRIAN Well, if you hit your wicket you more or less have to go out in most classes of cricket. Do you follow cricket in the papers? Do you have a particular hero?

DAVID Obviously I follow that lovely man, David Gower, because he's a trustee of my foundation and we know him terribly well, with Gary Lineker, who's also a great supporter. So that engenders an interest in cricket, when David's playing.

BRIAN So let's get down to the painting. Were you taught at school?

DAVID No, I wasn't. I always wanted to be a game warden. I was a total disaster in my early life. They told me they didn't want me as a game warden and then I decided to try and be an artist and I failed that one as well, because I was chucked out of the Slade School of Fine Art as being untrainable. I was about to drive a bus for the Aldershot and District Bus Company, because that was where we lived, when I met the man who trained me. I owe him everything – Robin Goodwin – the most amazing man.

BRIAN So what did he do? Did he take you under his wing?

DAVID Yes, he did and he gave me three years of intensive training. It was due to the RAF, actually. I never served in the RAF, but I started painting aeroplanes. Aeroplanes were my first love, because I'd lived in London in the Blitz and an eight-year-old spotty schoolboy like me in the Battle of Britain was terribly excited by World War Two and didn't realise that people were killing each other. And that engendered my love of aviation.

BRIAN Which was the first plane you painted?

DAVID Oh, Spitfires and Hurricanes and then a bit later Super Constellations and all those lovely old aeroplanes. I hate everything modern – I love everything old with propellers. I love steam trains, of course. But the RAF noticed my work and sort of picked me up and it was the RAF who commissioned my very first wildlife painting in 1960 and that changed my life.

BRIAN This wasn't the famous old elephant?

DAVID No, I did that one about a year afterwards – my famous Boots the Chemist one.

BRIAN They took it on and sold it. You went in for a pill or something else . . .

DAVID And you came out with an elephant. Two hundred and fifty thousand copies were sold – incredible.

BRIAN And it's achieved something on television.

DAVID It was on the wall in *Crossroads*. Fame at last!

BRIAN And in *Only Fools and Horses* – double fame. Was that one particular elephant?

DAVID No, I invented it, like the one on your chocolate cake. But that first elephant did me a lot of good, because it put my name around a lot. I'm very proud of it and very grateful, but a lot's happened since then.

BRIAN When you paint wildlife, do you actually go out there and do it? Or do you go and watch them and take photographs of them?

DAVID I take photographs. A lot of people are surprised when you say that, but Degas worked from a photograph when he was doing his ballet pictures, so I'm told. All a camera is to me is a means to an end to record the shape of something, because it's quick and convenient, but I have to take the photograph, because I'm there in Zambia or India or wherever, photographing and looking at tigers. I'm seeing them and that's what matters. Ninety per cent is seeing the scene and I take photographs of background bits of elephants' backsides and bits of tree.

BRIAN Are you brave and sit there while they're around?

DAVID The BBC filmed my life story years ago for television and they said, 'Let's film you walking up to two bull elephants. We'll find them in Zambia, nice and friendly bull elephants – with your easel.'

BRIAN   Are there such things as friendly bull elephants?

DAVID   They're all friendly. They're lovely, unless you shoot at them with an AK 47. I got within 60 paces of them and I was painting away with fourteen tubes of oil paint and linseed oil and turps and there was a team of fourteen of us, the whole camera crew. It was absolutely dreadful.

BRIAN   Did they decide to charge you?

DAVID   The cow the next day did charge us. It was so funny.

BRIAN   Are they more lethal than the males? It depends if they've got a little one, I suppose.

DAVID   You can't fool around if they've got young. The tragedy is you can't fool around with any animal, because you don't know if it's been shot at with an AK 47, or had its foot blown off by a land mine. All these things have happened and I've seen the results of this ghastly business.

BRIAN   To horrify us, an AK 47 is what?

DAVID   It's one of those ghastly automatic rifles which you can buy for 30 quid in Zambia. Now that human beings have stopped shooting each other, you can buy them off the shelf. And the dear old elephant's on the way out, like the tiger is and the rhino and that's why I'm such a passionate conservationist. Because I owe all my success to the animals and it's so easy to raise money through my paintings.

BRIAN   How serious is it for elephants or tigers?

DAVID   Well, I'm glad you asked me about the tiger, because only last week I got a press cutting from India about one poacher who's just slaughtered 21 tigers single-handed. And the tiger is now on the way out faster than we can possibly believe. It's frightening. They're probably down to about 1,800.

BRIAN They do that for the skins?

DAVID Yes. There are sick people in the world. They poach mountain gorillas. My wife and I had this wonderful experience with mountain gorillas in Ruanda last year and since then one of the silverbacks has been killed by poachers. They kill the gorilla, cut the hand off, it then goes solidified and strange people buy that for an ashtray. This will shock your listeners, but it's true. Can you imagine stubbing your cigarette out in a gorilla's hand? There are some incredibly sick people in this world, there really are.

BRIAN You did a famous tiger painting – you've done a lot of tigers.

DAVID Yes, I'm very lucky. I raised a lot of money with a painting called 'Tiger Fire' which went towards saving the tiger. We raised £127,000 in six weeks with the painting. I don't say that because I want thanks. It's so exciting, because I owe so much to the wildlife.

BRIAN I was wondering how you earn a living, because you give all your money to charity, very nearly, when you paint these things. Do you do the odd one for yourself?

DAVID Well, I'm sometimes in my studio, but this foundation that I've started has taken over our lives. The beauty of it is that it's tiny. There are only five of us and it's based in my own house.

BRIAN Who are you?

DAVID My daughter, Melanie, is the coordinator and we have a couple of other girls and Claire – she runs the trading company. We've given away about a million and a half pounds already in the first couple of years. The point is it's small, so if people support us they know where the money goes.

BRIAN And do you do new paintings or do you sell the old ones?

DAVID I'm painting all the time, anyway, as hard as I can. But it's so exciting trying to raise money. I did a little painting last year in two hours and it went for £11,000 that evening. I feel humble when I say that, because there are people who'd take two years to raise £11,000 with a flag tin in the high street, getting frostbite at the end of the day and five quid in the tin. That's the hard way to raise money for charity and I'm so lucky, because I'm painting anyway. I'm a compulsive painter; I'm miserable if I'm not painting.

BRIAN What about the rhino? There's the odd white rhino still.

DAVID In Zambia there arc seventeen rhino left. When I first went there there were two and a half thousand. Again because of sick people wanting rhino horn. Man is the sickest, most dangerous animal on earth. Man is the only animal that destroys through greed and ignorance and the poor old rhino is on the way out like the tiger is. We can't go on doing this. We've only got one world and we share it with all these other lovely animals. But I don't give up, because there are some wonderful children I'm meeting all the time in my foundation. It's the children that matter. They are so worried now what we do. So's the good old British public.

BRIAN How can they help you with your foundation? What do you want from them?

DAVID They join us, the kids. Gary Lineker is our captain and you can't have a better man than that. He's a lovely man. And they get a newsletter and we believe that if they support us they can get the incentive of feeling that they can help in retrieving the damage that my generation has done.

BRIAN Didn't you hire a helicopter to try and find the poachers?

DAVID I gave a helicopter. I raised money with a lot of other artists. We raised enough money in about twenty minutes to buy a Belljet Ranger helicopter.

BRIAN Did you catch any poachers?

DAVID Yes, it did.

BRIAN Is it illegal now for them to shoot tigers and elephants in these countries?

DAVID It's all strictly illegal, but while there's a financial motive to go and kill a tiger and escape capture they'll go on doing it. There are people who will do anything to make money.

BRIAN In all of this the king of the animals seems to have got away free. There are plenty of lions aren't there?

DAVID They breed like rabbits.

BRIAN Do tigers not breed like rabbits?

DAVID No, they're a different animal altogether. Lions are not endangered in any way and I don't think he's the king of the beasts, anyway. He's a scraggy old hearthrug compared to an elephant. When you see them lolling with their legs in the air – OK he's an impressive animal when he's angry, but you cannot possibly improve on an elephant. In my new book there's a lovely photograph on the cover of me four feet away from an enormous bull elephant. He's drinking from a waterhole. I went right up to him and my wife took the photograph. They're not dangerous.

BRIAN Have you got an affinity with elephants?

Are you good with them? I mean, if I went up to him he mightn't like me.

DAVID They'd love you, Brian.

BRIAN Don't look at my nose like that.

DAVID As long as they haven't been shot at by poachers, they'll leave you alone. Actually, in my case, I think they do know me. They say, 'Oh, God, Shepherd's coming again. Another picture in Boots the Chemist.'

BRIAN What's all the mystery of an elephant when it dies? They go to secret places.

DAVID It's all a lot of nonsense. I get worked up about this. There are a lot of scientists who are trying to find out a lot of answers to these mystical things about elephants. An elephant's been known to carry a tusk out of a dead elephant for 27 miles before it dropped it. Why pick up a tusk? Why didn't it pick up a leg bone or a rib? They've got brains bigger than ours and I hope we'll never find out, because it's lovely to leave them alone and just wonder. Same with the whale. That's got a bigger brain than we have. Wonderful things. They migrate from Alaska right down to California and back again and they don't use computers and navigational instruments.

BRIAN We've been talking about animals, but what about the railways? When did you get attracted to engines?

DAVID I think every small boy wanted to drive a train. But why Avril my wife's still married to me after 32 years, I don't know, because I bought two enormous 140-ton steam engines off British Rail and I've got a railway in Somerset and I promised faithfully last year I would not collect any more big toys. Well, about a year ago we were in Johannesburg when South

African Railways presented me with 220 tons of steam engine as a gift. Why? Because I asked them if they could give me one and they did and I'm bringing it home next year.

BRIAN   And where will it go?

DAVID   To the Somerset Railway.

BRIAN   How is that going?

DAVID   It's going very well, considering the recession. The lovely thing about it is it's a registered charity and when I go down there we talk about elephants. All the lovely public comes to ride on steam trains and they talk to me about elephants. The two are inseparable.

BRIAN   And everybody's an amateur on it, aren't they?

DAVID   Never use the word amateur, because we are more professional than professionals. They are volunteers, yes.

BRIAN   You mustn't deride the word 'amateur', because in cricket it was a great word.

DAVID   I don't deride it, but in the railway context, in the worst sense an amateur can kill people on a steam engine, because they're heavy things. But we can't do anything stupid, because we're run by all the regulations that BR are run by. You're hauling fare-paying passengers, so you've got to run it as a serious business.

BRIAN   What sort of mileage is yours? Where do you go?

DAVID   We go from the bottom of the hill to the top of the hill – two and a half miles.

BRIAN   I did a *Down Your Way* from there and you can have a meal on it. It must be a very quick meal.

DAVID   Well, we can stop. We've saved a bit of Britain's heritage. I'm sounding pompous now, but I think our heritage is important and in this age we're too damn keen to sweep aside everything in the name of progress. We live in a sixteenth-century farmhouse and that lovely old farmhouse will stand up long after all these tower blocks round the Oval have fallen down in a cloud of dust.

BRIAN Are you inspired, like Jack Russell, looking round the ground to do a painting of the Oval?

DAVID He drew my portrait, dear old Jack. He's a jolly good artist, actually. But no, I couldn't paint this, to be honest. It's just not my scene.

BRIAN You've actually done some portraits, haven't you?

DAVID I've done portraits, but nobody knows about them. The most exciting thing I've ever painted was a twenty-foot-long painting of Christ for an Army church. And nobody knows I do that sort of thing, you see.

BRIAN Who else have you done?

DAVID The Queen Mum. I had a fantastic time painting the Queen Mother.

BRIAN Does she come to you or do you go to her?

DAVID I'm not that important. I went to Clarence House and had six one-hour sessions with her altogether. It was an absolute riot, because we talked about Africa all the time and never did any work.

BRIAN She would have talked about cricket if you'd asked her, because she's mad on cricket.

DAVID I know, but we talked about HMS Ark Royal and other things I've painted, like Lancaster bombers. Then I painted President Kaunda of Zambia.

BRIAN He helped you quite a bit, didn't he?

DAVID He did tremendously and I love Zambia. He's no longer President but he's a dear friend of mine. A great conservationist.

BRIAN Has his influence helped?

DAVID   I like to think so. There are a lot of people in England who think that immediately a black country becomes independent they eat all their animals. In Zambia's case there was one national park when it was a British colony. There are now nineteen. They really are concerned and they're trying jolly hard with no resources, because they're very poor, these little countries. I'm very touched, particularly by the children. The children in these black countries are absolutely marvellous. They're fully aware of what we're doing and they're damn well going to do something about it.

BRIAN   What has been your impression of coming here to the Oval?

DAVID   First of all the lovely atmosphere, because I love atmosphere, whether it's in Africa to see elephants or here at the Oval. You can feel it. One of the stewards said, 'You're David Shepherd, aren't you? Have you got a cake for Johnners?' I said, 'Of course I've got a cake.' I daren't come near you without a cake.

BRIAN   It is a friendly game and I wish you'd come more often to it.

DAVID   I could catch the bug but conservation's taking up so much of my time.

THE 'BITER' BIT:
NED SHERRIN
INTERVIEWS
BRIAN JOHNSTON

WE FINISH WITH the most unexpected of all the 'Views from the Boundary' in which I have taken part since it started in 1980. Unexpected, that is, by me alone! Our guest was to be Ned Sherrin and I had done a good deal of homework about him, so that I could be fully clued-up on all his varied activities, on radio, TV and in the theatre. As usual, when play finished for lunch, we had a short summary of the morning's play and then went back to the studio for the news.

As it was being read, I settled down in my corner of the commentary box, and placed Ned at a microphone alongside me. I waited for my cue back from the studio . . .

I think it's a good idea for Peter Baxter to explain what then happened.

Peter Baxter:
To mark Brian's eightieth birthday, I thought we might surprise him by turning the tables on him at

Lord's. The problem was finding the right man to do the interview. It had to be someone who would be believable by Brian as a proper 'View from the Boundary'. Most of the obvious candidates had been on the programme already. Then I had the rare brainwave of Ned Sherrin. He liked the idea, but unfortunately, after accepting it, he revealed that his Radio 4 programme, *Loose Ends*, was to come that week from the north. He seemed such an ideal person to do it that, for the first time ever, I decided to switch the 'View from the Boundary' to the Sunday. To avoid Brian smelling a rat, I delayed telling him of the change until it was actually going to come out in the *Radio Times*. On the day I instructed Bill Rennells in the *Test Match Special* studio after the lunchtime news to hand back with the words: 'And now to introduce his guest who is taking a "View from the Boundary", here is Ned Sherrin.'

LORD'S, 21 JUNE 1992

NED SHERRIN We're turning the tables on you today, Brian. Today, this is your boundary.

BRIAN JOHNSTON What are you doing to me?

NED You're being interviewed – I'm not.

BRIAN I don't believe this.

NED Absolutely true. Aren't you going to be 80 on Wednesday? Haven't we been hearing about that all week?

How do I fill half an hour talking to you? Because

233

you've done 46 years. You must have counted up the number of hours that you've rambled on up here.

BRIAN Rambled is the right word, but of course I didn't ramble quite so much in the early years, because I did the telly, and one was meant then only to speak when you could add to the picture. And if you watched very closely, you didn't speak at all, really. That was the first thing we were told about television commentary.

NED Your first cricket team was Temple Grove (prep school) where you played with Douglas Bader.

BRIAN He was very popular, because he was a brilliant cricketer and every Saturday he used to get a hundred against another school and we used to get off prep every time he got a hundred. And he was a marvellous rugby player. He'd have played for England at both, I'm sure.

NED Then there was the terrible injustice of your Eton career – not being crowned with keeping wicket for the first team.

BRIAN I don't know about injustice, but a chap did stay on a little bit longer. He was nineteen and a half, I think. But I captained the second XI and as usual, I think, I had more fun doing that. The trouble was that when they came here to Lord's, we had two fast bowlers called Page and Hanbury and when you look in the records, he let 35 byes. Well, goodness knows how many I'd have let, but I had a quiet chuckle. But he was a very nice chap and we were friends.

NED And you had the sympathy of a great cricketer at the time, George Hirst, didn't you?

BRIAN George Hirst was the coach there and one of the most loveable characters you could ever think of. He took me under his wing, partly because just previous to the Lord's match I'd stumped someone down the leg side off him. He was a little round ball of a man then. He used to bowl left-arm round the wicket inswingers and I casually whipped off the furnitures, so he rather liked me and took me all round Lord's when I came up here. He took me up to the scoreboard and introduced me to everyone. He was a lovely man.

NED   The early hero was Patsy Hendren, wasn't it?

BRIAN   Patsy became a hero of mine when my brother threw me a cricket bat when I was about ten and said, 'You're Patsy Hendren and I'm Jack Hearne.' And I worshipped him from that moment. I used to get *The Times* before my father could get it and look at all the cricket scores. I then read in an advertisement one day, 'Why not take Wincarnis wine like E. Patsy Hendren of 26 Cairn Avenue, Ealing, London W5.' Well, who would give an address like that nowadays? Imagine Ian Botham doing it.

Anyhow he did and I wrote to him and said, 'Please, Mr Hendren, can I have your autograph?' And he wrote back with three little autographs. And the thing about that that has affected my life is that in 'Patsy' he never crossed the 't' and when he wrote 'Hendren', under the final 'n' there were two little lines. When I sign my autograph now, it's 'Johnston' without a crossed 't' and two little lines. So he had a great effect. He was a loveable man.

NED   One of your earliest doubtful jokes, too – the heckler on the Hill in Sydney.

BRIAN   I used to go up when he was scoring for Middlesex and he used to tell me all these stories and he said that in 1924, when he was fielding in front of the Hill on Arthur Gilligan's tour, Tommy Andrews skied a ball up to him. Patsy was hovering underneath and a voice shouted out, 'Patsy, if you miss this ball, you can

sleep with my sister.' So I said, 'What happened, Patsy?'
He said, 'Well, as I hadn't seen his sister, I caught the
catch,' which is a typical Hendren remark.

NED How many times have you had to tell that
one on *Test Match Special*?

BRIAN I don't think I've ever told it on *Test Match
Special*.

NED An original Johnston joke on *Test Match Special*.

BRIAN There are not many of those.

But he was very funny and he had this marvellous
story of when he was sitting in a railway carriage and
there was a very ashen, grey person sitting in the far
corner, with a white silk scarf round his neck, looking in
a terrible state and Patsy tried to cheer him up. He said,
'How are you?' The chap said, 'I'm miserable. Our side
only wanted one wicket to win the other day and I got
an easy catch at mid-on and I put it down and the other
side won. I feel absolutely dreadful.' And Patsy, joking,
said, 'Well, if I'd done that, I'd have cut my throat.' And
the chap said, 'I have.'

NED What about this trick which has never been
done on radio before, I gather, the ability to tuck your
right ear in.

BRIAN I'll take the headphones off. I used to be able
to tuck both in, but I think only one stays in now. I have
done this on Derek Nimmo's show and on Parkinson.

NED The top part of the lobe is going in. We've
still got to get the bottom part in . . .

BRIAN In hot weather it stays in rather longer.
Then I can flip it out by going . . . like that!

NED Beautiful!

BRIAN First time it's been tucked in on the air.

NED Now, I hadn't realised that you'd had a distinguished career by political association. You and Neville

Chamberlain were godfathers to the same child.

BRIAN That's right. Alec Douglas-Home made me and Neville Chamberlain joint godfathers of his daughter, Meriel. And I went to see him off when he went with Neville Chamberlain to Munich. He was short of a shirt and he was suddenly told he was going and he came round to William, his brother, who I shared a house with and said, 'Has anybody got a spare shirt? I've got to go off to Munich to see Hitler.' So we lent him a shirt, and we went down to Heston to see him off. They got into a tiny little aeroplane, the sort of thing you see at a display of Moths – all strapped up. They got into this and went off to Munich.

NED Is there one fragrant pre-war memory? You were shipped off to broke coffee in Brazil for a time. Were you captain of the Brazilian national side?

BRIAN No. I went to study the coffee bean. I didn't learn much about it. There are an awful lot of coffee beans in Brazil. But I did play cricket out there on the mat and my only real triumph was when an American cruiser came in and we took them on at softball, which is the equivalent to baseball, but I think the ball is slightly bigger, and I scored a home run. They have no mid-off at baseball and I hit the ball through mid-off and I got a home run.

NED Back home after the war, it was 1946 when you joined the BBC. Was that a chapter of accidents or a chapter of luck?

BRIAN A chapter of luck, because, when I was in the Grenadiers during the war, Wynford Vaughan-Thomas and Stuart McPherson came down to brush up on their war reporting in Norfolk before they went across to Normandy. They came and had supper in a wood with us and I got to know them then and I thought no more about it. After the war I happened to meet them at a dinner party and they said, 'We're short of people at the BBC, come and do a test.' They stuck me out in Oxford Street and they said, 'You ask passers-by what they think of the butter ration.' And if you ask silly questions you get silly answers. So they said, 'Not very good, but at least you kept talking. Come and join us.' So I said, 'Well, I really want to go into the theatre somewhere.' And they said, 'Come and join us for three months,' and I stayed till 1972 when I had to retire.

NED The television box had three distinguished names alongside yours early on: P. G. H. Fender, Aidan Crawley and Crusoe – Robertson Glasgow, the best cricket writer ever.

BRIAN Absolutely. And a great humorist. It didn't quite come over on the telly. He had a very sepulchral voice and when the producer said, 'Will you please give the score,' he'd say, 'For those who weren't listening when I gave it two balls ago.'

And Percy Fender – indignant, because he had a nose even bigger than mine and a chap up the line said, 'Will you please hold the microphone nearer to you, we can't hear you.' And nothing happened, so they said, 'No, we still can't hear you. Will you hold it so it's touching your nose.' And he said, 'I am!' And of course it was miles away from his mouth. He got indignant.

He was talking about Hayward and how he used to wear a panama hat when he was playing for Surrey and this was in the middle of a rather exciting hat-trick, I think. So the producer said, 'Stick to the cricket, Percy.' And he put his microphone down and said, 'Well, if he's so bloody clever, let him do it himself.' They were a bit irregular in those days.

NED   And poor Pauline – you postponed your wedding because there was a Test Match.

BRIAN   Well, we had to get married a little bit earlier. It was rather a good thing actually, because I had to be sure of being here for the Test Match. The colonel, her father, wasn't too pleased, because I proposed to her after a week and she gave me an answer after a month and we decided we had to get married before the cricket season started. So we were married within three months. But it seems to have worked.

NED   Where are these tattoos that she disapproves of so much?

BRIAN   I've only got one, just on my left arm, here, which is of two crossed cricket bats. I had it done when I was doing *In Town Tonight*. We went down to the Ship Builders Union or something, down in the East End and this chap with the little electric needle was so nervous as I was interviewing him that the bats don't look anything like bats and the little ball doesn't look anything like a ball. But it's on my left forearm and I can be recognised by that.

NED   We'd better examine, I suppose, the question of the gaffes. The famous one, I suppose, is 'The bowler's holding . . .'

BRIAN   That is the only one I didn't know I'd done. I got a letter from a lady who said, 'Mr Johnston, we do enjoy your commentaries very much, but you must be more careful. We have a lot of young people listening. Do you realise what you said the other day when Michael Holding was bowling to Peter Willey? You said, "The bowler's Holding the batsman's Willey." ' No one told me about it at the time.

NED   And then you got into trouble with the 'leg over' situation.

BRIAN   Well, this is Aggers' fault. It was the Friday of the Oval Test Match last season at the close of play. The producer, who bullies us like mad, said, 'Go through the scorecard.' So we went through the scorecard until we got to Ian Botham, who'd been out hit-wicket. And Aggers made a very long explanation of why he did it. 'And in the end,' he said, 'he just couldn't get his leg over.' And I said, 'Couldn't get . . .' I got as far as that and then I was more professional than I think I've ever been, because I went on reading the scorecard for about 30 seconds without going, but then I had to and I went wheezing away with laughter. But what didn't help us was Peter Baxter, stupid ass, said to Aggers, 'Say something.' Well, Aggers was hysterical and all he could get out was, 'Lawrence . . .' And he broke down after saying that. But the interesting thing in those giggles – and we've had lots in the box – we've always had a professional like Trevor Bailey or Richie Benaud on television, who would take over.

NED   Someone with no sense of humour, you mean.

BRIAN   No, someone disciplined. And we had Tony Cozier this time, who just sat silent, listening to it all. He should have taken over and said, 'Well, I'll go on with the scorecard.' So we were made to look rather stupid.

NED   Has Mrs Rex Alston forgiven you yet?

BRIAN   'Now from Southampton to Edgbaston, where they're playing on till seven o'clock. So over for some more balls from Rex Alston.' She didn't forgive me for a long time about that.

NED   Is it apocryphal, the one about Princess Diana going up the steps into the pavilion?

BRIAN   No, that was right. I was on Queen Anne's statue outside St Paul's for the Royal Wedding and I saw this carriage with the outriders and I said, 'Here's Lady Diana and her carriage will draw up below me. She'll be met by her father, Earl Spencer, and they'll walk up the steps into the pavilion . . . I mean the cathedral.'

NED   Then there was the funeral of George VI.

BRIAN   That was unfortunate. I was doing that for television with Richard Dimbleby. He was in St James's Street and I was at Hyde Park Corner. I thought, 'I must get this right,' and I wrote down and read it every night before I went to sleep. 'Here comes the procession, now, led by five Metropolitan policemen mounted' – and they'd told me they'd be on white horses – 'on white horses.' When the day came, I heard Richard Dimbleby say, 'Over to Brian Johnston at Hyde Park Corner.' And Keith Rogers, my producer, said, 'Go ahead, Brian, good luck.' And I said, 'Here comes the procession, now, led by five Metropolitan policemen mounted . . .' And they came round the bend and they were on black horses. So all I said was, 'Mounted on horseback.' So, Keith Rogers, on this very serious occasion, said, 'What do you think they're mounted on, camels?' And there I was trying to be very serious. And we had this awful business which is always recalled at state occasions of, when the cortège came by, having to stop myself saying, 'Here comes the main body of the procession,' which would have been disastrous.

NED   Wasn't there a time when you were suddenly commenting on a close-up of Yardley?

BRIAN   This was at Trent Bridge, the first time we went there for television, when Weekes and Worrell put on 280 odd and at about four o'clock I remember saying, 'Well obviously Norman Yardley's got to do something about this. I wonder what he's thinking?' And as we put the camera on him in close-up, he was scratching himself in a very unfortunate place. So I said, 'Well, obviously a very ticklish problem.' But his wife gave him the most terrible rocket when he got home. Poor Norman, what a lovely chap he was.

NED You were a sort of precursor of Jeremy Beadle in your radio career, weren't you? There were all sorts of practical jokes you used to play on people. There was the restaurant gag with Cliff Michelmore and two other commentators.

BRIAN It was rather extraordinary to see what people's reactions were. Cliff Michelmore was the host at a table and I was disguised as a waiter and we did things like giving everyone a nice bit of Dover sole except for the chap whose leg we were pulling. He just got the backbone with the head and the tail on. And Michelmore said, 'Are you happy with your fish?' And this chap said, 'Oh, yes, very good, very good,' and never reacted at all.

Another thing was at Victoria Station, when I had a mask on like a wolf, to see people's reactions and I heard people say, 'Oh there's a wolf there; must go and catch my train.' We put out the announcement, 'Will the people who have taken the eight eighteen train from platform six, please return it. It's needed first thing in the morning.'

NED It gives one faith in the imperturbability of the British character.

BRIAN Just outside Victoria Station Kenneth Horne and I tried to give money away. He was saying something about his old aunt having died and left him money and he wanted to distribute it, but people just wouldn't take it at all.

NED Did you enjoy tremendously the change from commentary on the television to commentary on the radio?

BRIAN Well, radio is a more natural medium and it's easier, because you have to keep on editing yourself on television, or you should do. On television, if you're very technically up on the game, you don't want to be told about the technicalities, because you understand it, and if you don't understand it, you don't understand the technicalities. So a television commentator's in a very difficult position.

NED How did you enjoy your first trip to Australia? Because it was quite late in life when you penetrated the colonies.

BRIAN I got a thing called 'grace leave' when I'd done ten years in the BBC, when they used to let you go off for three months. And I decided to go to Australia and the Beeb very kindly said, 'We'll use you while you're there.' And I went out – very posh – first-class in a Britannia and arrived 24 hours before the Test Match started in Melbourne. I went there and there was a chap commentating and they said, 'You've got to go on second; Alan McGilvray's aeroplane's late.' And when I started England were seven for three, which wasn't a very good start, and at that moment a pigeon dropped something from the rafters in that big stand at Melbourne. That was my christening in Australia.

NED This was the time when Benaud was captain and there were three bowlers who you accused of chucking.

BRIAN I never accused them at all, but the umpires should have. There was Meckiff and I remember seeing Slater, the off-spinner, who was bowling in the nets and I said, 'What a good idea, because so often people bowl in the nets. Much better to chuck, because you can be so much more accurate.' And this chap said, 'He is bowling.' Slater – we didn't mind about him, but Meckiff was a bit dangerous.

NED   How many tours have you done since then?

BRIAN   Well, I did altogether ten tours and one I was very proud of was when I was the neutral commentator for the last Test Matches that South Africa played for so many years – when Australia went there (in 1969/70). I was with Charles Fortune and Alan McGilvray.

NED   There's a very nice story of one of your favourite interviews with Uffa Fox, when you had a problem understanding how he, who spoke no French, could manage with his wife, who spoke no English.

BRIAN   That's right. I was interviewing him on telly and I said, 'How does it work?' And he said, 'My dear fellow, there are only three things in life worth doing – eating, drinking and making love – and if you speak during any of those, you're wasting your time,' which is a good philosophy. He was a lovely chap.

NED   How about umpires? I like the story very much of the Duke of Norfolk's umpire.

BRIAN   Well, that's an old classic, really.

NED   That's never stopped you before, Brian.

BRIAN   He was playing a match against the Sussex Martlets. Eleven o'clock start. At a quarter to eleven they were an umpire short, so the Duke drove down to the castle to get his butler, Meadows. He found him polishing the silver. 'Meadows, get your apron off. You're umpiring.' It was one of those days with a bit of drizzle. Not enough to bring them off, just making it slippery. The Duke came in at number ten and he was at the non-striker's end. The chap batting thought he'd better let him have the bowling, so he pushed one and said, 'Come on, your Grace, come one.' His Grace set off and he slipped and landed slap on his face in the middle of the pitch. Cover point picked the ball, threw it to the wicket keeper, who whipped the bails off, turned to the square leg umpire and said, 'How's that?' The square leg umpire, inevitably, was Meadows the butler. What was he to do? He drew himself up and he said, 'His Grace is not in.'

NED   Is it equally shop-soiled, the Bradman one when he was defending Australian umpires?

BRIAN   A friend of mine, called Tom Crawford, was arguing with Don during Peter May's tour. There had been a very good umpire on the previous tour called McInnes, but he was not quite so good on this tour. Tom Crawford was saying what we often say about our umpires at home – it doesn't quite apply now – that they're all old Test cricketers and they know what goes on out in the middle. He said to Don, 'The trouble with your people is, they learn all the laws, but they've never actually played first-class cricket.' And Don said, 'What about McInnes? He played for South Australia until his eyesight went.' Then he realised what he'd said.

NED   There's the Reeves and Robins one, too.

BRIAN   Robins was a bit fiery tempered and he'd bowled very badly and he said to Reeves, 'Take my —— sweater and you know what you can do with it.' And Reeves said, 'What, sir, swords and all?'

NED   Can you pick out a special Lord's memory?

BRIAN   Well, I suppose the best one was in 1969, when Alan Ward of Derbyshire was bowling in his first Test Match. Off the fifth ball of an over to Glenn Turner of New Zealand he hit him very hard in the box. He collapsed in the crease and the cameras panned in. He was lying there and you pretend he's been hit anywhere except where he has. Suddenly he got up, so I said, 'He's looking a bit pale, but he's very plucky, he's going on batting. One ball left!'

NED   I was hoping for an epic cricketing moment,

Brian. I wasn't hoping for another bit of sleaze.

BRIAN The epic was undoubtedly 1963. One of the great Test Matches, when Colin Cowdrey came out at number eleven with his wrist in plaster to join David Allen, with two balls left and six runs to win. Just before the start of this last over, my producer suddenly said, 'Right, hand back to the news at Alexandra Palace.' Luckily Kenneth Adam was then managing director of television. He was mad on cricket and he was listening at home and got on the phone to the news and said, 'Go back to Lord's at once.' So in the middle of saying something about President Kennedy, they said, 'We've got to go back to Lord's,' and we got back in time for the last over with David Allen playing defensively at the last two remaining balls.

NED Well, many happy returns of Wednesday, Brian.

By the same author and available in Mandarin

Someone Who Was

'I think I recognise you don't I? Aren't you someone who was?'

A bemused Brian Johnston was once greeted with these words by an unknown woman on Paddington Station. It inspired him to give this book, published to celebrate his 80th birthday, the title for a retrospective look at a life of variety and fun.

Brian Johnston here sets out in A–Z format all those events, people, places, anecdotes and jokes which have shaped and enhanced his life, and made him the elder statesman of cricket's *Test Match Special* team and Britain's most entertaining commentator.

'He's 80 now and still writes as he talks on the radio, easily and charmingly ... Let us applaud a remarkable innings and remember that after the frequently stale bread of radio sporting commentary, he does at least bring us cake'
                    Barry Took, *Evening Standard*

It's Been a Piece of Cake

A witty collection of tributes to Brian Johnston's favourite Test cricketers. These are pen portraits which are splendidly anecdotal, occasionally controversial and consistently shrewd in their technical appraisal.

Of course, there are one or two fine players he has had to leave out, but among those he has included are Patsy Hendren, Len Hutton, Denis Compton, Alec Bedser, Freddie Trueman, Ted Dexter, Geoff Boycott, Basil d'Oliveira, Alan Knott, Imran Khan, Viv Richards, Ian Botham, Allan Border – and many more.

Filled with his unparalleled gift of the gab, infectious sense of humour and unashamed fondness for chocolate cake, *It's Been a Piece of Cake* is Brian Johnston at his most talkative on the subject he knows best.

'As good-natured as the man himself, full of anecdotes and fond memories . . . one of his best'
Financial Times

A Selected List of Sport Titles available from Reed Consumer Books

While every effort is made to keep prices low, it is sometimes necessary to increase prices at short notice. Mandarin Paperbacks reserves the right to show new retail prices on covers which may differ from those previously advertised in the text or elsewhere.

The prices shown below were correct at the time of going to press.

☐ 7493 1649 7	**The Kop**		Stephen F. Kelly	£5.99
☐ 7493 1651 9	**Soccer City**		Shields & Campbell	£5.99
☐ 7493 1596 2	**A Game of Two Halves**		Stephen F. Kelly	£6.99
☐ 7493 1328 5	**Among the Thugs**		Bill Buford	£4.99
☐ 7493 0991 1	**All Played Out**		Pete Davies	£5.99
☐ 7493 0499 5	**A Strange Kind of Glory**		Eamon Dunphy	£5.99
☐ 7493 0888 5	**Oaksey on Racing**		John Oaksey	£5.99
☐ 7493 0293 3	**It's Been a Piece of Cake**		Brian Johnston	£4.99
☐ 413 35901 8	**Offiah (hardback)**		David Lawrenson	£12.99

All these books are available at your bookshop or newsagent, or can be ordered direct from the address below. Just tick the titles you want and fill in the form below.

Cash Sales Department, PO Box 5, Rushden, Northants NN10 6YX.
Fax: 0933 410321 : Phone 0933 410511.

Please send cheque, payable to 'Reed Book Services Ltd.', or postal order for purchase price quoted and allow the following for postage and packing:

£1.00 for the first book, 50p for the second; **FREE POSTAGE AND PACKING FOR THREE BOOKS OR MORE PER ORDER.**

NAME (Block letters) ....

ADDRESS ....

....

☐ I enclose my remittance for ....

☐ I wish to pay by Access/Visa Card Number

Expiry Date

Signature ....

Please quote our reference: MAND